W9-AFV-736

TENNIS SHOES ADVENTURE SERIES

TENNIS SHOES
AMONG THE
NEPHITES

TENNIS SHOES ADVENTURE SERIES

TENNIS SHOES AMONG THE NEPHITES

a novel

CHRIS HEIMERDINGER

Covenant Communications, Inc.

Cover illustration by Joe Flores.

Published by Covenant Communications, Inc.
American Fork, Utah

Printed in the United States of America
First Printing: September 1989

16 15   30 29 28 27 26 25

ISBN 1-57734-467-7

To my family, friends, readers, and fans.

And to my Savior, to whom everything I write or create belongs.

PROLOGUE

I didn't write this story. I realize it was written in the first person and the main character is me. Let me explain. I was going through my box of nostalgia some days ago. Mom had tucked it all away in the attic above the garage the year I went off to Brigham Young University. I found a manila envelope right under my seventh grade thesis on Louis Pasteur. Inside was a stack of erasable bond typing paper. The erasable characteristic was well abused; exhaust from the back end of a pencil was still trapped between many of the pages as if the manuscript had never been read before I blew off the dust.

Besides me, my best friends out of my thirteenth year also play big parts in the story. I have a theory. My Grandma Tucker passed away when I was fifteen. I have no way to confirm it, but my guess is that she's the author. The theory leaves a lot unexplained, but it's all I have.

The images in the story come at me like headlights. I should know what lies behind the light but I can't paint a picture in my brain. It's hard for me to believe that anybody, even my grandmother, could have pegged me so well. Nobody knew me like that. Thoughts are exposed in it that I never revealed to anybody.

Sometimes when I'm in that trance between laying my head on the pillow and falling asleep with classical music on the cassette, my thoughts become the music and the music becomes my thoughts; I see unknown faces and I hear snatches of unfamiliar voices. I don't know if it's déjà vu or revelation. I can't touch it—like a coin in cloudy water that shines when the sun hits it just right, but never for long enough to grab it. It occurs to me that our connection with the premortal world might be described the same way. They say we only use two percent of our brains. Perhaps the other ninety-eight percent is already filled.

I keep hoping someone will snap his fingers and it will all become clear. But if not, I have faith in veils and the parting of veils. Whether in this life or the next, I hope the images will be returned to me so I can pull my face off the canvas and see the painting from a distance. There must be so many more colors than words could ever describe.

Let me just say, if the main character is really supposed to be me, there was one slight misrepresentation. I don't remember ever being such a sarcastic little snot. That point remains for me the strongest evidence that the whole thing is fictional. No one could be that obnoxious. Not even at thirteen years old.

CHAPTER 1

My parents named me Jamie, a name I thought better suited for girls or French poodles. I much prefer Jim, and whoever tries to call me Jamie had better be much bigger than me or have endured two years of karate, because I've endured one.

I was born in a big town—Billings, Montana. My parents moved to Cody, Wyoming, when I was seven. Their motive was to keep me bored in my youth. There are no shopping malls. They have only one movie theater and it has no matinees. There's one main street called Sheridan Avenue. The buildings on Sheridan boast big fronts with big signs, but you can see from the alley they're only half that tall. That's why I always liked to walk down the alley more than the sidewalks. In the alley people gotta be honest. They don't dress in suit coats and ties. Their shirts hang out. People who work or walk in an alley always wear something with a hole in it. It shows you won't change for anybody.

Cody sits in the dust that settled between the Washakie and Big Horn Mountains. They call it the Big Horn Basin. Might as well call it a desert. Standing at our front gate, if I look east, I see the McCullough Peaks. They aren't peaks, really. Just hills the wind made jagged. There are only two colors in that direction. Grayish-brown and brownish-gray. Looking west, Cedar and Rattlesnake Mountains stand side by side, cut down the middle by the Shoshoni River. The way they tower so close to town, it ruins our sunsets. A highway goes between them. It's the only way to get to Yellowstone Park from here.

As far as my family rank, I'm second to the youngest. Mitch and Steven are in high school. Judd is in ninth grade. I still command a little sister, Jenny, though she doesn't take orders too well. My dad used to be a high school English teacher, but about the time I started fifth grade, he became principal of the junior high. So now that I'm a seventh grader, the teachers don't mess with me for a change. Back at Eastside Elementary, I can't count the times my sixth grade teacher, Mrs. Udderback (yes, that was her real name) had me drag my desk into the hallway for passing notes to Greg Shelby or whispering too loud, or for sticking the shiny point of a newly sharpened pencil slowly into the small of Garth Plimpton's back until he snapped forward and arched back, as if a couple thousand volts had just shot through him. Garth was a gawky-looking guy—skinny—with red hair and white skin and freckles on his arms. To top it off, he had green eyes. You could find Garth in the sixth grade yearbook under "Wimps."

It was me, Greg Shelby, Tom Slater, and Bob Jackovitch in those days. We called ourselves the Vikings. Plunder and destroy was our motto. The masses feared and hated us. We caused many recurring nightmares for kids who even gave us a slanted look.

The last days our legendary gang stalked our peaceful town were toward the end of my final year at Eastside Elementary. I blame my church for the disbanding. The Vikings decided to go on an overnight camping trip to Cedar Mountain. As we were leaving town, Shelby gave us all a wink, and detoured his Schwinn into Wing's Mini-Mart. Using the same note his dad had written to send him on an errand the week before, Shelby purchased a carton of Marlboros. You'd think the cashier would have noticed the overnight pack draped over his shoulder and guessed something was amiss, but Wing's employees weren't known for their IQ's.

Shelby kept his secret in a paper sack all the way to the campsite, delighting in our curiosity. Finally he brought it out and held it forward with all the pride of a new father. I got queasy inside when I saw what it was. While the other guys were patting Shelby on the back and helping him break all the seals between the carton and the first cigarette, I acted preoccupied building the campfire and said, "Later," without looking up. But nobody could ever hide a thought from a twelve-year-old. The ribbing and teasing began. Toward dark the harassment grew more intense and more personal, making it the longest camping trip of my life. By the time they finished, there was nothing left of my manhood. Then, fortunately, someone brought up girls. The words were crude, but I sighed with relief. If they had continued their persecutions, I might have been only minutes away from tasting tobacco.

Within two days, I was a lone Viking—no ship or crew. My family walked around me for a while. I was snapping at anything that moved. Mom and Dad tried to get me on the psychiatrist's couch to discuss my problem. I couldn't talk to them. I blamed them for it. The Church and I weren't on speaking terms either. In sacrament meeting that Sunday, they sang "There Is Sunshine in My Soul." Mrs. Gilchrist, with a neck like a turtle, was furiously conducting. The sound I heard resembled bleating sheep. When Bishop Winters talked, I could mouth nearly every word before it was spoken.

It all came to a head on my very last day in the sixth grade. I overheard Shelby and Slater discussing summer plans. When they saw me, they made an obvious effort to ignore my existence in the universe. But I caught their last words. They had to do with a lunch pail, a surprise, and a meeting after school under the west-wall fire escape.

When the bell rang, I wandered around the building myself, wondering if Shelby's lunch box might offer me a chance to redeem my reputation. As I stepped into the shadow under the fire escape, Shelby, Slater, and Jack-O were gathered around the lunch box in a circle that gave the appearance of a religious ceremony.

"I think you took a wrong turn, *Jamie*," Shelby said, profaning my name.

"I came to the right place," I said. "I overheard you. It sounded like this might be interesting."

"He's on patrol, Shelby," Jack-O warned.

"You looking for a party?" asked Shelby.

As I got closer, I could see the idol of worship. It was a can of cold silver. Shelby took the unopened Coors "Silver Bullet" out of the lunch box and stroked it like a kitten. Slater put his arm around my neck and pressed his sticky forehead onto mine.

"We're about to perform a satanic ritual," he announced. "We'd hate to corrupt a nice boy like you."

I forcefully gave Slater's arm back to him. "I was corrupt when you were suckin' Gerbers, Slater."

"Then you wouldn't mind doing the honors?" Shelby held the can toward me. It looked as big as an oil drum suspended there in front of my nose. I snatched it from Slater's hand. If I hesitated now, they'd denounce me with more spit and venom than ever before.

I popped the tab. The edge of the can sat cool against my lower lip. The brew fell right past my tongue, straight into my throat, one long steady stream. As the can drained, the gang began a chant that grew louder and louder.

"He's taking it all!" Jack-O protested, but Shelby held him at bay.

The final drizzle leaked down my chin. I lowered the hollow can, wiped, and studied the approval of my three best friends. The shadow under the fire escape seemed darker. My body didn't feel drunk, but my conscience felt plastered. The smiles left the three faces as I dropped the can and walked away.

Dad would be waiting to pick up Jennifer and me from school for a dental appointment. Turning onto the playground, I saw my family's new Chrysler LeBaron parked beyond the fence. Inside, impatiently watching for me, were Dad and Jen. I began jogging. The red LeBaron bounced up and down in my vision. Everything started moving in slow motion. It was like watching two carousels spinning beside one another in opposite directions. Pebbles crushing under my feet were unusually loud. The car seemed a million miles away and then, in an instant, it zoomed in close. As I climbed into the backseat, words like "What took you?" and "Where have you been?" came swirling around me. My father's eyes were glowing. I was nauseated. I had no control. It just happened—all over the backseat of the new LeBaron.

Everything is kind of blurry after that. All I know for sure is, I never saw a dentist. My dad recognized the problem immediately, having seen similar symptoms among his peers back in the Air Force. My first clear memory was my darkened bedroom, my face in my pillow. Next, I remember bright lights and impatient voices—my parents asking where they went so wrong that I should turn from all I knew to be just and holy, and corrupt my sacred body with an evil and pernicious nectar.

Sentence was finally passed. I was forbidden to see my friends until the end of the Millennium. My mother was convinced *their* influence had caused my questionable behavior the last couple of years. I failed to mention it had been *my* idea to egg Mrs. Udderback's Suburban, and *my* idea to abscond with all the pies at the ward's Christmas social. There were also restrictions against attending the Boy Scout carnival in Billings that weekend. I was planning to contract a virus the morning before departure anyway. Brother Jackson, the scout master with the Polygrip smile, conducting a bus choir in yet another four-part rendition of "Row, row, row . . ." would have been worse torture than lying in bed all day.

My punishments were relatively painless. I was actually grateful to pay my debt to society. It was the entire summer after my parole when life became unbearable. Since I was an ex-con, people got quiet when I entered the room. My older brothers became parole officers. They contested among themselves as to who would be the lucky soul to accompany me to the next stake fireside. The only peace I found in an otherwise dismal summer came from tossing hay bales for my Uncle Spence on his ranch in Burlington, a few miles south of Cody. Legend had it that he'd been quite the party animal as a young man. Aunt Louise claimed he was a full-fledged alcoholic—an accusation that caused Uncle Spence, when I asked him, to chuckle, "Louise wouldn't know an alcoholic from an epileptic."

I did enjoy the company of my Uncle Spencer. He had known the ways of the world and shunned them. He left me with the only worthwhile advice I got all summer: "If you want to sow some oats, Jim, there ain't a soul on this earth who can stop you. Just remember your roots, and gargle a lot of Scope before you come to the breakfast table."

The volcano erupted one night in August during a pork chop supper. That weekend, a high school kid had been killed on Sylvan Pass Highway while "under the influence." Nobody knew the boy personally—only knew *of* him. The dinner topics were lost youth and the evils of booze. I got really uneasy. Each person ended his sermon by throwing a glance in my direction to be sure I'd heard. I shoveled my mashed potatoes as quickly as humanly possible with plans to make a hasty exit.

My mother sighed and grew thoughtful. "I pray every day," she said, "that a phone call like the one that mother received never comes to this house."

I dropped my fork. The line was obviously meant for me. "Mom, I'm not an alcoholic, okay? Let me work on it."

"Not funny, Jim," my dad barked.

"Sorry."

My dad began one of his mini-lectures. "This is a serious issue. And a serious problem in this town—"

My temper was building. "May I be excused?" I interrupted.

Dad aimed his final point at me like a shotgun. "All we want to know is what we can do as a family to keep it from ever going that far."

"By getting off my — — back!"

I won't tell you the words that filled the blanks. Just know they sent my audience into an awesome silence. My dad's palm started to rise. He caught it before the slap was launched.

Then the most horrifying thing happened. Grandmother Tucker put down her fork and stood up. You had to have lived in my family a while to fully appreciate this moment. You see, my grandmother is—how can I put it—a fanatic of sorts. She tortures herself on behalf of the family. During a crisis, she locks herself in her room without food or water and goes on a marathon fast. Several days sometimes. It drives my parents nuts. She refuses to come out until the Lord "answers her prayers in vision." And she never emerges from that room without claiming he has. When I was nine, my cousin Reuben in Butte, Montana, was riding his dirt bike and got sideswiped by a pickup. His arm was run over by the car behind. They were afraid they'd have to amputate it, but Grandma came forth from the room with a solemn conviction that the arm would be saved. And it was.

Grandma went toward her room upstairs. I clutched my bangs, closed my eyes, and dug my elbows into the tablecloth while Mom pleaded with the old lady to not "do this thing."

"He's just going through a bad time—part of growing up. It's not worth risking your health!"

But Grandma wasn't listening. God would watch over her,

she said. Her bedroom door closed with an echo.

Though I kept my face on the table, I knew every event as it was happening. My mother, having returned, was giving my father a "shouldn't we do something?" look. My dad was responding with a "you got any suggestions?" shrug, followed by an "I'm losing patience with that boy" sigh.

"Now look what you've done, Jim" was right at the tip of my mother's tongue. She never said it though. In fact, nobody said anything. Forks were scraping plates again.

"Jim, eat your dinner," Dad said.

I felt robbed. My parents were playing "business as usual"—determined to let my conscience burn.

"May I be excused?"

My dad's voice said "Yes" with perfect pronunciation, like a jury saying "Guilty."

I wouldn't look anyone in the face as I went to my room in self-imposed exile for the evening.

I couldn't sleep. I tried desperately, but I couldn't clear my head of all the angry voices and haunting images. About two a.m., I gave up the fight and climbed out of bed. A light still crept out from under the door of my grandmother's bedroom. She was still at it. How could anybody pray that long? Once I had a goal to pray for fifteen minutes. I felt stupid with nothing to say after five. She was going on seven hours now.

My feet stepped delicately up the stairway. I was determined to knock, but my fist hung suspended at her door. It was hopeless. I turned around and started back.

Grandma's door whipped open and light burst into the hallway. Her arched silhouette stood in the doorway.

"Jamie, honey, come in," she called.

She seemed to know I'd been there all along. The lady had x-ray vision, I swear.

"Sorry, Grandma. I didn't mean to wake you."

"I was wide awake. Come in. I have something wonderful to tell you."

Uh-oh, I thought.

Her clammy hand grabbed mine and led me into her room. The place smelled "old," like always, but it was particularly nauseating this early in the morning. She sat me beside her on the bed. The old woman seemed more flexible—more alive than I'd seen her in years. She put her arm around me and we locked eyes. She'd glared at me this way once or twice before, but it had only been to tell me my eyes were "Tucker-blue."

"I want you to know, little Jamie," she began, as though I were a six-year-old, "that the Lord loves you very much."

The way my body stiffened, my discomfort must have been obvious, but Grandma only tightened her hold.

She continued, "He knows these are the most difficult years of your life. You're at the age when you know everything."

"I don't know everything."

"You even know that," said Grandma. "The point being that you've begun to think for yourself and question everything you've ever been told. It's good to do that. If we were to remain sheep all our lives, nobody would ever learn. You understand?"

"Yeah," I lied.

"The Lord is going to do something very special for you." She stopped talking.

"Like what?" I said, ending her dramatic pause.

"I don't know. He simply assured me he would do it. And he will. You can bet on it."

"That's great, Grandma."

She laughed inside. I could tell because her shoulders started to vibrate and air came through her nose in little bursts. Grandma knew every thought I was thinking.

"Now, it's late and we must both go to bed."

I moved to go. "Good night, Gra—"

She tightened her grip again. Those old eyes were glistening. They came out at me like 3-D.

"You're a special boy, Jamie. And you'll know it very soon."

She was scaring the heck out of me. My whole body was tingling.

"I'll—" My voice cracked and I cleared my throat. "I'll see you in the morning, Grandma."

I was already out the door when I heard her voice whisper, "Good night, Jamie."

CHAPTER 2

In three days, I'd begin the seventh grade. It was a bitter countdown, since I knew I'd be completely friendless. Church today was particularly dull. Old Man Simonton, in Blazer class, directed a question at me.

"Jim, how can we know the Church is true?"

A toughie. I'd only heard the answer recited by everyone and their dog since I was in the nursery.

"Read the scriptures and pray."

"Very good," the old man gloated, as if he'd deeply touched the hearts of an awestruck audience. I could have heckled him, but I felt sorry for the guy. He'd sweat and fidget through class, as if God himself were in the back judging his performance. Truth was, Old Man Simonton was terrified of any kid over ten years old. We never teased him like we did other teachers. Sister Nesmith, in Primary, was a riot to torment. She'd get apple-red and fuming. Her inch-long fingernails would pinch the offender by the ear, making him stand in the corner while she sought a parent. We'd seize these opportunities to draw terrible creatures on the chalkboard eating dismembered arms and legs. But if anyone misbehaved in Simonton's class, Simonton would have tears well up in his eyes. It was pathetic.

"And what scripture tells us, Jim, how we can know?"

"Moroni ten, three-through-five."

"Outstanding!" It was Simonton's favorite word. After some-body read the whole scripture out loud, the old man astounded us with the most difficult question of the day.

"So, how is the truth manifested to us?"

Silence. Nobody knew? Actually, we were just too bored to respond.

Finally, Garth "The Wimp" Plimpton broke the suspense. "By the power of the Holy Ghost," he stated.

I thought I'd turn and see a halo. I scowled. Plimpton smiled back, almost proud. He didn't get it at all. Total nerd.

Sacrament meeting was like an episode of Gilligan's Island: different guest stars, same plot. I entertained myself by sitting on Jennifer's dress, causing it to pinch her thigh. She complained to Mom, who immediately gave me a sharp, but whispered reproach. My face twisted into shock and innocence.

"Mom," I defended, "I haven't touched her! She does this every Sunday just to get me in trouble. She wants attention. Can't you see that by now?"

Jenny was open-mouthed, completely disarmed and confused.

"Jennifer!" Mom chided. "You keep to yourself. Both of you— keep to yourselves." She pointed her ears back at the speaker.

Jenny gave me a deadly squint. I returned a satisfied smirk. She faced forward, folded her arms, and stuck out her lower lip. The poor kid was no match for my superior wit.

It was the last Sunday for Dad to do his home teaching. His usual Aaronic Priesthood companion was on Labor Day vaca-tion in Glacier National Park. I was the unfortunate replace-ment. Our first stop was on Blistein Avenue. It was an older part of our humble town, considered by myself to be the closest Cody got to a slum. The name on the mailbox was none other than Eugene Plimpton—father of "The Wimp."

Tiny, fragile Sister Plimpton greeted us. The father's face was unfamiliar. Even in families where one parent was inactive or "non," they usually found their way out of the woodwork for Christmas or Fourth-of-July socials. I'd never set eyes on the man now enjoying a Bears vs. 49ers game.

"Good afternoon, Brother Plimpton," my dad called over to him cheerfully.

Without taking his eyes off the tube, Mr. Plimpton raised one hand and gave a cutesy wriggle of his fingers. Garth emerged from a back room, still dressed in his Sunday best: corduroy pants, an off-white shirt, and wide tie.

"Hello, Brother Hawkins." Garth firmly shook my father's hand, then turned to me, enthusiastically, "Hi, Jim!"

I gave him a nod, to be polite. After all, I was on a priesthood errand.

Sister Plimpton guided us all to a circle of furniture in the living room, separated from Brother Plimpton and the T.V. The volume on the tube was low enough that we could hear each other, but high enough that I could tell Joe Montana had thrown an interception. Dad invited Brother Plimpton to join in, not expecting him to accommodate, but feeling it best to be respectful.

"I'm listenin'," came the voice behind the Lazy Boy. "I'll offer my opinion when it's needed."

Dad began by asking how everybody was. Sister Plimpton was "fine." Garth was "fantastic!"—looking forward to starting junior high, and excited to have my dad as principal. Dad slapped his hand on my shoulder, rubbed it in, and stated that I was the last son he'd have under his jurisdiction as principal. He had a feeling I'd be a little more "lively" than the others, whatever that meant.

Dad's lesson was on "gifts of the Spirit" and how we all possessed one or more, whether we knew it or not. Dad said

Sister Plimpton's special gift was a powerful testimony of Christ and the gospel. Garth, he said, possessed intelligence and maturity. "Maturity?" I thought. Dad had mixed up his definitions. Mature meant "studly" or "macho" which Garth *definitely* was not.

Brother Plimpton decided he'd offer his two cents. He asked why certain gifts of the Spirit were never heard of anymore, like the gift of tongues. Dad explained that the gift of tongues was manifested all the time, especially by missionaries called to speak foreign languages. Brother Plimpton, more to be ornery than to understand, asked why you never heard about people in sacrament meeting manifesting the gift of tongues anymore. Garth interrupted.

"When God displays a miracle," he began, "it's for a purpose. The gift of tongues is to communicate. If everybody in the audience speaks the same language, why would the Lord manifest it? God is not an acrobat."

"What about Brigham Young? When he met Joseph Smith he spoke in tongues, didn't he? Everybody there spoke English, didn't they?"

Garth wore a smile, as if this wasn't the first time he and his dad had gone the rounds.

"On that occasion, Brigham Young spoke in the pure Adamic language. The purpose was to testify to Brigham, Heber C. Kimball, and all the others that they were in the presence of a prophet of God. Miracles happen all the time, Dad. But it's not likely you'll know about 'em if you're not where the Lord wants you to be, and doin' what he wants you to do."

Brother Plimpton chuckled and turned back to the game.

I found myself staring at Garth Plimpton. How could it be? I thought. Raised by an anti-Mormon father and a spineless mother, yet Garth loved the Church more than any kid I knew. I felt a little ashamed. But the feeling passed.

Dad finished his lesson. Closing with prayer was awkward. Brother Plimpton wouldn't join us. At least he was polite enough to turn down the volume on Merlin Olsen's voice a notch. Afterward, Sister Plimpton brought us into the kitchen for cookie squares. They were a bit hard. In fact, I could have used one to finish off a loose tooth. Dad and Sister Plimpton began a conversation on arthritis and related ailments. Garth leaned over to me.

"You like to study Book of Mormon archaeology?" he asked.

"Every day," I answered sarcastically.

"Come here," he invited, "I'll show you something."

I followed Garth into his bedroom. On his drafting desk there were three open books.

"Are we gonna see *Ancient America Speaks*, or something?" I asked.

"No. I'm talking about getting into the real meat. They really existed once, you know."

"Who?"

"Nephites. Every character in the Book of Mormon ate, slept, died, was buried—except, of course the Three Nephites, Nephi the Third, and possibly Alma the Younger, who may have been translated. Do you have a hero from the Book of Mormon?"

"Not particularly," I said.

"Mine is Ammon. Do you remember Ammon?"

"Is he the guy who chopped off all the arms?"

Garth corrected my rudeness. "I'd prefer to think of him as one of the greatest missionaries of all time."

All of his books were opened to pictures of rock carvings and paintings. "What's this stuff?" I inquired.

"They're called petroglyphs. They weren't painted by Nephites, just Indians. But it'll all tie together, someday. I *know* it will. I have firsthand knowledge."

"Oh, yeah? How's that?"

"Because I found something that nobody has ever seen. Nobody, except me. A discovery that could change New World archaeology."

"You found a rock painting?"

I reacted too eagerly. Garth seemed pleased to have caught my interest.

"Compared to what I found, those pictures are merely doodles."

"Where? Around here?"

"You want to see it?"

I shouldn't have acted so eager. Showing interest in something of Garth Plimpton's was beneath my standards.

"Sure. Maybe," I responded indifferently, turning the pages on one of Garth's volumes entitled *Encyclopedia of the American Indians, Vol. IV.*

"Well, we'll have to go sometime." Garth turned to leave the room. I was losing my bluff.

"How about today? I mean, how far away is it?"

"Today's the Sabbath," he said.

I almost lost my temper. Something as trivial as the Sabbath had never stopped me from doing something important.

"If you'd like, we could go tomorrow," Garth offered.

I followed him back toward the kitchen.

"Is it nearby?"

Garth turned back. "Show up tomorrow. Ten. Bring your bike."

Dad and Sister Plimpton walked out about then. Dad thanked her for her hospitality. We said our good-byes—Mr. Plimpton with another wriggle of his fingers—and left.

Back in the car, I asked Dad, "How come I've never seen Mr. Plimpton before?"

Dad looked at me—looked me up and down. He was deciding whether I was old enough to hear the answer.

"Brother Plimpton was 'X-ed,' Jim, years and years ago."

"Adultery?"

Dad gave me a double-take. "I believe he simply asked to have his name removed. I saw a lot of progress there today. I've never heard Gene Plimpton comment on anything. If he ever does come around, it'll be that son of his who makes it happen. Amazing young man."

I thought my dad's next comment would be, "Why can't you be more like that?" The comment that came said the same thing. "I'd like to see the two of you get together and become friends."

I almost told him about tomorrow's hike, but I couldn't give him the satisfaction. In fact, I probably would have called Garth later that day and canceled the whole thing if he hadn't found my weakness. I loved exploring and I loved ancient things. I kicked up an arrowhead once while walking through the hills behind my uncle's ranch. It was really only half an arrowhead, but it still sits inside a frame in my top dresser drawer—a prized possession. If Garth Plimpton had found something nobody else knew about, I wanted to see it. Maybe later, I could find a way to push Garth out of the picture altogether.

The next morning I hopped on my red Ross ten-speed and showed up on Garth's doorstep. He saw me through his kitchen window and gulped down his last bite of Captain Crunch. Garth pulled his yellow bike out of the garage. That bike was one of the reasons we'd placed Garth in a lower social class. It was an old style one-speed with foot brakes. Twenty years of rust, Crazy Glue, and twine held it together. The handlebars came off as he set it down on the driveway. He explained that the steering worked fine, but only if you held it just right and added extra body weight.

We pedaled eastward, up the Powell Highway, away from town. The McCullough Peaks loomed ahead and the Shoshoni

River ran parallel. About five miles out of town we turned down a dirt road running beside a big alfalfa field. Another mile and the road sloped downhill toward the river bottoms. The smell of sage would have sent my mother's allergies into warp drive. It was one of those days where the sun can't decide whether to shine or hide. Shadows moved like ocean waves over the land. Looking back, I'd say this day marked the end of summer. The breeze made it the best time of year to be hiking. It never entered my mind to call it hot or cold.

Garth was riding ahead when suddenly, he swung his legs higher than his handlebars and twisted to a halt, barely catching himself before eating gravel. I heard the problem before I saw it. A fat prairie rattler was coiled in the middle of the road, soaking up what little sun was available. I stopped my bike above it, which meant the snake was surrounded. We drew as close as we dared. The serpent was making its escape into the thick sage left of the road. One thing I had no patience for was an animal that wouldn't cooperate when I wanted to tease it. My fingers found a good-sized stone. Then my arm rose over my head in preparation for an air strike.

"No!" Garth shrieked. His voice was so intense, I froze— entirely confused. The rattler slithered into the safety of thick sage.

"What's the matter with you?" I demanded.

"You don't bother it, and it won't bother you," was his response.

"That thing is poisonous! It kills people!"

"Believe me, we're still winning the war. Come on, we'll stash our bikes." And with that Garth hopped back on his yellow embarrassment and rode the last twenty yards of trail.

Garth was genuinely weird. Why should I feel guilty for trying to kill a rattlesnake? If I'd sensed even the slightest air of phoniness about him—anything self-righteous—I might have slugged him. I didn't sense anything of the kind.

He led me toward a rocky ledge overlooking the river. The water level was lower than usual. Lack of snow the previous winter had even caused the city to restrict the number of weekdays that we could water our lawns. Garth claimed he'd walked along the riverbank on sections of bank that had never before been exposed. It was this condition, he explained, that made his discovery possible.

We climbed down the ledge by a trail Garth had already proven.

"It'll get a bit muddy from here on out," Garth warned.

About then his tennis shoes sank up to his ankles in black crud.

The smell resembled dead fish in a sun-baked bucket. We hugged the canyon wall to avoid the worst and deepest of it. Soon there was no bank at all. We were sloshing through four inches of Shoshoni slime, lifting each step with a terrible sucking sound and sending clouds of murky water downstream.

Eventually, the wall came to a corner and jutted out into the river.

"This is the worst part," Garth proclaimed while marching in up to his waist, keeping one hand on the wall for balance. The current whisked him around the corner and out of my sight. After inhaling deeply, I followed. With every step the cold river seeped higher up my jeans until the dark water line was even with my belt loops. Then the current sucked me in like a vacuum. It took more effort than I expected to keep from being dragged into the heart of the river. Somehow I pulled myself back toward the canyon wall where Garth was eagerly waiting, standing upon dry ground. A section of bank, about ten feet wide, rose up out of the current like a boat ramp and led into a thin crevasse. Garth helped me climb out of the water. I stood there for a moment, panting and dripping while Garth extended his arms and announced, "This is it!"

"Where?"

"You're leaning on it."

As I stepped away from the wall, the ancient painting became as clear as a billboard. Maybe the colors were faded, maybe the stone cutting was not as sharp as it once was, but the image was unmistakable.

A group of people carved in red and black, wearing many feathers and ornaments and carrying spears and knives, were chasing a smaller group of people, carved in white, into a cave. In the cave, stalactites and stalagmites like teeth surrounded the people. The white people were fleeing into the cave. Each white figure carried something in his hand that looked like a scroll. There were different symbols on each scroll. Curiously, the mural ended at a circular hole cut into the rock. I couldn't tell how deep the hole went. This hole was encircled by many colors—red, gold, white, faded blue, faded green, and black. It looked like a rainbow. White figures sought this hole, as if it meant safety or protection.

"Fantastic!" I exclaimed. My fingers felt their way into and out of the grooves. "Are we really the first people to ever see this?"

"Except for the artists, probably so," Garth stated. "For the last century, the river has been too high. To get into this nook you would have needed a rope. Why would anyone have thought to climb down here?"

"I'm impressed, Garth. Really impressed. We could be famous, you know that?" I was being pretty generous to myself by adding the word "we," but Garth didn't object. "Get our pictures in the *Cody Enterprise*. Maybe even the *Billings Gazette*."

Garth bit the inside of his cheeks. From the years of abuse I'd given him, I learned he formed that expression when he felt uneasy.

"Eventually," he said quietly, "but not yet. You've got to promise me, Jim."

I huffed. "Why not? This is something a scientist should be studying. Somebody from the Historical Center."

"If we tell someone, they'll rope it off. We might never get near it again. Archaeologists will come from all over the world to study it. I know they will. Nothing like it exists outside Mesoamerica."

"And you want to keep it a secret? Garth, we could be heroes!"

"We will, Jim. Trust me. Just give me some time to study it. I want to know what it means. I've sat here for hours memorizing it. I've ordered books to help me put the puzzle together. Look. This is the key." Garth pointed at the hole on the right end of the mural. "The rainbow hole where the white tribe escapes. It means something important, Jim."

"You ain't a scientist. What makes you think you could figure it out?"

"Jim, I brought you here as a friend. Don't let me down."

I looked away. "Right. It's our secret. You have my word."

And if you think I was sincere, I've got some swampland I could sell you.

We didn't say much during the ride back into town. I think he regretted having brought me. I don't know what the guy expected. When he'd called me his "friend" it jarred me a little. I hoped he didn't think we'd become bosom buddies. I just wanted to see the ancient mural.

If Garth Plimpton was lonely, he brought it on himself. He never participated in sports, had no sense of humor—from what I could gather, all he did was read, study, and do weird things, like explore never-exposed mud along the Shoshoni River. Grown-ups seemed to love him—teachers mostly, which of course made me dislike him all the more. I can't recall him ever being rude or unfriendly, but I can't recall him ever going out of his way to make friends, either. Why Garth tried to befriend me now was baffling. I'd have to disappoint him. Garth Plimpton was an "untouchable."

As we crossed into the city limits, the worst imaginable thing happened. Three boys on bicycles were riding in the opposite direction. By the time I recognized them, it was too late to hide myself. Greg Shelby, Tom Slater, and Bob Jackovitch—the Vikings—were already shouting greetings at me. I heard Jack-O ask, "Who's he with?"

I knew the moment Slater mumbled, "I don't believe it!" that he recognized Garth.

"What's going on?" I inquired as our bikes met on the gravel parking patch in front of the Cody Bowling Alley.

"What's going on with you?" The way Shelby asked the question was awfully accusing, glancing from me, to Garth, and back to me.

"We were hiking," I defended. "He was showing me something." I couldn't even say Garth's name.

"Good for you," said Shelby, dismounting.

Slater and Jack-O followed.

"Are you two friends now?" Shelby asked.

"We go to the same church," I answered.

Slater stepped in front of Garth and leaned on his handlebars. "Nice bike."

I felt the need to further explain, "I was making him show me some Indian ruins on the river."

I saw Garth bite his cheeks.

"How fascinating," Slater said with sarcasm. "You guys wanna play some pool? We'll even let you play, Garth, if you got some money."

Meaning, if Garth consented, he'd be responsible for all expenses.

"I think Garth has to get home. Don't you, Garth?" I said it partly to protect him, and partly because I didn't want him around. This was an opportunity to redeem my reputation over a friendly game of pool.

Garth spoke, "Yeah, you're right." He looked hurt. The others recognized my brush-off and approved.

"Probably got a hot date with Mrs. Udderback, eh, Garth?" As Slater said it, he yanked Garth's handlebars out of the socket. Slater held them up like a trophy. When Garth reached forward to retrieve them, Slater stepped just out of reach. Shelby and Jack-O were greatly amused. I half-smiled, trying desperately to regain the spirit of these things. It didn't seem that amusing anymore, having been where Garth was now.

"Come on, Tom," said Garth, "give it back and I'll be on my way."

About that time a hay-stacked truck was pulling away from Blessing's Animal Hospital next door, the driver having dropped off some creature for treatment. As it pulled its two front wheels onto the highway, the driver paused to look in both directions. Slater tossed the handlebars into the bed. Garth abandoned his bike and dashed after the truck, running nearly half a block until he got the driver's attention and convinced him to pull off the road.

"Aw," said Slater, disappointed that the performance had been cut short.

"Every wimp has his day," commented Jack-O, followed by a burst of laughter, as if he'd said the cleverest thing.

"Show's over," Shelby declared. "Let's play pool."

We parked our bicycles. Shelby led me into the bowling alley, inquiring about my summer. As we found the pool tables, Shelby boasted about all kinds of successful summer adventures with the opposite sex. I didn't believe a word, but it felt gritty even pretending to be entertained. The thought kept pumping me, I don't belong here anymore. All I could do was hope the thought would leave.

Shelby handed me a pool cue and put a quarter into the table. Slater and Jack-O arrived about then and sat on the end of the neighboring pool table, holding back another fit of laughter.

"What's going on?" I asked.

Slater pulled Garth's bicycle seat out from under his button-up shirt. He let go with a belly laugh so intense, I saw tears well up in his eyes. Jack-O and Shelby broke out laughing again as well. I felt nothing. Not even a smile would surface. My conscience was finally doing what it had been hired to do. I felt ashamed. It was a new feeling. At the same time, and this is hard to explain, it felt like a bubble had burst around me and I was free in a way I hadn't been in a long time.

I grabbed the seat from Tom Slater's hand and marched toward the entranceway.

Slater called after me, "He'll get home all right, Jim. His rump might be a little sore, but—"

They burst out laughing again as I walked around the corner, past the cashier, and out the doors. The gravel parking lot was empty. Garth was nowhere in sight. He'd escaped on his rickety bicycle despite the missing seat. I listened to the passing highway traffic and rolled the seat over and over in my hands. I had lost a friend I didn't think I wanted. It felt one notch lonelier than having had no friends at all.

Shelby came out the entrance and stood beside me. He gazed long and hard down the highway, dramatizing the fact that Garth was gone. Heaving a "ho-hum," he mumbled, "It looks as if he's finally up and left you. Oh, I wouldn't get all misty if I were you. You're bound to kiss and make up. The way it looked to me, Jamie, you two were meant for each other."

Every time in my life I've ever felt peace and satisfaction, it was usually in quiet moments with music or family. This moment had neither, but oh, what great satisfaction it brought to my soul to finally confirm my feelings toward Shelby. There was only one way to express this new conviction. It was by placing a carefully propelled fist into the center of Greg Shelby's face.

CHAPTER 3

The disinfectant my mother painted into the cut on my chin hurt worse than the punch that caused it. Greg Shelby's thumbnail had probably never been clipped or cleaned. So, to be safe, Mom insisted on putting medicine on the wound.

"Who won?" asked Jennifer, looking on through the bathroom door.

"Need you ask?" I pridefully huffed as Mom wiped away the excess.

Greg Shelby only connected with that one sissy, thumbnail punch. I laid him out with a second punch in the very same eye. It gave me a reason to look forward to school on Wednesday. I'd see my artwork on his face. As one-eyed Shelby was climbing back to his feet, Slater and Jack-O rushed out of the bowling alley to defend their leader. I swung Garth's bicycle seat and whacked Slater in the side of the head. He spent a couple of seconds counting stars. Using the seat wasn't the fairest of tactics, but it was three against one. I felt justified. I climbed onto my bike and pedaled off amid much profanity and promises of vengeance.

I called back, "I'll look forward to it!"

I didn't even know my chin was bleeding until I got home. The way my heart was pumping, I'm sure it made the cut look worse than it was. Seeing it now in the bathroom mirror, I was confident it would be gone in three days. At my insistence, Mom put the untorn Band-Aid back into the box. Band-Aids, I informed her, were for "woosies."

"I don't want to see any more fighting!" she said, as any good mother should.

When Dad got home, I got a similar lecture. When he learned that the fight had been with Greg Shelby, a brief glow of approval swept over his face. He knew now the Vikings were history. My brothers kept cornering me to recount the tale. By the time I got around to telling Keith, the story was sounding even better, but Jennifer, who had listened to every version, corrected any contradictions. Nevertheless, Keith, like the others, felt I deserved a hearty pat on the back. My spirits were up for a change—until Dad suggested I should seek new friends. Garth Plimpton was at the top of his list.

That night I slept with a simmering conscience. Apologizing was out of the question. If someone had done to me what I'd done to Garth, I'd carry a grudge until doomsday.

I woke up depressed. Maybe it was my state of mind that inspired Mom to organize an afternoon outing. At first Dad insisted he had a stack of paperwork that needed attention, but Mom prevailed. We took a picnic to the Buffalo Bill Reservoir. This was a ritual my mother performed at the end of every summer in celebration of nine wonderful months ahead with an empty, quiet house all to herself.

Uncle Spence and Aunt Louise tagged along. Behind their Dodge Ram Charger, Spence towed a fifteen-foot boat named *Orca* after the boat in the movie *Jaws*. Keith couldn't come, on account of football practice. Grandma stayed home and napped. Steven brought his newest "woman" so they didn't hang around long. Judd brought his dirt bike. Mom and Aunt Louise prepared the fixins. That left Dad, Uncle Spencer, Jenny, and me to take *Orca* out into the reservoir in quest for dinner.

The fish weren't biting. They never did on the reservoir. I don't think anyone much cared. We were there to feel the wind and the spray and to listen to Dad and Spence reminisce about their days in Cody High School, when dinosaurs still walked the earth.

From the center of the Buffalo Bill Reservoir you could see all of Wapati Valley. Mountains with names like Carter, Sheep, Rattlesnake, and Cedar watched over us like shepherds. Though I've seen that view a thousand times, I've never grown tired of it.

Uncle Spence pointed up at Cedar Mountain. "You been up to the cavern lately, Ron?" he asked.

"Not for years and years, Spence," answered Dad.

Near the top of Cedar Mountain, on the north face, there was a cavern. It had different names, depending on who you asked. I knew it as "Frost Cave." I'd never been up there. From what I understood, it was closed down and boarded up. The cavern had once been a tourist spot, complete with walkways and handrails. But upkeep was too expensive. The road to get there always looked different after spring runoff, causing even most four-wheelers to think twice. One year some people got hurt. The county blocked the entrance with a steel gate and left the walkways to rot.

"I was with you the last time," Dad added.

"Really? Now there's a story," my uncle began. "Your dad and I both took dates."

"Uh—" Dad interrupted. "They might be a little young for that story."

"Heck no," Spence insisted and didn't even pause. "You see, in those days, young bucks tried to con girls into climbing down into the deepest, darkest tunnel. The idea was to turn off their flashlights and practice some serious osculation."

"What?" asked Jen.

"Kissing," Spence explained.

Jennifer glared at Dad and blurted, "Somebody besides Mom?"

Dad's face was a deep, rosy color. "You're corrupting my kids."

Spence continued, "While your dad and his date were smoochin', me and my date stole the flashlights and disappeared. As your father groped around, trying to find us, we caught his date. The three of us hid from him for an hour."

"Closer to ten minutes," Dad corrected.

"I never heard your dad use more colorful language."

"Seems to me it was you that came out the worst," Dad told him. "Got a bump the size of a golf ball on your forehead, didn't you?"

Spence squinted his eyes in memory of the pain. "Ooo, I remember that. Hurt like a son-of-a-buck."

Spencer had a whole selection of words to replace cuss words. "Son-of-a-buck" sounded funny every time we heard it. The four of us laughed.

Spencer leaned back and soaked in nostalgia. "Yeah, I spent a lot of time in those caves as a kid, before they boarded it off. We used to search for the Rainbow Room."

My chest swelled, and a surge of blood rushed into every limb of my body. "The Rainbow Room?"

Garth's mural in the Shoshoni canyon flashed through my mind. My uncle grinned and leaned forward, as if to tell a ghost story.

"Legend had it that a certain tunnel went deeper than all the others—to a level lower than the rocky bottom of the Shoshoni River. This tunnel opened into a giant room, the size of several football fields. They said the walls of this room were phosphorescent, glowing every color in the rainbow. The ceiling sparkled with pure gold. Crystal-clear waterfalls poured out from the walls."

"Where did the legend come from?" I asked.

Uncle Spence thought a moment, shrugged his shoulders, and looked at my father.

"Don't ask me," was Dad's answer.

"Seems to me I heard it from an old timer," guessed Spence. "Maybe it was just a story old men told kids to make their eyes grow big."

"Did anyone ever find it?" I asked.

"Nope," Uncle Spencer concluded.

My father continued, "There was a tunnel that went awfully deep. Your uncle and I followed it down almost four hours once."

"It kept on going, too," Spence added.

"I was afraid we wouldn't have the strength to climb out again," Dad said. "In fact, that's why they closed up the place. A lone spelunker—climbing alone was stupid in the first place—climbed down in there and broke his leg in a fall. Search and Rescue took three days to find him."

"The poor soul nearly died of dehydration," said Spence. "The worst part was getting him out. The county decided to dynamite the tunnel and snap one of them big padlocks on the gate."

"They dynamited it?" I was appalled. "How stupid!"

"The cave was dangerous," Dad defended. "Sooner or later, somebody might have been killed down there."

"I'm with *you*, Jim," Uncle Spence agreed. "It was a sorry shame to dynamite the tunnel."

Jenny's pole gave a sharp jerk. She reeled in a fourteen-inch rainbow trout. It was the only catch of the day. She tried to make me jealous, shaking the dripping fish under my chin. But my mind was spinning with visions of Frost Cave, the Rainbow Room, and a part of Garth's stone mural.

As soon as we got home, I mounted my ten-speed and pedaled toward Blistein Avenue. Under my arm was a certain rusty bicycle seat. It was just getting dark when I put down my kickstand on Garth Plimpton's driveway. After I'd rung the doorbell, it was too late to turn back. I wiped my sweaty palms on my hips. There was a real good chance a door was about to get slammed in my face. Sure enough, Garth answered. A variety of expressions swept over his face. The first was surprise, the second was confusion, and the third, I wouldn't have believed it, was a smile—a *real* smile. He was glad to see me.

"Come in, Jim," he said.

I was speechless. Hospitality was the least of my expectations. I hemmed and hawed for a moment, forming the words. Then, as I handed back the seat, an apology limped out.

"I'm sorry, Garth, about yesterday. I wouldn't blame you, I mean, if you didn't want to talk to me."

"You *were* a jerk," he said. Then smiling again, "Come on inside."

Garth led me back into his bedroom. He stammered a little when he asked me a question.

"Did you . . . did you keep it a secret?"

"I did." All the tension left Garth's face.

"In fact," I continued, "I may have solved a major piece of the puzzle. I might know what the rainbow hole means."

Garth's attention was mine. He grew more entranced with every word while I laid the legend before him. Confident that I'd provided a truly important link, he began pacing his bedroom and thinking out loud.

"Maybe the old man who told the story to your uncle heard it from an Indian. There has to be a connection with Indian folklore somewhere. If what your uncle said is true, no white man has ever seen this room. None of them ever went deep enough. Have you ever been up there, Jim?"

"To Frost Cave? No."

"I explored it the summer before last."

"How'd you get past the gate?"

"Simple." Garth snatched a piece of paper and a black felt pen off his desk. "A cave entrance is shaped like this." Garth drew an arch and connected it on the bottom with a straight line. "A gate is square." He drew another line across the arch, near the top. "See the problem they overlooked?—especially for someone our size?"

I saw what he meant. There would be a space between the top of the gate and the ceiling of the cave.

"We just climb up and over. Piece of cake," Garth concluded.

"Yeah, but it doesn't make any difference. They dynamited the deep tunnel."

"Dynamited, huh?" Garth sat on his bed, intense with thought. "There has to be another way. That cavern is an anthill of tunnels. I can't believe there was only one route."

Garth's hands folded under his chin; the elbows balanced on his knees. Slowly his eyes turned upward.

"What are you thinkin'?" I asked.

"We're one step closer, Jim. But only one step. We haven't solved the puzzle. Finding the Rainbow Room. That's the key."

I grinned. "Count me in."

The expedition to Frost Cave was to be made on Saturday. We were sworn to secrecy. No half-caring parent would ever allow us to go. I knew it was a stupid thing to do. That's what I liked about it. I could see us getting lost, our faces ending up on some milk carton or drugstore poster. I lived for this kind of irresponsibility, but for Garth, it seemed out of character. The desire to make an important discovery outweighed his common sense. I had found a weakness in Garth Plimpton. Indeed, I was starting to like him.

Eastside Elementary had been a simpler world. Fortunately, at Cody Junior High, I had an "in." Most of the teachers looked twice when they read the name "Jamie Hawkins" off the role. That's right, I smirked inside, I'm the boss's kid. Dad had only been principal for two years, so I was the first "principal's son" the seventh grade had ever dealt with. Mrs. Dixon, my mousy reading teacher, pulled me aside after the bell rang to confirm my genealogy. Sugar words drooled down her chin as she spoke of my father. The year before she'd been considered for a transfer for lack of classroom control. Maybe she thought I had some kind of power to sway the school board if the problem resurfaced.

Mr. York, my biology teacher, read my name and studied my face. He was thinking, "So the principal's son might expect special treatment, eh? We'll just see about that." He went out of his way to be rude and embarrass me. "Speak up!" he barked when I said "Here." "Raise your hand!" he snapped when I answered a question. My answer was correct but "obviously lacked insight." This guy had fried his brain playing one too many games of child psychology.

Back in the hall, Greg Shelby appeared with a grape-colored shiner under his left eye. He pretended not to see me and walked in the other direction. I gloated all the way to my last class.

It was Social Studies—the only class Garth and I had together. He sat in the neighboring seat and we discussed our weekend plans. A few faces from the old grade school gave me looks of disapproval. I ignored them. The egghead was my friend.

For the next three days we spent our after-school hours collecting supplies. We found three flashlights. Garth went into his savings to insure an extra set of batteries for each. We found a rope—my dad had fifty feet of dusty nylon he'd never miss in the garage. We needed two hard hats. Batting helmets from Keith's closet wouldn't be missed until baseball season began in the spring. I also snuck a two-day supply of granola bars from our food storage. Candles, matches, and canteens were Garth's responsibility.

Friday afternoon we gathered all the provisions into my bedroom and did an inventory. Everything was neatly organized on my bed when Jennifer burst in. Failing to knock was a habit making her worthy of execution. Whatever statement she had come to make died in mid-sentence when she noticed our strange arrangement of gear.

"What are you doing?" she inquired as I blocked her view and pushed her back into the hallway.

"Nothing!" I shut the door, leaving Garth inside. "We're going on a hike."

"With flashlights and hats?" I'd carelessly left a baseball helmet on my head.

"Don't bother us, Jenny, and *knock* before you come into my room, you hear me?"

Jenny walked away, "All right. I'll just tell Mom you're going over to Garth's for dinner."

Fortunately, the small victory she had gained by misleading Mom about my dinner plans caused her to forget the gear.

Garth told me all he could remember about Frost Cave, admitting that when he'd been there before he hadn't taken the time to explore a great deal. We both knew that if we *did* find another route to the Rainbow Room, we might not get home until very late. Garth was as willing to take that risk as I was.

I lay awake the last hour before my alarm was set to go off. It was supposed to buzz at six a.m., but I grew impatient and popped out of bed at five minutes 'til. I dressed quickly and left the house, toting all my gear. Wearing backpacks and baseball helmets, Garth and I met in morning twilight in front of the Buffalo Bill Historical Center. We followed the Yellowstone Highway for three miles, passing motels and tourist sites all along the "West Cody Strip" until the last structure, the Bronze Boot Nightclub, shrank behind us. Another quarter mile and the foot of Cedar Mountain began to steepen. There was a rocky, unimproved road that switched back all the way to the mountain summit. Our bikes couldn't even traverse the first one hundred yards, so we hid them in a high clump of sagebrush and began our climb.

Forging our own shortcut, we climbed straight up the mountain, seeing the road only as one of its switchbacks crossed in front of us. We allowed ourselves plenty of rest stops and watched the flatlands grow broader. The lights of Cody, Wyoming, faded out as the sun rose behind McCullough Peak.

Reaching the timberline, we met the road again. It led toward a steep wall of cliffs. As we neared the cliff-line, the road thinned into a trail. Frost Cave was still hidden around the bluffs. Every plank on the wooden walkway was either broken or rotting. It was easier to walk along the ground beside the walkway, even if a few rocks slipped out from under our shoes and tumbled out of sight, causing a chain reaction on the ledges below that took part of the mountain closer to the valley floor. Higher up, a flight of moss-grown stairs was carved into the rock. We climbed up, around, and down onto a platform wedged into Cedar Mountain as if a giant arrowhead had been shot into the north face. At the tip of the wedge, a hole was exposed—the mouth of Frost Cave opened at us like the jaws on a moray eel attacking a camera on *Jacques Cousteau*. A rusty gate was cemented there; a long chain tied it shut. As Garth had said, there was a two-foot space between the highest bar and the stone ceiling.

"A cinch!" I commented.

Garth stepped forward into the eel's jaws and handed me his pack. Like a true primate, Garth scurried up the dozen feet of gate and hoisted his body over the top rail, dropping down onto the dusty cave floor. We took a moment to appreciate the prisoner/visitor feeling of looking through the bars. Then it was my turn. With one pack on my back and the other over my shoulder, I reached for the top bar and slipped each of them through the narrow space, dropping one, and then the other, into Garth's arms. When I landed, my knees buckled and I fell backwards onto my rump. A cloud of dust puffed around me. Garth laughed and prophesied we'd be much filthier before the day was over.

Our voices sounded hollow, as though we were standing in a train tunnel. I shouted "Hello!" and "Echo!" a couple of times. The outside light melted in to illuminate most of the inner room. The cave had been much abused in its days as a tourist site. Around the entrance, shattered bottles were thick. Ancient artifacts were everywhere. That is, if you considered fifteen-year-old pop cans to be ancient. The walls, even the ceilings (though I couldn't imagine how anyone got up there) were covered with the graffiti of the times: peace symbols, "Class of '61" logos, and various arrangements of profanity.

With flashlights in hands, helmets on heads, and packs on backs, Garth and I marched into the darkness of the main tunnel. On either wall smaller tunnels branched off in all directions. We planned to explore each one. First, we followed the main tunnel until it ended at the edge of a pit. Our eyes followed down the wall of the pit. Many catacombing tunnels began on different levels. The first jutting of rock wide enough to stand on was twenty feet below.

"Well," said Garth, "let's get started."

Garth dragged the rope out of his pack. A fat stalagmite with a broken tip made a convenient tying point. We hoped it would be the only time the rope would be needed, because if we wanted to be able to climb back out, it had to stay tied to that fat stalagmite.

I dropped over the edge, walking down the wall like a spider on a single web. There was a thin cave directly underneath the ledge, a dead end. To get past it, I had to suspend myself in mid-air for about five feet. From there I let the rope slide through my palms, easily reaching the next level. The end of the rope fell beyond, to the level after that.

Garth dropped next to me. Exploration officially began. After worming through tunnels for a good forty-five minutes, we concluded that every branch on this level either ended or circled into a section we'd explored before. The next level down kept us busy for nearly two hours. Skinny, twisting turns and tiny rooms stretched everywhere. Many generations of graffiti-artists had enjoyed the wall space. I was convinced Mike definitely *did* love Cindy. Their names were painted with a plus sign in between, every twenty feet or so. All the interesting formations had either been defaced or removed. You couldn't find a stalactite over three inches long, only broken stumps. If colorful crystal once covered the stone, hammers and chisels now left scars at every turn. No wonder nobody much cared when Frost Cave was closed down.

After exploring every possibility in the pit, we hoisted ourselves back up the rope and explored the other branches that led away from the main tunnel. At one point Garth and I stood in front of a pile of stones that looked anything but natural. This, we guessed, was where the dynamite had exploded. Our pathway to the lower reaches lay somewhere beyond the debris. Digging through the mess was a hopeless idea. Some boulders were larger than Garth and me put together. We explored every tunnel near the debris with increased energy, squeezing into every nook that even showed half a potential of opening up into a larger room. Thoughts of Winnie the Pooh in the rabbit's hole crossed my mind. One of the tunnels I climbed into was no wider than a two-by-two drain pipe. I must have crawled forty feet until the space around me had become so tight I couldn't arch my back or bend my knees. There was no way to turn around. An attack of claustrophobia was followed by a surge of adrenaline that sent me squirming desperately backwards until I could stand again and take in some deep breaths.

Six more hours passed as we searched for the one tunnel leading down and down. Nothing came close. My muscles were starting to cramp from exhaustion. Soon it would be dark outside. The warm supper waiting for me at home began to outweigh my lust for finding the Rainbow Room. As we wearily trudged back toward the mouth of the cave, Garth's face looked as discouraged as mine. We stepped into the light inside the gate. The sunshine revealed the dirt caking our faces. Our filth generated one last smile. Faces were long after that.

Walking down the mountain, Garth's only words were, "We missed something . . . something."

"What are we gonna do?"

"Come back next week," he said, and we climbed onto our bikes.

CHAPTER 4

All night I endured the same nightmare, crawling back and forth through spinning tunnels, never finding a way down, never finding a way out. I sat up in bed, frustrated. Continuing the search for the Rainbow Room was a most unappealing idea. If Garth still fought the desire, he could search alone. I forced my eyes closed until, finally, I was granted a sound, deep sleep. But when a ray of sun came through my bedroom window and awakened me, the passion was back, swelling furiously inside me. I would return with Garth to Frost Cave next Saturday.

Except for one occurrence, the following week was uneventful. I got in another fight with Shelby in the junior high library. I started it. Shelby has such a mouth. Two teachers braced us before I could blacken his other eye. We became the first students of the year to face my father, the principal, in his office. During the lecture, Dad pretended we weren't related. He almost suspended me from school—my own father! We got away with a stiff warning.

I felt lucky until that night at home. My brothers and sister thought it was Christmas all over again when Dad gave me dish-duty for the next two weeks. That was a mere love tap compared to his next punishment. My Saturdays would be reserved for yard detail.

Garth was genuinely upset with me for the first time. I almost thought he'd go back to the cave without me. Finally, he accepted it. But in my own mind, I was still formulating a strategy. I knew my father's weaknesses all too well. Friday afternoon I was busy brown-nosing. I hauled garbage, I scrubbed the dog, I set the table, I cleared it. It was when I started vacuuming the living room during a playoff game in the World Series that Dad sat forward in his easy chair and offered to lift my sentence—under one condition—I put that "darn" vacuum back in the closet and leave. Two minutes later I had Garth on the line. The second expedition was a "go."

Little ears were listening to my conversation. As I set the phone back on the receiver, Jennifer and her puppy-bright eyes sneaked out from around the corner.

"Does Dad know you're going to Frost Cave?" she asked.

"Of course," I lied.

She called my bluff and threatened to interrupt Dad's ball game and verify my claim. It took some skillful gymnastics to head her off before she got to the living room.

"Please, Jenny, I'll do anything for you. Anything."

"I want to go with you."

I was dumbfounded. "Anything else."

"Let me go with you. Please?" she pleaded, forgetting her upper hand.

"Jen," I stammered, "What if you were to fall down a pit and get killed?"

"What if *you* were?"

She had me. Through clenched teeth and crossed fingers, I agreed to let her tag along. She bounced up and down and requested to know her expedition duties. I pretended to be very busy. All the details would be provided during the six a.m. bike ride. I shut myself in my room and began to formulate another scheme. It was simple. I just wouldn't wake her up. Of course she would tattle, but I'd be long gone. The punishment was worth the risk.

At the unholy hour of 5:45 my alarm buzzed. I hit the button with the speed of a gunfighter reaching for his gun. After dressing without breathing, I tippy-toed past my little sister's room. Rolling my bike into the street, I began to pedal westward, watching the streetlights of Beck Avenue pass over my head.

There was a chilly morning breeze coming out of the canyon when I met Garth on the highway in front of the Historical Center. Zipping our windbreakers to the top, we began the familiar trek up the West Cody Strip, pedaling furiously against the wind. About the time we got to the Buffalo Drive-In, I happened to look back. A good half-mile of highway stretched all the way back to a bend in the road where the Ponderosa Motel sat. Just coming around that bend, I saw a lone bicycle fighting the wind. It was still too dark to make out the rider. A silly thought hit me, too silly to seriously consider. I even mentioned it to Garth, for a laugh.

"See that bike? Here comes my little sister," I said.

"Are you serious?"

"No, I'm not serious," I teased. "She wanted to come. I conveniently forgot to wake her up."

"Don't even joke about that." Garth sat high on his bike to accelerate the pace.

When we reached the Bronze Boot Night Club, the sky was a soft, deep blue with fading stars. I turned around again. That same lone bicycle was still trailing us. It was still too dark to tell anything. The early morning light made the rider look bluish, the same color as my little sister's jacket. I was sure it was just the light. Garth noticed me squinting and asked why. I shook my head and aimed my bike back into the wind to pedal that last stretch to the foot of Cedar Mountain.

We hid our bicycles in the same patch of sagebrush and began to climb. We soon reached the same stone that, one week before, had provided an excellent view of the rising sun and city. *Now* my heart sank. I could finally identify the rider who was coasting her bicycle off the highway.

"Great," I huffed.

"It is her, isn't it?" Garth demanded confirmation.

"I don't believe it. I wanna strangle her."

"Does she know the way to the cave?"

There was still hope. "I don't think so."

We kept low and avoided talking as we scurried up the mountainside, but silence was impossible. If we jarred loose the smallest rock it bounded all the way to the valley. We reached the timberline in half the time it had taken the week before. Exhausted, we collapsed against a couple of boulders. Several minutes passed before my breath returned enough so I could open my eyes and crawl back to the edge for a look down the mountain.

"You see her?" Garth asked.

I surveyed very carefully. "No," I said slowly. "Maybe she turned back. Oh, please, let it be so."

My hopes were shattered. I spotted that tiny blue jacket skipping along the road about two switchbacks below, unhindered by strain or pain. Faintly, I heard her singing. She actually had the nerve to be cheerful.

"There's gonna be a funeral," I said. "I mean it."

When we reached the point where the road narrowed into a path, I could still hear her rendition of "Give, Said the Little Stream" carried in the breeze. Garth and I, winded again, sat in the dirt and faced reality. The little twerp had beaten us. Our efforts to leave her far behind by hustling up the steep slope had weakened us to a speed of twenty feet a minute. It was only a matter of time. If she didn't catch us in the climb, she'd stand in the entrance of the cave, repeating my name to create an eternal echo until I came up from the lower reaches to answer.

"What if we tied her to a tree and came back to get her later this afternoon?" I suggested.

"Good idea, but we need the rope," reminded Garth. "Accept it, Jim. She's coming with us."

Disgusted, I tossed a rock at a weathered tree trunk and was even denied the satisfaction of hitting my target.

Finally, Jennifer came strolling up around the switchback. When she saw us, she stopped singing, paused, and began ambling toward us. When she was within calling range, her first words were, "You promised, Jim, so you better not be mad."

She was even wearing one of Keith's baseball helmets, as if she had anticipated my plan to leave her behind all along.

"Are you mad at me?" she asked again when I didn't respond.

"If you even once start to slow us down, I'll take your flashlight and leave you in the dark. I *swear*, Jennifer."

"I won't slow you down," she defended. "Since I can squeeze into a lot of places even you can't, maybe you oughta be worried about keeping up with me."

Garth admitted, "That's a good point, Jim."

"Then she can be your responsibility." I marched past Garth, on down the path, toward the cave.

Jen wasted no time trying my patience. Standing on the other side of the iron gate, Garth and I had to coax her for five minutes as she hung frozen—one leg over the top bar and the other refusing to follow, fearing she would fall. If something as simple as the gate was a hassle for her, I looked toward the rest of the day with great apprehension. She didn't have any equipment other than the helmet. Well, I take that back. She did bring her silly white rabbit fur purse. The foresight it must have taken to remember such an item was staggering. She took our only extra flashlight. As soon as she saw the granola bars she was suddenly overcome with an attack of hunger. I would have refused to give her one, but Garth was born with more compassion. Like a bunny at feeding time, she nibbled the bar all the way from the entrance to the multi-leveled pit.

Jennifer looked down at the deeper and deeper levels and nearly gave up the devoured granola bar.

"We're going down *there*?" she asked as Garth began to tie the rope around the stalagmite.

"Like I said, little sister, if you can't keep up, you know where the entrance is."

Her face took on the sternness of a sea captain. I shook my head and let out an exasperated sigh. Before Garth could ask what was wrong, I said harshly, "Nothing!" and took the rope in both hands, walking over the edge of the pit. Dropping past the first dead-end shelf, I slid until my feet were again firmly planted on the first level. Garth helped Jennifer into position. To every one of his patient instructions she quickly responded, "Okay, okay." My neck got sore from looking up. It seemed to take forever for her to put each step behind her. I sat and spun the flashlight on the cold rocky floor to entertain myself. Ten minutes later, she dropped next to me. She had such a big smile you'd have thought she'd conquered Everest.

"That wasn't hard at all," she gloated.

Garth joined us. Again we searched every nook and hole we might have missed. A few discoveries were made. One new tunnel looked very promising. It opened up into a large room with a ten-foot ceiling. No graffiti covered the walls. The formations were untouched. Some stalactites were six inches long. Unfortunately, the room had no offshoot tunnels.

"Maybe there is no Rainbow Room," my sister suggested, drawing snarls from both Garth and me.

"You know the way home!" we said in unison.

She kept further pessimism to herself.

Two hours later, Garth and I began to harbor doubts as well. We climbed up from the second level, back to the first level, no closer to finding a route.

"Well," said Garth, with little courage remaining, "there's still a lot more holes off the main tunnel to search again."

With that, he began climbing out of the pit. I wanted to call up to him, "Let's bag it, go home, and see the rest of Saturday morning's cartoons," but exerting some discipline, I held my tongue.

I let Jennifer climb up the rope next. She was much more agile now. Toward the top she was showing off, taking giant steps. Her little rabbit fur purse fell out of her jacket and hit me in the nose.

"Jennifer! Can't you hold this stupid thing between your teeth?"

She reached the top and stood next to Garth, shining a light down, extending her free hand over the edge. "Throw it back, Jim," she demanded without remorse.

Receiving no apology may have influenced my aim. I tossed it skyward with little concern for where it landed. To her annoyance, it landed inside the shelf, just below the top.

"Jim!" she whined and climbed back over the edge, pulling herself into the little dead-end shelf and disappearing from view.

Garth and I waited. She did not re-emerge. I called her name. My voice echoed off the cavern walls. I'd had it. How could Jen even imagine that I was in the mood to tolerate a practical joke?

I began the hand-over-hand ascent up the wall of the pit, reciting half out loud, and half in my mind, a vicious speech designed to send her squealing home. I reached the shelf and shined my light inside.

It was as clear now as it was the first time my beam had moved across that inner wall—the little shelf went in about ten feet and ended. Yet Jennifer and her purse had vanished. Garth must have seen my face turn white, even from above.

"What's going on?" he called.

Suddenly my little sister's blonde hair and fair face poked upwards out of solid rock. The illusion was perfect. Actually she came up from behind a thin underpass hidden behind a slight rise in the shelf floor. The way the shadows played off my flashlight, there was no way I would have ever noticed it.

Jenny displayed her purse, saying, "There's a big tunnel down here. Have you guys explored it already?"

"Garth!" I shouted, but he was already on his way down. We followed my little sister into the thin cave that cut back underneath the floor. It opened up, after a sharp downward stretch of a dozen feet, into a wide tunnel that steadily descended into the heart of the mountain.

We forged a spiraling trail through spotless tunnels where the formations were perfect. Many of the stalactites dripped water at a rhythmical pace. One that we came upon gave up a fat drip every three seconds, uninterrupted for the past thousand years. The thought of such a perfect pattern caused me to slide my hand down the tip and shake the water from my fingers. It failed to drip for fifteen seconds—the only vacation the formation had had since the beginning of time.

We kept moving through the cold inner veins of Cedar Mountain and, in consequence, we kept warm. Endless walls of pink and white crystal kept my eyes entertained. Four hours must have passed before Jennifer finally commented on how far we'd gone. We ignored the comment and kept on going.

There were parts of the tunnel where deep holes to the left or right made us dizzy. A sloppily placed shoe might have led to a chain reaction that would have killed us all. I followed Garth, who was meticulous in his footing. Had I been in the lead, my impatience might have led to an accident.

After a couple more hours (I was losing track of time now; nobody had the foresight to wear a watch), everything began to close in on me, though the tunnel ceiling was a good ten feet overhead. I wondered if I would be able to remember the way back when the time came. Without warning, Jenny began to cry. She leaned back against the wall, sank down until her knees came against her chest and hid her face in her arms. I rolled my eyes at Garth and squatted next to her. It's the first time I remember putting my arm around my little sister.

"How much longer?" she sobbed. "We've missed dinner by now, Jim. They'll be wondering. They'll be worried."

I looked to Garth for an answer to that question.

"No tunnel goes forever," was Garth's response. "We've come so far. Just a little further."

"Do you want to wait here?" I asked Jenny. I tried to say it with compassion, but she took it as an insult.

"No!" she snapped, and the tears went back into her head. She bounced to her feet and marched past Garth.

Our mood was very dark the rest of our journey—our sense of security was starting to crumble. I had completely forgotten the emotion that had brought me deep inside the guts of this mountain. Spending the night was inevitable. I was grateful that we had remembered matches. Then a few minutes later it hit me—we had no firewood anyway! We would freeze to death without a fire. I was at the point of a full panic when I saw that Garth had stopped. The tunnel had ended. Well, it hadn't ended, but it thinned into a tiny crawl space that curled upward. Garth stood calmly gazing up the hole. He seemed so at peace I might have guessed he was staring into the face of an angel. When I stood beside him, I felt what had caused his stillness. Jennifer joined us.

"Warm air," she said to describe the sensation that brought blood back into our cheeks.

We climbed up into the hole. This time, I led the way. It was only a few yards further when the beams on our flashlights lost all definition.

We turned them off, putting them in Garth's backpack. There was no need. The enormous room that lay before us glowed and sparkled with all the energy of sunlight shining though colored glass—gold and red and orange.

The three of us were like tiny insects focusing our eyes on a far-off wall that must have been a mile away. Between us and the wall, three waterfalls, at different distances from us, bubbled icy-cold liquid out of the ceiling. On either side, more falls framed the cliff upon which we stood. Fifty feet below, a mighty river gathered all the water, sucking the drainage for several hundred yards until the river churned into a black tunnel, flowing to the center of the earth for all we knew.

A new "Wonder of the World" lay before us. We gawked with the same breathlessness that an astronaut must have had when he first stood on the surface of the moon.

Our faces naturally turned toward each other. No evidence of the exhaustion we all felt showed in anyone's face. I sent my sister an "I told you so" smile. She returned a smile of gratitude.

Jenny was the first to follow the urge we all felt to walk across the chalky white ground between where we stood and the edge of the cliff. Garth and I watched her go.

I saw Garth, out of the corner of my eye, open his mouth and bend forward to grasp the air, as if intuition was suggesting he should call Jenny back. But he stopped himself and no sound came out of his mouth. It was three, no—it was only two seconds later, that a terrible shriek drowned out the sound of the mighty waterfalls. Unknown to us, the ground upon which Jenny stood was no more than a thin crystal shelf overhanging the river. In one horrible instant, the ground around Jennifer collapsed. Her scream sank with her.

In terror, I cried my sister's name and lunged forward. Garth and I now stood upon the rim, looking helplessly into the white current. A whirlpool had caught her. Her struggling was useless and the river twirled her in an angry circle, dragging her toward the cavern where the river disappeared.

The panic I felt, knowing that in a few more seconds my eleven-year-old sister would sink into that black tunnel forever, ignited my brotherly instincts. My actions were involuntary. I leaped off the cliff, thinking somehow that I had the power to rescue her. The same insanity had also overcome my friend Garth. He fell after me and, with wheeling arms, we dropped fifty feet, slapping into the icy, rushing water. I realized I was powerless. The river had no conscience. It had captured a rare prey inside its throat and was preparing to swallow. The light of the Rainbow Room grew dim through splashing water. I was pulled into the cave, choking and swallowing huge gulps. The current had become very powerful and fast. The will to fight for air was leaving me. I faded in and out of consciousness from that moment on. I remember a fleeting image of the light returning, like a near-death experience. The water became green and warm. I remember breathing again and coughing water from my lungs. Then I fell asleep for what could have been anywhere between an hour and eternity.

CHAPTER 5

I woke up spitting sand from my lips, my eyes blinking. Squeezing my fist, I filled it with dark, smooth mud. My chest lay flat against a bank of earth. There was water lapping against my hips; my shoes were submerged. The rest of my clothes were stiff, having dried in the sun. To my right, my sister was sprawled in the same position, a brown button of dirt on the end of her nose. She was still unconscious, her body tangled in and around a patch of reeds growing along the edge of a blue-green lagoon surrounded by a black-green jungle.

I rolled onto my back and squinted at the sun, hoping the heat would burn focus back into my eyes. Nothing changed. I shut them tightly and tried again. I opened my eyes the second time and found the sun blocked. A shadow covered my face. Garth's silhouette perched overhead and studied me for signs of life.

"How do you feel?" he said.

"Garth," I asked, "Are we dead?"

He wouldn't answer. With his hand as a visor, he gazed across the lagoon. Offshore about twenty feet, the water bubbled and erupted. This caused tiny ripples to lap against the shore. An underground spring filled the lagoon with cooler water. Had we come up through that spring?

Garth wiped the smudge of dirt from his forehead and tried to straighten out the tangle in his hair with a sweep of his fingers. An icing of dark mud covered the front of his yellow Nike shirt.

I dragged my body from the water. My tennis shoes squeaked and drained. The scene around me was chilling. This is Africa, I thought. I'm in a *Tarzan* movie.

"My name is Jamie Hawkins. I live in Cody, Wyoming. I go to Cody Junior High School," I mumbled to myself.

I was interrupted by a twittering bird—beautiful, like nothing I'd ever heard. Looking for the bird, my eyes focused on the roots of the mighty jungle trees. They jutted up from the earth like a candle out of its own glob of melted wax. A velvety-green skin covered the bark. I looked up the trunk in time to see a strange squirrel dart behind a limb. It had a long upturned nose and a ringed tail. The little head poked back out from around the limb, eyes peering, as interested in us as I was in him.

I'd never imagined so much green in one place at one time. It wasn't just the greens either. There were deep reds and browns, yellows and oranges. The jungle floor was covered with giant leaves the color of emeralds. The earth was like chocolate. The one missing color was gray. Wyoming gray was nowhere in the jungle.

I only recognized one plant. Certain trees had scraggly bark leading up to a canopy of fingered leaves. These had to be palm trees; I'd seen them on postcards. Under the canopy hung yellow-brown globes that were certainly coconuts.

"It's a vision," said Garth.

"Then we're all having the same vision," I responded.

"When Joseph Smith and Sidney Rigdon wrote the 76th section of the Doctrine and Covenants, they both had the same vision."

"Then what's God trying to tell us?"

The sound of my voice caused Jenny to stir. I went over and helped my little sister to her feet. When her jaw dropped upon seeing the surroundings, it was clear the vision had three participants.

"Where are we?" We left it to Jennifer to ask the obvious.

"The center of the earth," I said half seriously. "Either that or Africa."

"It could be South America," added Garth. "The Amazon. It might be even New Guinea or Australia."

I couldn't believe he even wasted his energy guessing. If I'd have said we were on another planet, it would have been just as valid.

"Jim, I'm sick." Jenny cupped her belly in her right hand. The other hand rose to a pair of swollen lips as she stumbled into the edge of the trees and emptied water from her stomach.

Garth was sorting the remains from his backpack. My own pack and my windbreaker had been sucked right off my shoulders in the underground river. Two of the flashlights were drenched and useless. The other one was waterproof. The light still worked. The granola bars resembled creamed oatmeal, unsalvageable. Garth's large Eagle pocketknife had survived. We also retained the plastic match box, with about twenty-five dry wooden matches. That concluded our grim list of supplies.

We wandered along the lake's edge for half an hour, watching the birds and squirrels jump from tree to tree. The sky had gathered a few clouds. I didn't think there were enough clouds for a downpour, yet pour down it did. The surface of the lake became riddled with tiny holes. Again, our clothing was drenched.

We found a footpath leading into the jungle. Thinking the trees might serve as umbrellas, we started to follow the path. A hundred yards down the path, the rain stopped. Warm runoff from the high jungle leaves continued to drip on our shoulders. The evaporating water created a steam that screened the sun. Salty sweat melted down my forehead and dripped off the tip of my nose.

A little further on, the jungle path ended. Below my feet stretched a stone-laid road. Though crusted with dirt, it was solid evidence—civilization existed in these parts. It was a kind of cobblestone and it made the jungle appear as though it had an arched tunnel cut through it. The rain came and went so fast that the road didn't have time to cool. Steam seeped up from the hot stones. It reminded me of the mudpot walkways in Yellowstone.

"Which way?" Garth asked.

I chose the direction. Nobody argued. My decision was to travel deeper into the jungle, away from the lake.

All this walking was getting to me. My tennis shoes were damp, so each step ground a bigger blister on my ankles. Judging by the shadow stretching across the cobbled road, the sun was getting low. A hollow noise started to churn in my stomach. It was Jennifer who complained of hunger first. I resented her grumbling, since she'd eaten the last dry granola bar when we were back in reality.

As if things weren't bad enough, the rain came down again. We sat on the edge of the road. Our hair dripping, our heads drooping, we looked like a litter of lost puppies.

Garth reached into his hip pocket and brought out the Eagle pocketknife. By force of habit, his thumb tested the edge. Then his eyes scanned the palm trees overhead.

I knew what my friend was thinking—but I hated coconuts. Any time I'd ever found coconut flakes in my mixed chocolates, I put the bitten sample back in the box. My mom said she'd never known a pickier eater than yours truly. I gagged on green peppers. Onions turned my stomach. I could eat peas only while pinching my nose. This moment was a first in my life. I truly didn't know where my next meal was coming from. Choice was a luxury I no longer had. Mom would gloat.

Garth stood under a palm tree, looking helpless. I asked to see his knife at the same time that I snatched it away. As any good Tarzan would do, I stuck the knife between my teeth and bowed my legs around the trunk. Pushing upward, I focused my eyes on those yellow globes.

Twenty feet later, the coconuts dangled at arm's length. I looked down and panted, to prove my effort. Garth and Jenny stood anxiously below, like hounds under a treed coon. Awkwardly, I chopped at the first coconut until it dropped to the jungle floor with a heavy thud, bursting open with an explosion of coconut milk. A second one fell, and then a third.

After shimmying down the tree, I found my two companions kneeling before the open one, licking a gooey white film from their fingers. It was all they could scrape from the coconut's inner shell without a knife. We took turns chopping, prying, and then chewing the coconut chunks.

By twisting the blade, we bored a hole in the top of one of the unbroken coconuts, chugging the sweet milk inside. Nothing had ever been quite as satisfying.

Three gutted coconut shells were left in the jungle dirt. Reenergized, we moved on, sucking at the coconut stuck in our teeth as we went.

Only a hundred yards farther, a small portion of ground had been cleared. But the ground wasn't naked. It exhibited four very distinct structures—houses. Or huts if you prefer. They were circular, built of thatched branches with a kind of plaster in between. The pointed roofs were laid with dried palm leaves, layer upon layer. The doors were built of criss-crossing sticks. Behind the huts was a large garden separated into sections by short fences of stones. There was corn, although the stalks had been stomped to the ground. There were other crops, also uprooted. The clearing was carpeted with yellow and tan leaves. A thin pathway of deep-red earth led to each door.

As we closed in, the wind slapped us with the smell of rotting meat. A large pile of animal bones lay near the path, picked almost clean. Other garbage was mixed into the pile: husks of corn, fruit peelings, and broken pottery. A few birds fluttered away with scraps in their beaks. Ants and flies helped themselves to what remained. We passed a structure without doors—just wide entrances on either side. Perhaps most of the stink came from the half-cooked carcass propped over a cold fireplace within, crawling with every unmentionable form of life. This particular construction had a hole designed into the ceiling to let smoke escape when preparing meals—meals, I hoped, that were normally less decomposed.

Everybody seemed to have up and left, maybe a week ago, maybe earlier. Things were a mess. Nothing was in place. My mother wouldn't have been impressed with a woman who left her home in such condition, whatever the excuse. I found a shiny green pebble in a silver setting lying right in the dirt. There was a hole in the top, as if it had once hung as a necklace. I wanted to show my treasure off to Garth, but his hands were busy examining a rock slab, about the size of a bread box. Upon it was an hourglass-shaped stone. Garth curled the stone into his hand.

"A corn grinder," Garth declared. "Indians call 'em *metates*."

Stepping onto the central hut's stone porch, I called "Hello"—not because I expected an answer, but to make it look a little less like trespassing when I pulled open the door and invited myself inside. Jenny followed me in. Two hammocks were strung from wall to wall. Each was lined with soft gray and white fur, as soft as rabbit—maybe it *was* rabbit. Oh, it looked comfortable. So comfortable I began to feel dizzy.

My legs collapsed and I rolled into the hammock. Jenny rolled into another one. At that point my day ended. I shut my eyes and listened to the rain start up again, purring peacefully upon the roof of the little jungle hut.

Late that night, I was awakened by the quiet peep of my sister softly crying. She had crawled into my hammock and cuddled beside me. Her body temperature made the muggy night more unbearable. After curbing my first impulse to push her out, I figured if I ever needed an example to prove I had compassion, I could use this.

"Jenny," I whispered, "you OK?"

She swallowed. "Are we being punished, Jim?"

"Punished? By whom?"

"By God."

"No," I answered. And then I thought about it. "Why? Did you do something really wrong?"

Sniffling, she nodded, "A lot of things."

"Tell me one."

"You remember over Memorial Day when I babysat for the Carters? I forgot to pay tithing. Three and a half dollars."

My sister could be such a flake. "That's nothing. I owe almost fifteen. Maybe more. I lost count."

"God *is* punishing us." My sister was confident.

"No, no, no," I scoffed. "Garth pays every penny. Probably even *fifteen* percent. So why would God be punishing *him*?"

"He must have done something else. He never told his mom and dad about going to Frost Cave. That's breaking the fourth commandment—'Honor your father and your mother that your days may be long upon the land.' So he was sent to a different land."

"If that were true, every kid I know would be here with us. We could have a party. So go back to sleep."

Jenny let out a long sigh. "Jim, will we ever get home again?"

"We'll figure it out tomorrow. Good night, Jen."

I lay awake until Jennifer stopped stirring. Her breathing slowed to a steady rhythm. I could hear Garth in the other hammock. Crickets chirping in the jungle surpassed his snoring, like a million tiny whistles. Back home, up North Fork Valley, singing crickets meant the forest was empty, safe. Nothing wild was about. That thought filled me with security. I could close my eyes again and drift away.

Bright and early, we were working our dried and stiffened tennis shoes soft again upon the cobbled road. The puffy clouds were floating. No more rain came for the time being.

The further we walked, the more houses and farms we saw. Huts came in all shapes and sizes—round and square—I saw one that was rectangular with two round rooms built on each end. Often the plaster was painted—pale red and off-white, some yellow, some green.

A variety of colorful clay pots, urns, and dishes sat around the yards on wooden tables and stone benches. Under a palm canopy that sat along the road, I touched a frame with five snake skins, stretched and tied. The serpents must have been very fat—the skins were three to four feet long and at least ten inches wide. Each skin's pattern looked like finger painting. The taxidermist had left the heads attached. The snakes' eyes seemed to be looking at me. It was eerie.

There were a couple of turkeys running loose through the neighborhood. The skinny birds were excited to see us, trotting on over, expecting a handout.

Every patch of ground was stripped. Not a bean on the stalk. The gardens had been uprooted deliberately. I wondered why. It was like somebody knew we were coming and decided to starve us out.

Above the doorway of one hut, we found husks of drying corn. Garth cut it down. We picked off the kernels, chewing each and every one. The hungry turkeys made us feel selfish. They would have changed their attitude if they knew I was considering them as a second course.

We were acting like alley dogs. The three of us looked miserable—dirty, sticky, and smelly. What else could I complain about? Oh yeah—the weeds along the paths had deposited stickers under my shoelaces that were driving me nuts. It was useless to try and pick them all out.

I climbed another palm tree. Afterward, we sat in a quiet circle in the shade, chewing the contents of four or five more coconuts. While Jennifer was methodically lapping every gooey drop from her fingers, something in the jungle caught her eye and she stopped licking.

There was somebody there. Although we could see only snatches between the trees, we were sure a person was walking casually toward the main complex of houses. We crept into the brush and vines for a closer look.

At first I thought it was a boy since the figure was so short. But on closer investigation, it was a man—an old man. There was a walking stick in one of his hands and a netting filled with fresh fruits and vegetables in the other. If the fruit had grown around here, it must have been his own private stash. Covering his body was a white pullover of sorts—made of gunnysack-like material.

His skin was very tan. His hair, a mixture of black and gray. The lines in his face and the knobbiness of his limbs confirmed his age.

We ran from tree to tree, following him while trying to keep ourselves hidden. I stepped in a rut and accidentally ground some stones together. The old man stopped. We scrambled to hide, but he didn't bother to turn around. He waited a moment, then continued.

We pursued. As we drew a little closer, it became clear that his walking stick was used for more than balance. He was blind—or darned close to it.

He stopped again. The tip of his cane plunged into the dirt and those skinny legs halted. Keeping his back to us, he started to speak.

"I hear you," the gravelly voice began. "Am I worth it? I don't know as I'd be much of a prisoner. If you want a quetzal feather you'll have to do me in. Though I'm old and blind, I promise to put up a worthy fight. Probably kill half of you. No matter how harmless I may seem, you better know the blood running in my veins is that of a Nephite."

CHAPTER 6

He introduced himself as Onin, a Samite by birth. It didn't take him long to decide we weren't Lamanites. He used our reluctance to speak as proof.

"Lamanite warriors love to interrupt any time a Nephite opens his mouth," he said.

"Nephites," he added, "love to talk and find it particularly annoying to be quieted."

Had he known why our tongues were tied, he'd have been the quiet one. My body became an icicle when he used the word "Nephite." The old man was sincerely convinced he was one, and proud of it.

I'd heard that word used all my life—inside the walls of my stake center, in family home evenings, and in morning readings, sitting sleepy-eyed in my living room—Mom reading the Book of Mormon chapter after chapter. It was a ritual that lasted almost two years, until Mom got sick, and the habit was never reestablished.

Onin was also convinced we weren't Nephites.

"No Nephite in his right mind would be wandering in this country in such small numbers."

He asked how many were in our party. But before Garth could answer, Onin raised one hand and looked thoughtfully toward the sky, tapping two fingers on his chin.

"Three," he determined. "Where are you from?"

Once again, he wouldn't wait for a response. The guy thought he was Sherlock Holmes.

"The north. And you're hunting. Am I right?"

We looked at one another, choosing silence. Our silence only encouraged him. The old man grinned confidently.

"Are you hungry?" he asked.

"Yes," Jennifer squeaked.

Jenny's voice caused a rise in those bushy eyebrows. His two fingers went to tapping his chin again.

"A woman! And a child, for that matter—ten, maybe eleven years old. I've heard it said, the mighty men from the north are companioned by mighty women. Still, that's a very long journey for a youngster. Are you all hungry? Come to my home," Onin invited. "We'll have papaya and beans."

If I'd had a choice, I'd have taken breakfast at McDonald's, but as dull as my diet had been the last twenty-four hours, this stuff sounded great. After entering his hut, the old man used his cane to direct us into a circle around a modest stone fireplace. Blindness didn't seem to slow his hands in preparing a meal for four. I'll bet he'd meant the food he'd just collected to last him three or four days. Our host was being a little more generous than I probably appreciated.

"You're in bad country," Onin declared. "The East Wilderness is no place for man or beast now that the rains seem to be lettin' up. A plague is coming."

"You mean a disease is coming?" asked Garth.

"Yep. The disease is hate and the carriers are the children of Laman. They hate Nephites. Have now for better'n five hundred years. I'd have thought the legend would have carried even to your country."

"We know the legend," Garth assured him.

" 'Course you do." Onin presented each of us with a bowl of

food: brown beans, cold but soft, and a half-cut of fruit that looked pinkish and mushy.

"Where's everybody gone?" I asked.

"You missed 'em by eight days. Most of the able-bodied men went to Nephihah or to Moroni. The rest to Zarahemla. Those bound for the capital wanted me to tag along, but I think my days on that trail are over. Was a time when I used to walk it once a season. It doesn't matter. To kill an old blind man is the act of a coward. When the Lamanites come, worst I'll probably get is a little spit and a lot a cussin'. I can return the same. Don't want to, though. Gotta watch my tongue. The wife is listening." He made that last statement pointing upward with his finger.

Onin continued, "I had a son once—just like you two. He was a war hero. A soldier under Captain Lehi. Fell in battle on the Sidon seven years ago, in the service of God."

I was shoving food down my throat so fast I didn't catch the meaning of Onin's statement. But not a word from the old man's lips got past Garth. A morsel of food that he had balanced on his wooden utensil dropped back into the bowl. Garth's bright green eyes were distant. He walked to the doorway and stared off into the jungle, sweat tumbling down his forehead.

"The Lamanite king is Amalickiah," said Garth.

"Yes, Amalickiah," Onin replied. "Now there's a name worth cussin'. Hate to see that snake get famous."

"I know where we are," whispered Garth, "and I know when we are."

The bits and pieces were adding up in my mind too. I'd given up on Santa Claus and the tooth fairy, and I never did believe in Wonderland or Oz, but I now believe in the Land of Mormon. Did we travel in time? Was this some kind of vision? I might never know. But today I was sitting in a Nephite's home, eating Nephite beans. A Nephite breeze was blowing through the doorway, making the bangs dance on Garth's forehead.

Onin looked a bit confused by Garth's tone. He tapped his fingers on his chin. Sherlock was not to be beaten.

"Lost, eh? I'll tell you exactly where you are. This here's the East Wilderness of the Land of Zarahemla. The virgin country. I was here before the settlement program. In those years you couldn't walk to the river in broad daylight without a bow. The land belonged to the Nephites, but the Lamanites didn't care much about borders. I couldn't keep a flock of turkeys together for more than a moon before half my birds were missin' or killed. It was a grateful day when the army finally drove 'em out."

The old man went on and on, mostly about his son, the great warrior. Onin mentioned, in passing, that he had met and spoken with Captain Teancum on several occasions. Teancum was a local hero of sorts, reared most of his life in a nearby valley called Jershon. He said even the great Moroni had been through these lands several years before, recruiting. But Onin was sightless by then and couldn't describe his face to us. He said it was the only time he regretted the Lord taking his vision.

Jenny asked about the possibility of a bath. Garth and I were getting used to the grungy feeling. I almost told her "when in Rome, do as the Romans." After all, Onin didn't use any kind of deodorant. Yet, a dip in cool water did sound good. Onin waved his hand more or less eastward.

"Any trail across the road'll take you to the river."

It was more of a creek, but it did look refreshing. The water that rumbled around the rocks was a pale gray color, not too appetizing for drinking, but good for soaking. It looked like any river back home in the spring. Only Wyoming runoff was more brownish. Brightly colored moss and flowers grew on all the boulders. Lizards leapt from stone to stone. Downstream, the villagers had built up a dam. As a result, a neck-deep pool had been created. I yearned to have my sticky body surrounded by every gallon.

My sister wasn't pleased when Garth and I peeled down to our briefs, and charged the water like Teddy on San Juan Hill. Even as filthy as she felt, her modesty insisted she wasn't getting in until we got out. She planted herself on the bank of green lawn surrounding the pool, shutting her eyes until we were under.

In unison, Garth and I yelled and did swan dives, disappearing under the cool gray surface. I propelled myself upwards, causing a wonderful explosion. Then I swam freestyle and Garth swam breaststroke over to the stone dam.

Boulders had been piled up to make the dam. On the other side, the creek wound through the greenery. Boulders below the surface served nicely as chairs. A velvety moss on the submerged stones made a comfortable cushion. Garth and I stretched back our arms, laid our heads in a couple of grooves between the boulders, and let the cool current rush around our necks.

I happened to glance at Garth and caught him exhibiting another one of those thoughtful expressions that made me nervous.

"We gotta get outa here, Jim."

"I know," I said.

Garth changed my interpretation. "I mean out of this land."

"Why?"

"Amalickiah is coming. Onin said the Nephites have only been gathering in the walled cities for a couple weeks at the most. So it hasn't happened yet."

"I'm not following you. Who's Amal—er—that guy you said, and what's about to happen?"

"Trust me. We need to get outa here."

Garth swam back. I didn't appreciate being left hanging.

Sis finally got her turn in the water. Garth and I sat on the bank, our backs to the pool.

"There's just one thing that really bothers me," he began.

"Yeah, what?" I humored him.

"The Book of Mormon wasn't originally written in English. It was written in Reformed Egyptian. And that was only because the Nephites thought Hebrew wasn't as easy to put on plates."

"So?" I hoped this scholarly hoopla had some point behind it.

"So why doesn't Onin speak Hebrew? Or at least some Nephite form of Hebrew? Onin speaks English. In fact, if his voice were a little deeper, I'd think he was my grandfather. And how is it that he understands us? It doesn't make sense, Jim."

"You're losing it, Garth. Wake up, Mr. Potato Head. This whole thing doesn't make any sense. Remember?"

Climbing back into my smelly clothes kinda took away the fresh feeling I got from the pool. Arriving back at Onin's hut, we found the old man asleep in his hammock. Garth interrupted him in the middle of a deep snore and asked directions to the City of Moroni.

"You'll get there midday tomorrow if you stick to the road," he yawned, "Or if you take my trail you could be there tonight."

"Where does your trail start?" Garth asked.

"It starts right here, but I guarantee you, my boy, you'll find yourself neck deep in swamp if you try to take it without a guide."

"We have no guide," I informed him.

"So you haven't."

Onin closed his eyes again. I wasn't even sure why a blind man felt he had to.

"Let me nap through the heat a while," Onin slowly drifted away, "then I'll take you there. Tomorrow's the Sabbath. It'll be a welcome change to spend it with people."

One instant later, he was out.

The cliché of "blind leading the blind" ran through my mind. The idea of spending another afternoon hoofing through the jungle didn't thrill me. My temper was raw. When we stepped out of the hut I laid into Garth.

"What are you trying to do to us? We've done nothing but walk for two days!"

"I've got blisters on every toe!" Jenny added.

"What's so important in Moroni?" I demanded.

"We have to warn them, Jim. In a matter of days—maybe hours—the Lamanite army, under Amalickiah's command, will overrun this whole country. Moroni is the first city to fall, that is, if it hasn't fallen already."

"How do you know?" I had to ask.

"It's all in Alma, chapter fifty-one. The rainy season is ending. The Nephite soldiers are gathering in the cities. For months they've been building fortifications and digging ditches for defense. Look around you! Everybody living in farm settlements like this has evacuated. Don't you understand? They know Amalickiah is coming. They just don't know where he'll strike first. We might save the whole city!"

I felt myself swallow. "Wouldn't we be tampering with history or something?"

"It doesn't matter," Garth insisted. "We're still accountable. Just because in the last days the world will be desperately wicked doesn't mean we don't do our part to fight it. Just because Joseph Smith knew he would be killed by the mob didn't mean he shouldn't defend himself. We *have* to go to the City Moroni. We need to find Captain Moroni. There are things we know that could save thousands of lives!"

Not things I knew. Things *Garth* knew. I barely had an inkling of what he was talking about. Walking into a war zone wasn't my idea of a pleasant afternoon. Then something started to well up inside me. I raised my shoulders and stood up straight. Captain Moroni, I repeated in my mind. Garth was serious. The name of Captain Moroni stirred up visions of courage and might that very few men could equal. One year a four-star general rode in Cody's Fourth of July Parade. I shook his hand. He looked me right in the eye and growled, "Do you love your country, son?" I nodded yes, and answered, "Uh-huh," and left my mouth hanging open. The thought of shaking the hand of Captain Moroni sent my imagination spinning in circles.

I can firmly report, I had a change of attitude. If Garth had suddenly decided against the trip, I'm sure I would have insisted. Unfortunately, Jenny didn't share the enthusiasm.

"I won't go!" she stammered. "I'm *not* going!"

"You want to stay here alone?"

"Jim, *please*," she begged, "I'm afraid."

I put my arm around her. "We'll protect you, Sis."

The old "big brother" ploy was losing its touch. She pulled away.

"I want to go home!" She collapsed and started to blubber.

Little sisters. They drive me crazy. No sense of adventure. After an hour she unwillingly consented to come. Really, she had no other option.

Onin emerged from his hut, smacking his tongue on the roof of his mouth. He carried his cane and wore a leather pouch over his shoulder—a Nephite canteen.

"If you need water, there's a barrel around back."

"Do you have any more water pouches?" Garth asked.

Onin was surprised by our lack of travel gear, considering the distance we'd supposedly come. Nevertheless, he supplied each of us with one of his own water pouches. Onin had also packed a hefty supply of papaya and jerky.

I imagined what would happen if Onin could see the contents of Garth's backpack. I'd seen jungle movies where the natives were shown radios or rifles and went nuts. I'd bet Garth's flashlight would have had the same effect.

I soon missed the luxury of the Nephite paved road under our feet. Onin led us into the jungle—I mean *really* into the jungle. Most of the time we couldn't see the sun. Our legs were constantly hurdling massive tree roots crossing the trail. The old man repeatedly asked us to describe what we saw.

"Swamp on both sides," I would answer.

"Good," he would respond.

He echoed that answer for the next two hours. At first it was reassuring, then it got tiresome.

"Are you sure you know where we're going?"

"I've taken this trail a hundred times, boy," he snapped. "'Course I'm sure."

I started to feel claustrophobic, like in the cave. If only I could climb the trees, just to see the sky again and breathe it in. Every other step, a spider web snapped across my nose and stuck to my cheek. There were always splashes along the swamp's bank fifteen or twenty feet ahead—something escaping into the murky water, creating ripples in the mossy surface, leaving a black hole behind. I never saw what was creating the splash. I wasn't sure I wanted to know.

To my relief, the trail began to take us out of the low swamp and into a hilly forest. We climbed up and down one gully after another, never knowing what lay even ten yards ahead. It began raining as it usually did at this time of day. My soaked clothes stuck to my body once again.

To tell the truth, I actually enjoyed the rain. I felt like the bath I'd taken earlier was just to change sweat. The weather in this land was the pits—like a steam bath! I'd never get used to it.

There came a moment, late that afternoon—I couldn't guess the time without seeing the sun—when the birds became much less noisy. Maybe they were always quiet at this time. Maybe it was because the rain had stopped, I don't know. But when I realized how quiet it had become, I stopped.

My hesitation caused some concern for Garth and Jenny. When Onin didn't hear our footfalls, he stopped as well. I expected the old man to grumble, "What's the holdup?" He said nothing—took a step back toward our position and stood perfectly still.

Garth wanted to ask me what was wrong, but he didn't. Jenny also stayed silent. We just looked at one another for an uncomfortable amount of time, an embarrassing amount of time.

The branches were still dripping rain from the earlier cloudburst. I could hear every drop break against the ground. The hot earth caused a mist to hang low throughout the jungle. The deeper into the trees I focused my eyes, the thicker the mist appeared.

Then I saw the shapes; human silhouettes that floated in the distant mist like angels in a cloud. But they were not angels. The figures were dark and still. They watched us like mountain lions watch an aimless fawn.

One of them began a chilling scream. The others joined in. If the screams were meant to confuse and frighten us, the tactic worked. Eight warriors, armed with spears and bows, surrounded us on every side. They wore strips of skin about their loins. Black had been painted onto their chins and chests. A filthy and unwashed crop of dark hair stood straight up from their heads like a bushel of grain—bound with a leather strap. To be honest, I found the hairstyle extremely silly. But under the circumstances, I didn't laugh.

These, I was certain, were Lamanites.

The tallest one was nearly six foot. A couple of them were no taller than I was. But with those weapons waving in my face, they *appeared* much taller. To get us to stand closer together, one of the miserable cusses slapped me in the face with his spear, just below the obsidian point. I'm sure it left a bruise.

One of them gave Onin a shove. "This one is a Nephite!"

Our fair complexions made it clear to them we weren't locals. Almost immediately, grubby fingers were poking and pinching the material of our clothes. One of them rubbed his fingers along Garth's arm, as if he were trying to wipe off the freckles.

The one who appeared to be the filthiest yanked on a strand of my little sister's blonde hair. "Look at this one!" he grunted. "Golden!"

You'd have thought the guy had never seen a blonde before. It didn't occur to me that maybe he hadn't.

"What do we do with them?" one Lamanite asked of the group.

"They're spies," another replied.

Onin laughed. "They think we're spies." Onin seemed to think he was translating their words. He continued, "I'll wager every one of them can speak Hebrew. They mumble that Lamanite gibberish to unnerve us."

"Quiet, Nephite dog!" Onin was slapped.

"Leave him alone," the tallest Lamanite commanded. This one was younger, mid-twenties maybe, but he had the voice of authority.

"You three are not Nephite. What are you?" the tall one asked.

"We're American," Jenny bragged.

They weren't impressed. I don't think the title had much clout in these parts.

"We're from the North," Garth explained.

"What are you called?"

"Jim Hawkins," I humbly answered. "This is my sister, Jenny."

"Your sister?" repeated the filthy one and turned to Garth. "Is she your wife?"

The way that greasy slime was glaring at Jenny, I was hoping Garth would answer "yes" thinking it might protect her. Then I happened to notice that the Lamanite was gripping an obsidian knife as he asked. I cringe to think what might have happened if Garth had followed my instincts.

Garth looked a bit embarrassed. "No." He shook his head. "She's just Jim's sister."

People must get hitched awfully young around here, it occurred to me. Jenny was only eleven years old. Maybe she could pass for twelve, but Garth Plimpton, with that baby face and freckles, didn't look a day over thirteen.

Another Lamanite addressed the taller one. This guy had painted a red bull's-eye right in the center of his chin. "Middoni, she could be a gift for the king. Our kinship might regain his graces."

Middoni nodded thoughtfully. The filthy Lamanite was still grinning rudely at Jenny. I could tell she was somewhere between fainting and slapping him in the face. The grin was erased when Onin unexpectedly whacked him in the face with his walking stick. It was a hefty whack. Old Onin was one surprise after another.

Blood streamed from the filthy Lamanite's nose. He threw Onin to the ground and laid the obsidian blade against his throat. The Lamanite was so angry I could see the veins bulging in his neck.

Middoni's firm hand grabbed his comrade's shoulder.

"He's old and blind, Amgiddi. The curse would be heavy."

Amgiddi regretfully backed away. Middoni continued, "Well leave him. He'll die in the jungle. These three spies will come with us. You could be right," he said to the guy with the bull's-eye on his chin. "The gift could redeem us."

They didn't waste time. Jenny, Garth, and I were herded off the trail and into the raw jungle. I turned and got one last look at Onin. He was standing again, holding his cane in the air. "God bless Captain Moroni!" he yelled. "God bless Captain Teancum!"

Upon hearing those names, the Lamanites spat in the dirt. Since Onin was blind, the display must have been for their own comfort. The old man faded from view, but we heard his voice chanting for some time. "God bless Judge Pahoran!" was the last cry I could make out before Onin's voice faded out completely.

"Where are you taking us?" Garth had the guts to demand.

"Shut up!" Amgiddi barked. "Your next words will be spoken before our Great and Terrible Lord, Amalickiah."

CHAPTER 7

Shortly after our capture, Jenny collapsed from exhaustion and stress. Middoni carried her the rest of the day. Garth and I trotted along with a spear directed toward our backs while its bearer, Amgiddi, complained endlessly about the inconvenience of bringing us along. Jennifer's life, he insisted, was the only valuable one among the three—so why not leave the bodies of the two boys behind? Fortunately, Middoni disagreed.

That evening we slept in the dirt under the jungle stars, cuddled together. Lamanite guards were posted throughout the night, each taking his shift. Poor Jennifer was out like a light. She didn't seem to be taking this well. I was worried about her.

Garth's brain was still doing a mile a minute. He had a theory and he whispered it to me.

"We have the gift of tongues," he said. "That's why they understand what we're saying. In our own ears it still sounds like we're speaking in English, but to them, it sounds like we're speaking in whatever language they're most accustomed to."

"How do we understand what they're saying?" I asked.

"We also have the gift of the interpretation of tongues. We understand every word they say, and they understand every word we say—even if they don't understand each other."

"How do you figure we got these gifts?" I asked.

"The same way anyone gets a spiritual gift. It has to be given to you from On High. Before the Tower of Babel, there was only one language. I believe God has recreated that setting for the three of us. We've been very blessed."

"I don't feel particularly blessed at the moment," I replied.

It became Middoni's shift. He sat back on a thick dead log. A beam of moonlight found a hole in the jungle branches and illuminated his face. Middoni was the only one among the eight, it seemed to me, with a level head. When the other warriors tried to strip us of our belongings, he defended us again. Since we weren't armed, he insisted there was no reason we shouldn't carry our own things.

Now, the stern and unmoving Middoni looked troubled. I saw Garth's hand feeling inside his backpack. He found a piece of jerky and called to Middoni.

"Want some meat?" Middoni's concentration was broken by Garth's voice.

"No," he said. "Sleep. We'll be marching again before the sun is up."

Middoni returned to his pose in the moonlight. Garth decided to try his luck with another question.

"What will they do to us?" he asked.

"You will be tried as spies," Middoni said.

"But we're not spies," Garth asserted.

Middoni paused before responding. "Then you will go free."

There was no confidence behind Middoni's promise. In truth, I don't think he expected us to see freedom again. I sensed a thread of guilt in his voice.

"Are you from the land of Middoni?" Garth asked.

"No!" Middoni was insulted. "There is no longer such a land. They became Nephites."

"Garth—" I nudged my friend to back off.

He kept quiet for about a minute, then he whispered to me, "The land of Middoni was converted by the sons of Mosiah, remember? I thought that's why he was friendlier."

"Friendlier?" I asked. "That's probably why he hates us."

Garth ignored me. "Still, if that's so, why would his attitude be different than the others? All eight of these guys are more than likely in the same kinship. Yet I sense a different spirit about Middoni."

"Garth, please. I'm begging. Shut up."

Garth persisted. He sat up and called back to Middoni, "Have you ever met a Christian?"

I'd befriended an imbecile. I couldn't have imagined a greater blunder under these circumstances. Middoni arose and walked toward us. The moonlight flashed on his drawn obsidian blade.

"Talk again," Middoni threatened, "and I'll slice out your tongues. I promise you."

Needless to say, we were perfectly quiet after that—except for a short sarcastic statement that I whispered very close to Garth's ear. "Different spirit, huh?"

Before the sun was up, we were marching again. Our eight slave-drivers maintained a dizzying pace the better part of the morning. Jenny gave out again, twenty minutes after sunrise. Once more, Middoni became her taxi. The jungle began to thin around midday. Grass and tall leafy scrub took the place of trees. I saw hundreds of iguanas. I'm not kidding. They were everywhere.

We forged a murky river, or should I say, we swam it. Out in the middle, the water reached my armpits. Climbing onto the opposite bank, the Lamanites tore leeches off their legs with the same lack of concern that I would give to swatting a mosquito. My hands were trembling as I pulled one of the slimy worms off my wrist. Garth found one attached to his ankle. Carrying the pack overhead had protected his arms.

It was hard to shake the disgust. There was a knot in my stomach as I pinched and felt every square inch of my body to be sure I was clean.

We hadn't traveled fifty yards into the scrub on the other side of the river when a city of tents filled our view, pitched at random, sometimes in circles. Fires were built in the middle of most circles. Thousands of Lamanite warriors were making preparations for war. They fashioned and sharpened weapons: clubs, spears, bows—I saw one warrior swinging a weapon that looked particularly fierce, testing its weight. It was a club; the edge exhibited a jawline of obsidian blades on either side. The warriors wore a variety of colorful bracelets on each ankle. Their loincloths looked like (dare I say) big diapers. The majority had their hair tied on top, like Middoni's kinship. Others wore it cut in a perfect circle around their head, like a nerdy 60's rock star. Some soldiers were repairing or fitting a kind of protective armor for their chest and arms.

The clothing consisted of fabric and animal skins, sewn together with sand in between the layers. Other Lamanites were gathering and arranging food. Iguanas were hanging every-where—still alive. Their top and bottom legs had been hooked together by twisting the claws, forming a painful-looking hog-tie. Some lizards were turning over a spit. When I saw one being eaten, I lost my appetite. The carcasses of many small deer were being skinned. If Garth hadn't pointed out the fact that deer didn't get any bigger in this part of the world, I might have concluded these scoundrels only killed yearlings. As our party walked through the camp, we drew a lot of stares. Several times, a man walked up to Middoni and asked where the "tall, pale children" had come from.

"Where's the king's tent?" Amgiddi asked one in return.

The man pointed us in the proper direction. As we walked away, I saw him draw the attention of others, pointing at Jenny upon Middoni's shoulders. "Do you see? Hair of gold!"

We arrived at a circle of tents in the center of camp. All the tents were brightly colored with intricate designs and symbols painted onto the surfaces. The tent that stood in the middle of the circle was the largest of them all. A dozen men could have slept inside.

Lamanite runners had gone before us, announcing our arrival. A man emerged from an outer tent surrounded by many servants. He was dressed in a colorful costume and wore a head-dress with many feathers and precious stones, as I might have expected from a Lamanite leader. But his face was different. His features were less Indian-like. Actually that's not a very good description. I suppose he could have easily passed as an Indian, based on what I had seen in my limited wanderings. But his nose was smaller, his face was longer, and his skin lighter. Many characteristics were altogether different from those of a Lamanite. He was as tall, if not taller, than Middoni.

Our party stopped. Middoni set Jennifer down. She rubbed her eyes and hid behind my shoulder. Middoni approached the man.

"Our Lord, Ammoron," Middoni chanted. "May I speak?"

Ammoron answered, "You may not rise or look in my face. Neither you, nor your kinsmen. The curse on your family is not lifted." Ammoron raised his voice and stretched his arms, drawing the attention of all onlookers. "This is the family whose cowardice brought such great shame upon this nation at the Battle of Ammonihah—a battle never fought—because of the weakness of this man's father."

Middoni replied, but kept his eyes toward the dirt. "Captain Hamuel was not my father, my Lord. He was my uncle."

Ammoron was insulted. He kicked Middoni right in the face. Middoni fell back and held his bruised cheek in his hands.

When it came to Book of Mormon names, my vocabulary was limited to about seven people—Nephi, Lehi, Laman, Lemuel, both Moronis, and Mormon. There's no way I would have recognized the name of Ammoron. But for Garth, the sound of Ammoron's name sent a jolt through his body, turning him ghostly white.

"Is he the king?" I asked.

"No. The king's brother," mumbled Garth.

Ammoron continued ranting at Middoni. "If Captain Hamuel had not been killed at Noah, I would have placed a knife in his heart myself!"

Middoni regained his composure, and again bowed before Ammoron.

"Yes, of course," recalled Ammoron. "You are Middoni, are you not? Son of King Antiomno. Heir to the throne of the forgotten kingdom of Middoni."

"Please, my Lord," Middoni pleaded. "We have come to present a gift to the king, that the kinship's curse may be lifted."

Ammoron noticed our presence for the first time. Stepping forward, and stopping about five feet away, he gave his servants a disapproving glance. They noticed the indiscretion. Several men sprang forward, forcing the three of us onto our knees, in the same bowing position.

"Aren't children taught proper manners in your land?" Ammoron said to us. "In this land, commoners kneel to royalty."

Out of the corner of my eye, I caught Garth lifting his head to look into Ammoron's face. One of the servants slapped him on the crown.

"Avert your eyes," the servant commanded.

I could sense that Garth's conscience told him this man deserved no respect whatsoever. I was afraid Garth would cause trouble, just out of principle. He was a fanatic, remember? Fortunately, he kept his sights in the dirt.

"Where are they from?" Ammoron demanded.

Amgiddi answered, "My Lord, our group was one of the scouting parties under Captain Jacob's command, assessing strongholds around the City of Moroni. We were returning to report our findings. The two boys and the golden-haired girl were traveling with a Nephite. The Nephite was killed. The girl was brought as a present to King Amalickiah. The boys are spies and should be executed as such."

"What is the burden on this one's back?" asked Ammoron, pointing at Garth's pack. Garth defensively grabbed the shoulder straps. Ammoron smiled and directed a servant to bring it to him. Obviously, if this boy valued it enough to try and prevent it from being taken, it was worth a closer look. Reluctantly, Garth allowed the pack to be removed from his shoulders. Ammoron rolled it over admiringly in his greedy hands.

"How is it opened, boy?" he requested of Garth.

Garth hesitated to answer. It didn't matter. Ammoron figured out the zipper and pulled it back.

"Fascinating," said Ammoron. "Where can I find more of these? I want one for each of my chief captains."

Before Ammoron had even finished his offer, his curious fingers had latched onto the flashlight. This was the moment we'd all been waiting for. Ancient had finally met modern. Sparks were about to fly.

"What is this?" Ammoron demanded.

Garth swallowed. I shrugged, with a dumb look shrouding my face. Ammoron grew impatient.

"Answer me, boy!"

In a flash of brilliance, an idea popped into Garth's mind. One that would postpone our immediate execution.

"Let me show you," Garth put out his hand. A servant transferred the flashlight from Ammoron's palm into Garth's.

"This is a magical light used to see at night," he said. Garth pushed the switch forward and the bulb of the flashlight burned a dim yellow. It wasn't very impressive, because of the brightness of the sun right then. Nevertheless, the crowd gasped and stepped back. Ammoron's face displayed as much surprise as everyone else's.

"Is this a magician's trick?" he asked.

Garth switched off the flashlight, "Anyone can do this," he said. "But only if we teach them how."

He placed the light back into Ammoron's hand.

"Or," said Ammoron, "if you were watching closely and saw the trick."

Ammoron pushed the switch forward, as he'd seen Garth do. The light didn't work. Garth had loosened the head of the flashlight before returning it. The villain felt humiliated. He threw it forcefully onto the ground, shrieking. I found his behavior particularly immature. Not that I was about to tell him so. Ammoron dropped the pack as well.

"Return it to them," he ordered. "Take the girl. Adorn her properly. We'll present her to the king at the feast tonight. Guard the boys. Bring them also to the feast, with their little bag of tricks."

The pack and flashlight were piled back into Garth's arms. We could only hope the flashlight still worked after Ammoron's abuse. Jennifer latched onto my waist. Several Lamanites had to peel her away. She bit down hard on someone's hand. The man wailed in pain. The others laughed, admiring the little girl's feistiness. They dragged her into the circle of tents.

"No!" I screamed. "That's my sister!"

I was held fast.

Ammoron was about to retire to his own tent again. I watched Middoni make one last attempt to approach him, crawling like a dog, avoiding direct eye contact.

"Lord, it is our hope that the curse may be lifted from our kinship," Middoni pleaded. "Certainly this gift will please the king."

"I think you're right, Middoni," Ammoron agreed snidely. "But adding one wife to the king's harem is hardly recompense. Perhaps we could forgive the sins of your uncle, but the shame that your father brought upon this people can never be forgiven. Report to Jacob. Get out of my sight!"

Ammoron walked back into his tent, leaving Middoni with his elbows still planted in the dirt. Though arms and bodies surrounded us, I did catch the expression on Middoni's face. It was pure hatred. He hated this man more than Garth did. And Garth was hard to beat. Frankly, right that moment I hated everyone. I punched a Lamanite twice in the ribs until my wrists were seized more tightly.

Garth and I were forcefully taken to another part of the camp. They left us with the pack, as Ammoron had commanded, but our clothes, which they found equally interesting, were declared free game. Every item was stripped off our bodies, down to each sock and each shoe. The only thing I retained was the green necklace ornament. I kept it hidden in my fist, hoping later it might kick in as a good luck charm. Up to now, it had miserably failed. Our clothes were replaced by one of those Lamanite diapers. I felt ultimately stupid, and probably wouldn't have worn it at all, if the Lamanite in charge of my wardrobe hadn't grunted and shown his teeth when I looked as if I might toss it aside. A pair of Lamanite sandals were also thrust in my face. Garth and I did the best we could to fit them properly for walking; it was a matter of wrapping them around our feet and ankles the right way. The two of us whiled away the remainder of the afternoon in a dark, humid tent, under heavy guard, slapping bugs off our bodies.

Garth filled me in on the true character of Amalickiah and Ammoron—the two conspiring brothers whose charisma had destroyed a host of souls; whose lust for power had inspired Captain Moroni to rend his garment and raise the "Title of Liberty." That was one Book of Mormon story I actually remembered. Garth recited the Title for me, word for word, for conversation's sake. Any other time I'd have plugged my ears or sounded off a dirty limerick to balance it out. But I listened to Garth recite that scripture from the edge of my seat. I was right in the middle of it all! The impact of those words rang in my ears like a mighty anthem.

"In memory of our God, our religion, and freedom, and our peace, our wives, and our children."

CHAPTER 8

It was after dark when Garth and I were finally rounded up for the royal feast. We had managed a few hours of sleep before we were rudely awakened and summoned.

Our warrior escort took us into the circle of tents and brought us under a canopy that sheltered an area for dining. Distinguished guests were gathered, sitting on a carpet of palm-woven mats, conversing and waiting patiently for the meal to begin. I counted eighteen men under the torchlights, heavily adorned with bracelets, feathers, and wide necklaces. This eighteen didn't include the many servants and maidens busily running errands and arranging dozens of food items. Garth and I were not the last to arrive. The King was missing. A place at the head of the mat, decorated with garlands of flowers, was reserved either for him or the Queen of England. Jennifer wasn't around either. Ammoron directed our escort to seat us at the other end of the canopy, in the dirt. It was not our honor to eat directly with royalty. None of the men seated on the mat resembled the common Lamanite warriors throughout the camp. Their features and complexions were similar to Ammoron's.

"Zoramites," Garth declared. "And Amalekites. Not a one of them is a Lamanite."

Their garb was no less than Lamanite Sunday best, while the two of us wore just this diaper and a flimsy pair of sandals. They must have feared it would outclass our hosts if we had stayed dressed as we were in twentieth-century raiment.

I'd been wondering what they'd done with our stuff. My wondering was over. I noticed a warrior seated on the end wearing my shirt! Underneath his cape I could see the blue and white stripes. The shirt was a size too big for me, but it fit this guy perfectly. Sure enough, down the line, another one was wearing Garth's shirt with "Nike" over the breast pocket. Garth pointed out yet another who had slipped into his corduroys. They were a bit "high water" at the cuff, but the waist fit snugly. Over his feet were Garth's socks. Soon we had accounted for every item of clothing, right down to my pair of white high-top tennis shoes, worn by a latecomer who proudly kicked up the dirt as he approached the others, drawing compliments. The shoes were on the wrong feet and the laces were tied around the ankles, but he had the general idea.

At that moment, the flap of the center tent was tossed aside. A man stepped out. All conversation under the canopy ceased. Every soul in sight maneuvered into bowing position. The face of this man was still in the shadow. He walked across the circle and came into the light under the canopy.

His hair was tucked under the skin and skull of a jaguar. Its teeth sat comfortably against his brow, green stones replacing the jaguar's eyes. Beautiful feathers of blue and green circled from ear to ear. The jaguar's head hung onto a cape of yellow and black fur, dropping all the way to the ground when the man stood straight. Dozens of other colorful feathers were arranged on bands encircling his arms and legs. The showy headdress bounced and swayed as he seated himself on the mat. The paws of the jaguar, claws still intact, came over his shoulders and crossed his bare breast. The lowest hanging necklace had a chunk of gold designed into some kind of animal, another jaguar maybe, also with green stones as eyes. The leather straps on his footwear were wrapped all the way up to his knee.

This guy could have passed as a movie star. He was taller than any man I'd seen so far in this land: 6' 1" or 6' 2". His chest and shoulders were broader than his brother's. At his consent, everyone arose.

"Eat, my captains!" Amalickiah announced. "This may be the last grand feast for a while. Tomorrow we march triumphantly through the gates of the city Moroni."

Cheering and hooting went up from the group. Anxious hands tore into the wide selection of fruits, vegetables and meats. One captain raised his tall clay goblet into the air.

"Bring these tomorrow. Fill them to the brim with Nephite blood! There's a drunkenness from it that will top this wine's!"

Laughter resulted from his comment—a frenzied, twisted laughter. It made me cringe.

Amalickiah's eyes found me through the crowd. He watched me for several seconds, sending the most uncomfortable chill through my body that I've ever experienced. The moment those eyes locked onto me, I felt weaker, as if energy were being drawn from my limbs. The feeling was real. I know it, because when he turned away and looked back again, the sensation returned. This man hadn't uttered a single word to me, yet I feared him. It was all in the eyes. They were large and dark—coal black from where I was sitting.

Amalickiah chatted and smiled with his brother and the chief captain on his right. I did manage to hear one of his statements. He commented to his captain: "Jacob, your calves seem to have outgrown their Quetzal bands. Interesting leggings. Where did you get them?"

This Jacob guy happened to be wearing my blue jeans. The Zoramite had compensated for their ill fit by splitting the entire seam of both legs, piercing holes in the material, and tying them together with leather straps. He stood and strutted proudly before his king, drawing laughter.

"These are the garments of our guests . . ." Ammoron pointed at us, "who were captured by a scouting party and are suspected of spying."

"Spying," Amalickiah repeated. "Really? Bring them here."

"One is coming toward us *now*," said Ammoron.

I hadn't noticed my sister approaching simply because I didn't recognize her. They had her wrapped in a bright green gown. Her hair had been braided and caught up on top of her head. Flowers and feathers were interwoven to accent her blondness. She was wearing dark red lipstick, and her eyes were painted. The only time I'd seen Jenny in makeup before was as a genie on Halloween. Mom wouldn't have approved. She didn't think it proper for any girl under fourteen to wear makeup. I agreed. I was embarassed for Jenny. When she noticed us, she turned her face, trying to hide. Two other women, dressed much simpler, brought her before the king. They made a few last-minute fussy changes in her hair and left her standing alone, in front of a gawking dinner crowd.

"So, this is the golden-haired beauty," said Jacob.

"She's my gift to you, brother," Ammoron announced. "Add a few years, we could use her to bargain with any king for his entire kingdom."

Amalickiah called to her, "Come here."

My little sister looked mesmerized. Her eyes were locked into those of the king. Amalickiah had one hand extended toward her. Slowly, she moved forward. She didn't give him her hand, but the king took it anyway.

"This one may take a part in my own harem," he said.

I felt my fists clenching. Garth, seeing the strain in my face, grabbed my shoulder, attempting to cool my steam.

Ammoron was laughing. "Another guest to please the queen?"

Amalickiah scoffed. "King Onihah's woman has grown many lines in her once fair face." He touched my sister's cheek. "This is a face I could look upon for twenty years—maybe twenty-five."

Amalickiah seated my sister next to himself. Servants placed food before her. Amalickiah motioned her to eat. She hesitated, then began nibbling.

Amalickiah looked at us again and spoke to Ammoron.

"Tell me, brother. Why am I surrounded by children this evening? Pale children. Are they freaks?"

"I was told they come from the North. The spotted one is a magician. You!" He pointed at Garth. "Show us some of the tricks in your bright blue bag."

"I can show you many tricks," Garth began, "for the price of a meal."

Garth's high, boyish voice, trying to sound authoritative, caused some laughter.

"Feed them," Amalickiah ordered.

A variety of bowls and plates were dropped on the ground before us. There were nuts and seeds, unsalted and uncooked. There was squash. There was popcorn! Genuine popcorn, unsalted and unbuttered. There was a spice on it that tasted sort of sweet. I was handed two kinds of cooked meat. One was deer. The other, according to the servant, was peccary. Having no idea what kind of animal that was, I set it aside.

I found a red chili pepper on one plate. Once I'd placed red peppers on my "untouchable" list. Now, I savored biting into that little devil and feeling my mouth catch fire.

Three minutes was all we were given to stuff our faces before Ammoron was again insisting on a magic show.

Garth looked somewhat at a loss. He unzipped the back pack and found the aluminum container with the matches in it. Carefully, he unwrapped the electrician's tape around the edge while a fidgeting audience waited. Garth's style and grace lacked showmanship. The Zoramite captains looked dreadfully bored until Garth struck a match on the side of the container and made fire. They were impressed, but not ecstatic.

"I've seen better," said Jacob.

"Bring those here," Amalickiah ordered after Garth struck a second match. At least the king was entertained.

Garth revealed his trick. Amalickiah tried it. After one awkward attempt, he too, brought forth a flame.

The captains were much more impressed when Amalickiah did it, and they applauded.

"What do you need in order to make more of these for my army?" Amalickiah asked.

Garth fumbled. "To be honest, I don't know, exactly."

"A performer who doesn't know his trade?" Ammoron scoffed.

"They're made by the people of my land," Garth said.

Amalickiah watched Garth's eyes. "I hope you're not lying, young man." Amalickiah's threat was almost friendly. "Are you sure you can't make them? I would pay you well."

"I would have to return to my people," Garth insisted.

"Your people are quite the artisans. The clothing you have graciously donated to my chief captains is woven with unusually high quality," complimented the King.

"Show him the light-stick," Ammoron demanded.

Garth signaled me to do it. I brought it forth from the pack and flicked it on. Now I got the reaction that would make any performer gloat. I shined the beam through the middle of the feast, into Amalickiah's eyes. Everyone shielded their faces, and leaned back, as if they expected to be burned or blinded.

"He's disappeared," announced one of the captains as I shined the light his way. I'm sure he was just reacting to the effect one has when looking straight into a flashlight, seeing only blackness around the bulb.

Amalickiah arose and came toward me. I shined the light onto his belly, hoping the beam might slow his intimidating approach. It didn't. He snatched the flashlight from me and tossed it from hand to hand like Luke Skywalker with a light saber.

Amalickiah shined it across his men, then spun to illuminate the side of his tent. "Brilliant!" he said, "It's like the sun at midnight. A fire that burns without heat or pain. How is it made?" Amalickiah demanded. Those enchanting dark eyes held me prisoner.

"I don't know," I meekly admitted. "They make millions of 'em, but I never learned how."

"Millions?" Amalickiah was surprised, but he never lost his perfect composure. "Where are your people from?"

I knew my answer wouldn't make any sense, but I was about to lose control of my bodily functions. I'd forgotten how to bend the truth with any creativity.

"Cody, Wyoming," I said.

"How large is this land?" he asked.

"About five thousand people."

I caught a glint of relief in Amalickiah's face. Perhaps he was afraid my people might be too mighty to bargain with. "I have never heard of this land, Cody, Wyoming" he said. "It must be far north indeed."

Garth decided to stick with Onin's theory. "We were hunting and became lost in the wilderness."

Amalickiah ponderously walked back toward Garth, a conniving plot forming in his brain.

He began, "I feel I must explain to you my reasons for gathering this army on these borders. Earning your confidence might deliver a mighty blessing, both to your people and to mine.

"My people are engaged in a holy war," he declared, "against a perverted nation. I know their sins, because I was nurtured among them, barely escaping the stain. They are lazy and weak—kept in a state of confusion by their government. They have no king. In fact they have no leaders. Power is horded by bickering judges, captains and priests—all suing for greater control. As a result, the people are in poverty, the children, starving. But they don't rebel because they are kept drunk—not with wine—but with a vile religion. Promises of salvation and riches granted by an unseen heaven blind the people. They await an unborn god that will destroy their enemies. So their circumstances worsen. Yet they are forced to perform public rituals of gratitude for their lives of filth and abomination."

Amalickiah made this speech for the benefit of his leaders as much as for us. They nodded and supported their king with supreme reverence. Amalickiah looked longingly toward the Nephite lands and continued: "I loved my people. I wanted to end their misery and offer them hope. Many supported me in my dream. But before I could speak to the people, the priests took to their towers and falsely accused us of many sins. They made us look like villains. In the name of religion, my followers were tortured and killed. Some of the men you see here are all that remain. They escaped with me and my brother into the wilderness."

Towering over Garth and over my sister, Amalickiah recounted the many crimes he felt had been committed against him. He said he loved the Nephites, they were a great people, just miserably misguided. They loved their families and yearned for the freedom a righteous king could provide. He spoke of the days of Benjamin and Mosiah—kings who had led the people in their highest moments. His dream was to restore the people to those happy times and crush those who grew fat off the labors of others.

"Tomorrow we are returning to our homelands," he concluded. "We bring with us the Lamanites, Lemuelites, and Ishmaelites. They are a strong nation and they share our hatred for injustice. Other peoples and nations join us daily. If you would see it in your heart and in your conscience to allow me to assemble an army escort, we would take you back to your land and purchase tools such as this for every soldier. You would be richer than any merchant or tradesman. Among my people you would be nobles for the rest of your days."

Things weren't sitting right. Were the Nephites really that bad? It couldn't be so. They were the good guys. That's what I'd been told in church my whole life. Maybe some of what Amalickiah was saying was true. But it couldn't all be true. Whatever else Amalickiah might be, he honestly seemed to believe that by giving the Nephites a king, he would better their lives. At this moment, everything black and white seemed very gray.

I looked at Garth. His eyes were cold, his breathing deep and heavy. Garth's face was made of stone. He spoke and the cloud began to clear. "You're a liar."

Time froze. I don't think when Garth formed the words in his mind, he intended to speak them, or at least, he didn't intend them to be heard. But he did, and they were. Everyone heard; they just wondered if they had heard right.

Amalickiah himself raised an eyebrow. Ammoron's eyes were dagger-thin and his teeth were grinding. "How dare you speak to a king with such disrespect," he growled.

A touch from Amalickiah's hand stayed his brother's impulse to lunge at Garth. "He's a boy," Amalickiah defended. "Boys say foolish things."

The king sat down. He seemed perfectly calm, much calmer than any of his men who were poised to draw their blades. Amalickiah resumed eating, pretending only half an interest in anything Garth had to say.

"On what point have I lied, boy?" Amalickiah invited and popped a berry into his mouth.

"You *wanted* to be king," said Garth.

"Yes," Amalickiah admitted. "And the *people* wanted me to be king. Even at this day my supporters in Zarahemla rally for my return. I will not disappoint them. The nations will unite under Lamanite dominance. After all, the ancient right of kingship belongs to them. They recognized my eminence at once, welcomed my leadership with open arms."

"No," Garth insisted. He was shaking. More was behind his tongue, but he paused. I thought he'd swallowed the words. Then I saw a power well up in Garth Plimpton. He delivered his speech.

"The Lamanites already had a king. You stirred up their king into desiring another war against the Nephites. Most of the Lamanites knew better. They wanted to keep peace. The Lamanite king let you take his army and force the pacifists to take up arms. But those wanting peace organized into an army of their own, with a man named Lehonti to lead them. They fled to Onidah. Lehonti's army camped on Mount Antipus. Your army was in the valley. At night you sent three secret embassies to ask Lehonti to meet you at the foot of the mountain. He wouldn't come, so you went to him and you offered him victory even before the battle was fought—on one condition—that he'd make you his second in command. Betrayal number one."

Every Zoramite and Amalekite under the canopy was taut and ready to spill blood. I was amazed that they allowed him to continue. But Garth seemed to have a glow about him. If any man had touched him at this moment, they might have shriveled away.

Garth went on uninterrupted. "Then you killed Lehonti by slow poisoning and took command of both armies. Betrayal number two. But your scheme was just beginning. When you got back to Nephi, the Lamanite king went to greet you, thinking you'd accomplished his command. He wanted to give you a hero's welcome. But you sent your guards on ahead. As the king was extending a hand of fellowship to them, he was stabbed to death, right in the street. It was murder. And you planned it. Betrayal number three. But it's not over. You convinced everyone that the king's servants committed the crime and preached justice and revenge. The people's support fell right into the palm of your hand. There was only one heart left to deceive. The queen. It didn't take much to woo her, so—"

"This is blasphemy!" Jacob stood and shouted. "Never has any man dared profane—"

"Silence!" Amalickiah demanded. Garth had brought the Zoramite's temper to the edge. His neck was taut and his eyes were flaming. The composure he had attempted to portray earlier was cracking away. If all his words prior to this moment had been clothed in silk, each one was now dipped in poison. "Whatever filth has whispered these black lies to you is a villain and a traitor. Who is it? I want his name."

I noticed that the Lamanite servants had stopped to listen. Only when Ammoron yelled at them did they return to their errands. Garth's words had been disturbing.

"No one told me," Garth answered the king.

Captain Jacob catapulted between Ammoron and Amalickiah, latching onto Garth's bangs and forcing him onto his knees, tilting his head back to expose the boy's neck to his blade.

"He wants his name!" Jacob repeated.

"Jacob!" Amalickiah's voice froze his chief captain. "Do not spill blood at my feast. Sit down or retire to your tent."

Grudgingly, Jacob released Garth with a shove.

Suddenly, the King's expression changed, as if a dark revelation had entered his mind. He knew something now. But what could he know? He looked upon us with an eerie recognition, like enemies meeting again after a lifetime.

"You're not from the North," he said, "and you have no people. You are spies. Spies of the cleverest kind, sent to sow treason and rebellion among my army."

Again he faced the east. Thousands of campfires caused a glow to climb up from the earth all around the royal tents. Drums were beating throughout the Lamanite camp. I heard yelling and chanting. The Lamanite army was full of energy tonight—violent energy they expected to vent the following day.

Amalickiah called to a servant, "Bring the priests!"

The servant went between the tents and disappeared.

Amalickiah recaptured his perfect composure, and passed sentence upon us.

"Before a great battle will be fought, this people will seek the grace of their great spirit, the Sun. This God's appetite has only one pleasure. He feeds on the blood of our slaves and reprobates. For weeks the warriors have gathered victims for a great sacrifice. When the first corner of light from the rising sun strikes the priest's altar, the blood will begin to spill. Since they have dedicated only one altar here in the wilderness, they believe the first victim is the most important "

Amalickiah now stood over Garth. "The Sun would likely find your blood the most pleasing of all. This people would consider it their highest honor if you would fill that role. Be assured, a greater honor has never been granted in your kinship. Your companion will follow."

He pointed to me, then he stepped toward my little sister. Tears without sobs were flowing down her cheeks.

"The maiden will not be sacrificed," Amalickiah declared. He touched a strand of her hair.

"Please . . ." Jenny whispered to him. "No."

Amalickiah went on speaking, pretending he hadn't heard any plea. Yet he smiled at her with such kindness. In other circumstances, I would have never distinguished his manner as anything but compassionate. Certainly, a being this evil had never felt such an emotion.

He touched her chin. "She has the complexion of a queen. I

will raise her up to be such. In a year or two, after the child has blossomed into womanhood, there will be a wedding the likes of which has never been known in all the land. It will be the wedding of a king whose power and glory stretch the length and breadth of all the earth."

The servant returned. He was followed by five figures. The figures may have once been men, but any resemblance they may have once possessed was entirely gone. This is how I would have envisioned demons from right out of a terrible nightmare. Each wore only the barest of loincloths. Their bodies were adorned in necklaces and bands. There were other ornaments as well. Bones. Whether they were animal or human, I hope I'll never know. Their long black hair was deliberately unkempt—clotted together with dried and drying blood. In fact, blood covered much of their outer skin, front and back, painted into designs and patterns. A good portion of the blood was their own. All of them were badly scarred. Their ears had been cut and shredded. Some of the wounds were new, as if they'd spent the evening hurting themselves or hurting each other. I don't think I could ever thoroughly describe the smell. It was death. I'll never smell anything more putrid.

"Take them, bind them," Amalickiah ordered the priests. "These two will be your principals in tomorrow's ceremony."

"Yes, my Lord," a priest answered.

Jennifer cried out and tried to break away. Jacob and Ammoron wouldn't let her reach us. My arms were forced painfully high behind my back. I tried to keep my eyes on Jennifer. I wanted to call something to her—"I love you"—anything! but over the shrieks of the priests, she'd have never heard me anyway. Besides, they grabbed my hair and forced me to look away. They kept my head bent down and my back arched forward as we were led into a part of the camp where there were no fires and the night was particularly cold.

CHAPTER 9

"The Book of Mormon seemed like a much nicer place," I mumbled in the darkness.

"It depends on the century you come in at," Garth replied.

A splintery stick had been propped behind my shoulders. My arms were stretched across it, strapped down at each end. Another strap wound around my neck to keep the stick in place. Two ropes, tied to the roof, kept me upright. My weight was fully carried by my knees. Blisters were grinding into my kneecaps.

Garth and I were among ten other men and one woman. All of us awaited ritual sacrifice at first light. The others never spoke, but after the priests left and took their torches, the darkness was kept alive with the sound of their breathing. One of the condemned men moaned the entire night. The moan always lasted three or four seconds. Then there was silence until he sucked in enough air to moan again. The woman sobbed lightly, like a little girl, though she was probably in her fifties. When we were hauled into the tent, I remember seeing her eyes, glossed over, empty. The fight had long since gone. After a while, she faded off to sleep. It grew quiet in her corner of the dark.

I hated Garth. I had to blame somebody. If he hadn't spouted off, we might have gone free.

Who was I kidding? If we'd have consented to Amalickiah's offer, we'd be marching to Cody, Wyoming, tomorrow. Upon discovering that no such place existed in this day and time, we'd have been in the same predicament. Our only chance had been to escape—but in this jungle we didn't stand a chance at outwitting Lamanite pursuers. I sighed and forgave my friend without him ever knowing I'd held a grudge.

Then I prayed. I was sure Garth was doing that anyway, so in the blackness, I joined him. I prayed like I've never prayed before. If every half-hearted prayer I'd whispered in God's ear up till now had been ignored, this night, he would hear my words. I didn't care how fancy they sounded to him. I didn't care that I repeated myself over and over. My words were going to rocket into the heavens to find my God wherever he was hiding.

After several hours I felt a peace come over me. The pain wasn't as bad on my knees. Nothing told me I would go free or return to my family. I just felt loved, and in the whole scheme of things, it was suddenly clear that was all that mattered. With that peace upon me, I was able to doze.

The night had reached its most silent moment when I snapped back to consciousness. I heard something Was it a cry? I couldn't place the source. It seemed to me it didn't come from inside the tent.

Suddenly, the tent flap was tossed aside and a Lamanite warrior entered. Middoni? Uncertain that this wasn't a dream, I watched Middoni locate Garth and me among the condemned. There was a knife in his palm and a bow strapped over his shoulder. Was this his moment of vengeance? Perhaps he wanted to credit our murders to himself, rather than the priests. I held my breath as Middoni lifted the knife to my arm and cut the leather strap.

Middoni continued to sever the other straps as he whispered, "I've killed two of the priests. I fear the second one's cry may have stirred the others."

I was free. With difficulty, I stood. Blood rushed into my lower legs, making them itch most uncomfortably. I wanted to massage them with my palms. But any touching would only intensify the raw pain. Middoni began to cut Garth's bonds.

"Why are you doing this?" Garth was naive enough to ask.

"Suffice it to say, I've changed my allegiance," Middoni said. Garth was free.

"Hurry!" Middoni started toward the entrance.

"Wait!" Garth insisted. "The others!"

The other condemned souls were awake, staring at us through glazed eyes. One of the men spoke in a very thirsty voice, "If you run, the sun may fail. The gods would curse you with misery the remainder of your days."

"If we stay," I responded, "we'll be cursed for our stupidity."

If I thought my words were clever, they were wasted on deaf ears. These people actually considered sacrificing their lives to be a bittersweet privilege. The man who had spoken began yelling as loud as his dry voice would allow. The others began howling and clamoring with him, as if the whole group had become mindlessly possessed.

Desperately, Middoni grabbed Garth's arm. "Come on!"

As I stumbled forward, my legs collapsed. Middoni caught me and hoisted me back onto my feet. The Lamanite warrior pushed us through the tent entrance, scolding himself for letting too much of the night go by. There was a faint morning glow in the east sky. I could see the silhouettes of the trees mixed with the stars and the dim embers of Lamanite campfires.

There was another scream. A priest lunged at Middoni. It was the most piercing twist of a human voice that I'd ever heard. Through a skillful defense, Middoni dodged the priest's thrusting blade and embedded his own into the demon's belly. The priest fell to the ground, writhing. It was a horrible scene, but it brought a surge of adrenalin into my limbs.

Another incarnation melted out of the blackness. His scream was equally insane. Middoni placed an arrow in his bow with remarkable talent, and sent the angry missile in the general direction of the charging shadow. The arrow hit its target and the priest buckled under.

The Lamanite camp was stirring now. I saw the vague movements of a few warriors coming out of their tents, responding to the noise.

Middoni began to run toward the river, only half caring whether we were following or not. His plan had obviously not gone smoothly. It wasn't until he had stretched his lead by ten yards that he even remembered we were with him. He turned back and waited for us with furious impatience.

"I fear we've lost the head start I was counting on," he said, making it clear with several sweeps of his arm that it was critical we move faster.

"What about my sister?" I asked.

"Are you crazy, boy?" Middoni demanded. "Follow me!"

Though I felt nothing from my knees to my toes, somehow I was able to run. Garth, only a little behind me, was also blessed with newfound strength.

We made it to the river bank. Middoni walked into the water slowly, cautiously, suspecting the river might be scanned by lookouts. My teeth began chattering, a combination of the water, my nervousness, and the crisp morning air. We swam across, keeping our heads low, following Middoni's example. No leeches attached themselves to us. Maybe leeches didn't like this section of the river. As we climbed onto the opposite bank, a hollow, deep trumpet blared in the Lamanite camp. It repeated.

"Here they come," Middoni announced.

We continued an exhausting pace for thirty minutes, maybe forty-five. I was only steps from collapsing completely when I finally called to Middoni, "I can't—!" I didn't even have enough breath to finish my statement.

Middoni understood. He wasn't happy about it, but he consented to stop. Garth and I were panting and coughing uncontrollably. If there'd been anything left in my stomach from the night before, I'd have lost it. Maybe we'd have been better off with the Lamanite priests. I wanted to sit down and place my head between my knees, but Middoni, like a good P.E. coach, wouldn't allow it.

"You'll stiffen up," he said.

Garth had found a sturdy tree to lean against. I stole his idea and found a trunk of my own. With my head tilted back, I waited desperately for my breath to return.

Middoni, barely winded, paced once or twice. Something was on his mind. Out of the blue, he offered us an observation. "You're Christians. Am I right?"

I popped open my resting eyes. Both Garth and I tried to read his expression. What possible motives would an A.W.O.L. Lamanite have for asking such a question?

"Yes," Garth answered him, "We're both Christians."

"My parents were Christians—are Christians," Middoni said. "I haven't seen them since I was a boy. I don't know if they're still alive."

This was an interesting development. The mystery behind Middoni's behavior included more than just a bout of resentment against Ammoron.

"My father was Antiomno. He was a Middonite—king over all the valley. When I was nine, I went to the land of Jerusalem to spend a season with my uncle. They said the Nephite missionaries came into my homeland that year and made my father a Christian. I was ashamed. My uncle, and the people of Jerusalem, approved of my shame. I never returned. My parents emigrated with many others to the lands of the Nephites."

"What did Ammoron mean when he said your uncle had shamed the Lamanites?" Garth inquired.

"When I was sixteen, my uncle became a chief captain in Amalickiah's army. He disobeyed the King's orders at Ammonihah and failed to attack. The Nephites killed him at Noah. Since he wasn't alive to be tried for his crimes, my kinsmen were punished in his place."

Middoni looked distant, broken. This morning he'd severed all remaining ties with the only people and culture he'd ever known. The pain of that realization rushed over his face like a gust of cold wind. He glared at us again with mixed emotions.

We were breathing deeply now, long and slow. Our lungs were shrinking back to their normal size. Middoni couldn't maintain direct eye contact with us for very long. He timidly glanced away again and again.

"I think we can travel more slowly now," he said.

The first beam of sunlight broke—the beam that was to have marked our execution. I mumbled a few words of prayer, words of gratitude. We traveled on, crossing through the same country as when we arrived. The scrub and grass were behind us. The jungle was growing thicker and the land became more hilly, making a gradual climb. There were mountains in the distance.

Middoni always kept us several yards to the rear, seldom turning to say anything. One time Garth called to him.

"Maybe your parents are still alive, in the land of Melek. That's where the Christian Lamanites finally settled. Do you know how to get there?"

"No," Middoni answered.

He didn't seem interested in carrying on a conversation. If Middoni had any plans or ambitions left in his life, I couldn't have guessed what they were. I read no clues that told me he had any intention of becoming a Nephite, or even a Christian. He seemed to be following some instinct that told him that whatever happened, our lives and our safety were somehow important.

After another hour we could hear running water nearby. We climbed a short rise through some very leafy undergrowth and found a thin, sparkling stream in the gully on the other side.

"Drink," Middoni directed us. "We don't know when we may drink again."

The three of us crouched down and put our lips into the stream. After a few swallows I turned to Garth.

"What day is it?" I asked.

Garth thought a moment. "Tuesday."

I half-chuckled, "I had a book report due today in Mr. Bell's class on *Where the Red Fern Grows*."

"I don't think you'll get it in," Garth confirmed.

The water tasted clean and cold, like any mountain stream in Wyoming. Middoni cut his drink short. Leaping to his feet, he walked in circles, studying the ground around us.

I glanced at my own hand in the soft dirt. There was a sandal print next to it. Middoni found many more like it.

"People camped here last night," he said.

Considering it was only about an hour after sunrise, they couldn't have been gone long. Garth and I followed Middoni, looking over his shoulder, trying to see what he was seeing. Middoni indicated a patch of greenery that looked pressed down, like a picnic blanket had been spread out.

"Three of them slept here," Middoni claimed. He took a few steps to his left. "Three more here."

Middoni leaned over and picked up a patch of drying palm leaves.

His face grew stressed. "Nephites."

"How do you know?" Garth asked.

"Lamanites do not travel with woven sleeping mats. We fashion a new one every night."

We scanned the jungle for movement. There was a good chance the campers had been awakened by our approach and had taken to the trees. They might be watching us now from somewhere in the foliage. This probability frightened Middoni more than us. He fought an urge to take cover in the brush. Because of this tension, it was particularly startling when a familiar voice called out.

"Middoni!"

It came from behind us. A figure was standing on the leafy ravine above the stream. His face was unclear. The morning sun, still very low, sat directly behind him. But we could perceive a loaded bow in his arms.

As we shielded our eyes, the face became recognizable. It was Amgiddi, Middoni's kinsman. His arrow was not aimed at us; it was aimed at his relative. Amgiddi was sweating heavily. His legs and arms were scratched and cut. To have caught us he must have endured an incredible pace, crashing through branches and thorns. He knew the trail that his cousin would follow.

"The kinship is dead, Middoni. All of them. They tried to kill me as well. They knew it was you, my cousin. One of the priests survived your wounds. They attacked our tent like butchers at a slaughter of dogs."

Middoni knew the weapon was directed at his heart. Yet he made no attempt to unshoulder his own bow in defense.

"Why, my cousin?" Amgiddi pleaded through a choke of tears. "Why did you betray your family?"

"You're *not* my family!" Middoni screamed. "The kinship divided when I was nine years old!"

"Is that what it is?" Amgiddi was shocked. "My father raised you as his own son. He respected your bloodline and gave you the kinship when it should have been mine. If it hadn't been for him, today you would live as a Nephite! The son of a liar! Cursed in life and death by their lying god."

"Now we are cursed in life and death by our own people," Middoni said.

Middoni's words struck his cousin deeply, but Amgiddi's anger was past softening. Amgiddi released the bowstring. The arrow struck Middoni's chest with a thud and a crack.

Middoni fell onto his face, almost dutifully, without wincing. He gave up the ghost with a sigh and lay still. I looked into Amgiddi's eyes. The regret that he endured while murdering his cousin was not the same emotion that I saw now. He looked down on Garth and me with ferociousness. Spilling our blood would be satisfying, instead of painful. Another arrow was placed in the string. The black tip was pointed between my eyes.

In what I felt were my last seconds of life, I was torn between backing away or collapsing to bury my face. As a result I did nothing. I just watched my executioner seal my fate.

Before the bow discharged I saw a blur—a wisp—flying through the air to rival the arrow of Amgiddi. He was struck in the heart. The arrow came straight from heaven. I couldn't fathom the credit belonging anywhere else. Amgiddi dropped his weapon and clutched the wood projecting from his chest. Unlike Middoni's death, this Lamanite's final seconds were dramatized by a desperate fading moan. Amgiddi tumbled through the leaves and rested near the tiny rapids of the stream. The kinship was now extinct.

Amgiddi never saw his assassin. I turned toward the source of the arrow, and there stood our benefactor, still wielding a loaded weapon. His breast was shielded by a thick, quilted tunic decorated with many feathers. His left arm was wrapped by an even thicker padding of the same material. His complexion wasn't that of a Lamanite.

Seven other warriors, garbed in the same quilted armor, came out from behind trees and shrubs. Every hand carried its own ready weapon.

"Albinos?" one asked another.

"No," he said. "Their eyes aren't pink."

One man approached us without hesitancy. He gripped a long sword with a bright silver blade, directed downward. This man did not fear children. I got the impression he didn't fear anything.

"Who are you?" he demanded.

I kept with the usual story. "We come from a tribe in the North. The Lamanites took us prisoner," I said.

"Are your people enemies to the Lamanites?" he asked.

I said, "In a way."

The group became more passive. Bows were shouldered; knives were replaced in their sheaths. Two of the men kneeled to examine Middoni's and Amgiddi's bodies.

"Are they dead?" asked the man standing before us.

His men nodded. "Yes, Captain."

The captain turned back to us. "I heard the talk. Why did this one help you escape Amalickiah's camp?"

"We're Christians," Garth answered.

Compassion welled up in the captain's eyes. Garth had chosen his words perfectly.

"Are you Nephites?" Garth asked.

Smiles formed on the faces of the group. "Yes," the captain confirmed.

Garth looked up and down this man they called "Captain" with awe. "Are you Captain Moroni?" he asked meekly.

The Nephites laughed. The captain was humbled by Garth's question, but he remained in good humor. "I'm afraid I'm not that famous. My name is Teancum. I'm a Mulekite by birth."

CHAPTER 10

His face was hard but his eyes were warm. A long, flat nose started between a pair of bushy eyebrows and ended with a set of large nostrils—not abnormal, just big for his face. There were two scars: one high on the right cheekbone, and another, smaller, under the eye. A few worry lines were starting to show on his forehead. This was the face of the legendary Nephite captain, Teancum.

Nephites didn't much resemble the husky bodybuilders in all those paintings. They were actually rather slender. Although Teancum's build was somewhat bulkier than that of his companions, if I'd have chosen a sport in which he excelled, it would have been the triathlon, not weightlifting.

Teancum asked how old we were. We told him.

"You're awfully big boys for thirteen years," Teancum decided. "They say the cold, dry North breeds large men."

At 5' 3", I fit in rather well as a Nephite—only slightly under average. Nearest Garth was a Nephite warrior in his mid-to-late teens. At 5' 4", he and Garth were identical in height. Upon request, we revealed our first names. Teancum introduced the other six men.

"These are my kinsmen. My brother, Moriancum." He indicated the archer.

"Forgive me," Moriancum said, referring to the frightening threat he'd given us earlier with his bow.

"My cousin Jerem and my cousin Sellum," Teancum continued.

Jerem and Sellum nodded.

"My nephews from Nephihah, Pachumi and Mocum, and their father, my wife's oldest brother, Gallium. Even though he's my brother-in-law, I call him Uncle."

"He does that to make me feel old," Gallium winked.

"And finally, my son, Teancum the Younger."

"When did you boys eat last?" Gallium asked.

"Last night, but only a little," I said.

"If we had time, I'd fix up something real special for you." Gallium reached into a pouch on his waist. "Let this suffice for now."

More jerky. Nephites hadn't quite perfected jerky. It was not like our nicely packaged jerky sold in the big glass jars in the mini-marts back home. If I ever got home, I knew I'd look at a helping of junk food in a way that might be judged a sin. Kinda like a heathen bowing down to an idol.

Teancum stood over the body of Amgiddi.

"More warriors couldn't be too far behind this one," he said. "I've got a feeling you two boys have caused quite a stir in ol' Bloodeye's camp. We better start moving. Fill with water, everyone."

Water pouches were dipped into the stream. Teancum's son came between us. He was about nineteen, I guess. Almost the spitting image of his father, except for a lighter hair color and less distinguished "crow's feet" around his eyes.

"What are your kinship names?" he asked.

"My full name is Jim Hawkins."

"Garth Plimpton."

Moriancum, Teancum's brother, repeated them to see how they felt on his tongue. "Very different," he added.

"Are all your people as white as you?" inquired Mocum, Teancum's nephew.

"Most of them," Garth replied.

"Even the women?" Pachumi probed.

Mocum was sixteen. Pacumi was eighteen. Their questions were the kind of things I'd expect my older brothers to be dumb enough to ask. My mouth was too stuffed with jerky at the moment to answer. Gallium thought we might have found their questions rude and came to our rescue.

"Let them eat, my sons," he told them. "These are trail stories. They probably have as many questions about our people."

Captain Teancum added, "I also want to know if they've heard any whisperings about Amalickiah's plans—when ol' Bloodeye intends to attack."

"Today," Garth said. "His plan was to march on the city of Moroni today."

Teancum pinched his upper lip under his lower lip and nodded. "I knew it would be either today or tomorrow. The city Moroni would have been my first conquest as well."

"They don't stand a chance. They'll be crushed!" Moriancum stated.

Teancum turned to him. "Our small numbers wouldn't change anything. The reserves in Jershon would be massacred. We'll return from Zarahemla with the remainder of our kinship and an army behind us—at least ten thousand men to add to the meager ranks in Jershon."

"More cities will have fallen," Moriancum said.

Teancum grew mildly impatient. His words were firm. "And if we fail to inform Captain Moroni and bring greater forces, Amalickiah could seal off the narrow passage, and then it's just a matter of time and the entire nation will have fallen! It's the only choice, my brother."

Moriancum nodded. He saw Teancum's point, but his face displayed deep regret for the unsuspecting people of the city of Moroni.

"Do you intend to send word to Jershon?" Teancum the Younger asked his father.

"Are you volunteering, my son?" Teancum inquired.

Young Teancum nodded, "I am. On the way I can warn the city of Nephihah. Let them make whatever preparations they can."

"I can go with him," Jerem offered.

"Good," Teancum praised. "Tell the reserves in Jershon to hold tight. The journey to and from Zarahemla should take twenty days—no more."

"Yes, sir," responded Teancum's son in a stiff, military tone. "We can reach Nephihah by tonight—Jershon, day after tomorrow."

"That'll be fine," Teancum said. Then he sighed, "Your mother will likely strangle me when she doesn't see you at my side."

"Tell her I love her," the younger Teancum said. "If we're going to make it before dark, we'd better leave."

"Right," Jerem agreed.

Teancum and his son embraced. It wasn't really a hug. They held each other's shoulders firmly and looked into one another's faces. I read the unspoken thoughts: "I'm proud of you," and "I know, Dad." Then Teancum the Younger and Jerem slipped into the jungle.

"You may come with us to Zarahemla," Teancum invited us. "It is the capital city of our people, and in recent times, accustomed to accommodating refugees. I'm afraid a few seasons will pass before you can return northward. A great war is erupting in this land. The northern highways are very dangerous."

"You don't think the boys will slow us down, Captain?" Sellum asked Teancum. When a person makes a comment like that, it doesn't give you a real positive first impression of him. To Teancum, Sellum's question was not unexpected.

"I suspect they've done considerable traveling already. They have no choice but to keep up. Their chances alone aren't high."

I found myself walking over to Middoni's silent body. I hoped he somehow knew my gratitude. He may not have understood why, but he had saved our lives.

"There's one more of us," I said. "My sister is still held prisoner in the Lamanite camp."

Teancum was sympathetic. "I fear for her."

I wanted more than sympathy. "Will you rescue her?"

I was afraid my request might insult him. After all, this was Teancum I was talking to. The legend. Of course he would rescue her. Teancum could do anything.

"It's impossible," he replied. "The whole of my people are threatened at this moment. I'm sorry."

Without a pause, Teancum called to his men and announced the party's departure. I stood there in shock. Teancum and Moriancum moved toward the rest of the group, busily finishing last-minute arrangements in their travel gear. I was close to tears.

"He's a fake," I whispered to Garth. "That's not Teancum. The Teancum from the Book of Mormon would have helped us."

"He *is* Teancum from the Book of Mormon, Jim," Garth tried to comfort me. "When you weigh Jennifer against the fate of a nation, does his choice surprise you?"

I almost slugged Garth. Fortunately for him, I'd already directed my resentment toward Teancum. The party was ready to embark. Mocum waved for us to follow.

"I'm not going with them," I told Garth. "I can't leave my sister."

"There's nothing we can do, Jim. We *have* to go with them," Garth pleaded. "We'll die if we stay here."

I knew Garth was right. There was a deep pain in my heart. The legendary Teancum had turned out to be not much of a hero at all. Resentment brewed inside me. Reluctantly, I followed behind Garth, and the two of us traveled with the Nephites.

We began to climb toward higher elevations—toward a range of ominous looking mountains. Fierce clouds twisted around them. There would be more rain ahead.

As we walked, I fiddled with my green necklace ornament, thinking about Jen, not much in the mood for conversation. One of Teancum's nephews, Pachumi, broke the ice by asking me what I had in my hand. I showed it to him.

"It's jade and silver! Where did you find it?" he asked.

"Lying in the dirt."

"Would you like some tether so you can hang it about your neck?" Pachumi asked.

"Sure," I said, "If you've got it."

He handed me a piece of string from one of his pouches. I threaded it through the ornament and slipped it over my head.

"Thanks," I said.

Because of the gift, Pachumi and Mocum suddenly felt they had the right to throw out a barrage of questions.

"What do they call your people?" Mocum asked.

"Americans," I said.

"Was America a great man?"

Pachumi's question didn't make sense to me at first. "What do you mean?"

"America," Pachumi explained. "The man who founded your nation. Is he revered by your people?"

"We're named after a man named Amerigo Vespucci," Garth replied.

"What a silly sounding name," Mocum laughed.

"He was an explorer," Garth added.

"What did he explore?" asked Pachumi.

Garth thought a moment. "I don't remember."

Seeing Garth stumped by anything was unusual. Mocum and Pachumi took advantage of the moment.

"If you don't remember, he must not have been a great

man," Mocum concluded. "The founder of our people was Mulek. He was a great man. The son of King Zedekiah of Old Jerusalem, the city across the sea. He brought our ancestors here to save them from destruction."

Pachumi took over. "His descendant, Zarahemla, founded the great capital to which we are traveling. It's a beautiful city. There is a temple there and a great palace for the Chief Judge. They say there are over fifty thousand people."

"Denver's bigger than that," I said. "Over a million."

I had him on that one. It felt good. Pachumi huffed. He turned to Mocum, and acted as though he was trying to speak privately. But I understood every word.

"It's a tall tale," he comforted his brother. "This one is a storyteller."

"I'm serious," I insisted. "I've been there. If you wanna hear a tall tale, I can do better than that."

The brothers' heads turned quickly, eyes wide.

"Did you understand what I said?" Pachumi asked. "Do you speak Coarse-Tongue as well as Hebrew?"

Moriancum, who'd drifted in and out of our conversation, now listened intently.

"We've understood every word spoken since we came to this land. It all sounds the same," Garth admitted.

With that statement, Teancum stopped. That meant the whole party stopped. They looked impressed, but I couldn't tell if our strange talent was judged to be admirable or evil.

"Do you understand what I'm saying now?" Moriancum tested.

Garth hesitated. "Yes."

"I was speaking common Jaredite," Moriancum said. "How is it that you know so many languages?"

"I don't know," Garth shrugged. "It all sounds like English. The language of our people."

After pondering a moment, Teancum turned back and everyone began walking again.

Finally Teancum said, "I must introduce you to the Chief Judge in Zarahemla. You boys possess a strange gift. Perhaps a very valuable gift."

Our journey continued up a mountainous trail referred to as the Zarahemla Road. I started to notice trees that looked like a kind of pine mixed in with the tropical foliage, not much different from what you might see in Wyoming. To my biology teacher, Mr. York, they may have looked entirely different. Nevertheless, the scenery made me feel more at home.

I'd have never guessed my feet could carry me this distance. After all, I was a city boy. The most grueling Boy Scout hike I could remember only took us about eight miles. When we finally broke camp, I was utterly exhausted. My blisters had formed blisters.

Gallium supplemented our menu of corn biscuits and dried fruit with a variety of roots and seeds that he'd gathered along the trail. He brewed a bitter tea out of leaves. Honestly, it tasted like powdered sagebrush. We were still too close to the Lamanites to build a fire, so everything we ate was cold.

Palm leaves were laid out for Garth and me, since we had no sleeping mats of our own. The daylight faded quickly. After group prayer, the others laid their sleeping mats around us and we nestled into a tight circle.

Teancum gazed up at the thousands of stars and said to Garth and me, "I wish you could see Zarahemla during a happier time. I was born there. When I was a boy my father settled my family in the East Wilderness. The city has changed greatly since my youth. It has grown larger and it has grown colder."

Moriancum added, "The East Wilderness has been affected by that same chilling. Last year we marched against the rebellious inhabitants of an entire land. The battle was swift and the people were reinstated, but they could switch allegiance at the snap of a finger. The Lamanites need only make the people of the land of Morianton an offer sweet enough."

"God is frowning upon us," Gallium said soberly. "That is our problem."

"If what you say is true, my uncle," Teancum stated, "that is our *only* problem."

Gallium began quoting a scripture, "'Whoso should possess this land of promise, should serve him, the true and only God, or they should be swept off when the fullness of his wrath shall come upon them.' Our ancestors, the mighty Jaredites, wrote those words."

Garth identified the scripture. "'The Word of the Lord to the Brother of Jared.' Those are Ether's words."

Gallium was astonished by Garth's recognition. "Does your nation possess the words of Ether? I thought the only record of his words was kept by Helaman, our prophet, seer, and revelator."

"Well, Nephi said it, too," Garth quoted, "'If it so be that they shall keep his commandments they shall be blessed upon the face of this land, and there shall be none to molest them, nor to take away the land of their inheritance, and they shall dwell safely forever.'"

Garth was showing off, and getting a little bit carried away. They were sitting up now, their mouths gaping.

"Are you a prophet?" Mocum asked. Garth became embarrassed, and felt ashamed for creating the wrong impression.

"No," he admitted.

The confusion Garth had stirred didn't settle easily. Teancum looked most suspicious.

"You say you come from a land farther north than our people have ever traveled, and yet you have memorized the words of our ancestors? How is this possible?" Teancum insisted.

Everyone waited to hear. No secrets would be tolerated any longer. Teancum knew we were hiding a lie. He wanted answers. Garth felt we had no alternative but to tell the truth.

"We know many things about your people," Garth began. "We've studied about you since we were little children."

"Are you of God or the devil?" Teancum demanded.

"Neither," he defended. "We come from a place and time a lot farther away than we've admitted."

"Time?" questioned Teancum.

"We haven't been born yet," Garth said. "We won't be born for a couple thousand years."

"This is nonsense!" Sellum barked. "You are sitting before us!"

The concept was totally incomprehensible to them. They knew nothing of time machines or *Back to the Future* to help them understand. Garth's words were a mishmash.

Garth tried to explain. "Imagine waking up one day and suddenly you're in Jerusalem. Lehi and his sons surround you. They're getting ready to travel into the wilderness to avoid the Babylonian destruction. Mosiah, Benjamin, Alma—none of them have been born yet. It's not a dream. You're actually living at the time they were living. That's what's happened to us. I can't tell you how it happened, but it has. We know so much because the writings of your prophets have been translated into our language and written in a book. The book tells us all about your wars and struggles. It even tells us—"

"Speak no more of this!" Teancum interrupted. "I don't understand how this can be. Only a prophet would know if this is of God. In Zarahemla, you will tell all of this to the Prophet Helaman. He will know what is to be done. There will be no more talk tonight."

Teancum rolled over. Nothing more was said, though I knew that none of them fell asleep soon, and probably would not fall asleep until time and fatigue calmed their boggled minds.

"Do you think I jumped the gun?" Garth whispered to me.

"Big time," I answered.

When I awoke, the stiffness in my body was not as bad as it had been the mornings before. The worst pain was caused by the scabs on my knees. Gallium mixed a green jelly-like ointment and massaged it into our knees. The ointment moisturized the scabs so they wouldn't split and bleed.

By noon the rocky trail had become very steep. More rain fell, much colder now. During our only rest stop Gallium approached us, stammering for a moment until he could bring himself to ask an unusual question.

"In your day, has the Christ already come?" he meekly asked.

"Yes," Garth said. "He came."

"Did he save all men?"

"He did," Garth answered. "All who would believe in him."

Tears started pricking Gallium's eyes. He smiled and thanked us.

Late that afternoon, the trail leveled off. We walked along a grassy plateau in the midst of the mountains. We could see a vast valley to the south. The climate looked much different— dry, almost a desert. The sun was getting low. It reflected on a distant river, turning it into a shiny, silver snake.

"The Sidon River of Zarahemla," Moriancum announced. "Civilization at last."

CHAPTER 11

For the first time, we built a fire. Gallium announced plans to prepare a special treat. Water was heated. I watched him take a pouch and pour tiny brown beans into his palm.

"Cocoa beans." He looked at me, closing one eye. "Do they have hot cocoa where you boys are from?"

"You bet!" I said. "Are you really going to make hot chocolate?"

Finally, something familiar would sink into my taste buds. After camp chores were done, the seven of us weary travelers waited around the fire, watching Gallium add his final touches to the brew. The heated pot, filled with brown and bubbling water, was transferred into a pottery cup. The cup was passed around the circle—first to Captain Teancum, then to Mocum and Pachumi. Their tongues caught every drop that tried to escape down the side. Every man whose turn passed before mine smacked his lips and complimented Gallium on his cooking. I expected no less than ecstasy when I poured the warm liquid onto my tongue. Instead, my face puckered up like a prune and I blew a spray of brown steam back into the coals.

"What is this stuff?" I whined, and continued to spit.

"What's wrong with it?" Gallium frowned.

"It's bitter!" I scoffed. "Don't you guys use any sugar?"

Garth started laughing so hard he had to lie on his back. Nobody else understood the joke, but they all were grateful to have more cocoa left for them.

The sunset made the ribbon that Gallium had called the Sidon River glow like a stream of lava. We watched the darkness fade across the valley.

The next afternoon, Moriancum pointed out the city of Sidom and its outlying villages in the far distance. I could see some of the settlements, in spite of the haze. Gallium said it was a big city. A lot of people claimed it was larger than Zarahemla, though no one had actually done a census.

"A lot of non-Nephites down there," Moriancum commented. "There are many good Christians, but unifying their warriors for battle is difficult. So few speak our language." Moriancum looked at Garth and myself. "Gifts like the ones you both possess could be very useful . . . if you are willing."

Garth wanted to go to Sidom, but Teancum insisted it was too far out of our way. In my opinion, Teancum was a hardnose. One hundred percent professional soldier. I didn't care for the guy all that much. His family seemed to love him though. At least they respected him. Even his own brother called him "Captain," as did everybody else. I wasn't sure if it was a commandment or an endearment. Mocum spent an hour enthusiastically recalling his heroics in battle. I listened to the story of how Teancum stopped the flight of Morianton and his men when they tried to escape to the land northward. His tale included exciting details of the battle in which Teancum slew the dissenter, Morianton, in a perilous duel of steel swords. I asked Pachumi why Teancum was the only one in our group who possessed a metal sword. Pachumi told me metal was very precious. The common soldier's "sword" was a club with obsidian blades.

The mountain forest through which we traveled had an eeriness all its own. I passed a spider web with a spider in the middle as big as my hand. I stopped twice and stared off into the trees, convinced my eyes were playing tricks. I could have sworn I saw somebody. After I'd stopped three times, Gallium put his hand on my shoulder.

"Don't worry about 'em," he said. "They've never been known to bother us outright. They'll steal from the nearby villages now and then, but other matters take priority with the Nephite people these days."

Gallium walked on ahead and began talking with his sons before I could ask him to explain.

Moriancum spotted a deer as we were settling into camp. Without a moment to lose, he took his bow off his shoulder and went after it. A half hour later Moriancum walked into camp with its carcass and proceeded to clean and groom the animal for eating. Although the finished product was in serious need of A-1 sauce, I heartily approved of the meal.

That night, around the campfire, I found the opportunity to ask Gallium about the forest people.

"Amulonites," he said.

Moriancum further explained, "Their ancestors are Nephites, but their father, Amulon, rejected God and raised up an apostate branch among the Lamanites. That is, until they took it upon themselves to judge their fellow countrymen— especially the Lamanite Christians. The Amulonites got a little carried away in their persecutions. Their countrymen turned on them. Wars and executions have made them almost extinct."

"They're an evil people," Gallium somberly added. "The few that are left live alone in this wilderness, like were-jaguars. They thrive on filth and darkness, hunted and killed by any Lamanite who learns their true ancestry."

"What's a were-jaguar?" I had to ask.

Pachumi answered. "It's a Jaredite legend. A woman of the woods gave birth to a beast—half-man, half-jaguar. A race of were-jaguars rose up, wandering in the wilderness casting evil spells and shedding blood. The Jaredite cults believed they were supernatural. They controlled the rain during the growing season—"

"Enough of that," Teancum interrupted. "It's sorcery. Speaking of such things brings a dark spirit to the camp."

I couldn't sleep for the longest time. Every rustle of wind through the trees sent a shiver up my spine. When I finally fell asleep, nightmares encircled me—nightmares about half-men, half-jaguars, stalking me through the jungle in the dark of night, trying to tear me to pieces with ferocious, overgrown claws. In the dream, a were-jaguar grabbed my shoulder. My eyes traveled up its body until I saw its face. It was the face of my little sister, Jennifer.

I bolted up and called Jenny's name. Sweat was dripping down my neck like ice water. My yelp was not very loud. Nevertheless, it awakened Teancum. Since the coals of the fire were still quite bright, I could see his face clearly—those deep brown eyes studying me. Uncontrollably, tears started to flow down my cheeks.

Teancum pulled his sleeping mat close to mine and wrapped his arm around my shoulders. The chief captain held my head against his chest while all my imprisoned emotions were permitted to escape. I tried to weep quietly. It would have been embarrassing to wake up Garth. I fell asleep there, I don't remember quite when. No one else awakened. It was a secret moment between myself and the Nephite captain that I never told anyone.

The following day we forded dozens of creeks and streams as we left the elevated forest shelf and sank into lower elevations. The green hills ahead began to appear checkered. Farms and gardens had been tilled right onto the steep slopes. The corn was tall and green. I noticed some of the hillsides had tilled ground, but grew no crops.

"Why aren't they planted?" I asked. "Seems like a waste of land."

"A field will only bear fruit for a few seasons," Gallium explained. "God must renourish the earth."

I began to see houses again—humble farm huts, built above the trail to steer clear of a traveler's footfall. I saw children! Nephite children pointed toward us from a ridge overlooking the road, laughing and shouting. Seeing soldiers was a thrill for the country folks. The farmers stopped working. The women stopped scrubbing clothes in the stream.

Houses and people became more and more numerous. The structures began to look more and more sophisticated. There were flower gardens, wells, wooden roofs, stone walkways—even dogs barking. One boy had a pet on a leash that looked like a cross between a monkey and a raccoon. Mocum called it a "coati."

We were entering the Nephite capital, Zarahemla. The road became wide, paved with cobblestones. The Sidon river ran parallel to the city, flowing slow and greenish-brown. Zarahemla was a long city, built up on either side of the river.

Garth pointed out a tower with a white flag hanging out the window. There was writing on the flag. We asked Pachumi what it meant. He couldn't tell us. It must have referred to something which happened while they were gone.

After we crossed the Sidon River by way of a wooden bridge, a high city wall loomed before us, much of it still under construction. Heaps of earth were piled about. Cut timber was stacked in designated places. Around the wall a type of moat had been dug. River water had seeped into it, making the bottom into a pool of mud. Lookouts were perched all around the city wall. As we entered the gate, we were greeted by a unit of soldiers. Teancum embraced the unit leader.

"Captain Teancum! You look well," said the soldier.

"Teomner, I see that your family has promoted you."

"You knew it was going to happen. Thank you for your

recommendation. I command one hundred men," Teomner proudly announced.

"One day it may be ten thousand," Teancum said. "Congratulations! The Zeniffites should be very proud. Is Moroni still in Zarahemla?"

"They're *all* here," Teomner said. "In the palace. Lehi, Gid, Solomon, Antipus. They've been in council all afternoon. Your face will be a welcome sight."

Teancum sent Gallium and his sons to the family settlement to announce his arrival. Sellum was commanded to buy Garth and me a new set of clothes.

"They look like Lamanites in those clothes," Teancum declared. "Send them to the palace as soon as they are properly attired."

He and Moriancum departed swiftly.

Much of the city was protected within the walls—especially the most important structures and points of interest. This included the Zarahemla marketplace and town square. It had hundreds of shops along many streets, bustling with thousands of shoppers.

"Pity we couldn't have arrived a few hours earlier," Sellum lamented. "The plaza would have been almost empty while the merchants napped."

Everywhere I focused I saw canopies and cages, tables and piles of goods. The people bartered with cocoa beans. A few traded goods for goods—I saw one man exchange a bundle of firewood for a colorful blanket. If gold or silver were used to buy something, a merchant pulled out a set of graduated measuring cups. Each measurement had a name attached to it. I heard the biggest measurement for gold called a limnah. The biggest cup for silver was called an onti.

The Nephites were a lively people—very busy. I'd say for every man that I saw, there were two women. So even anciently, a woman's place was in the mall. Many of the women had toddlers in bundles over their shoulders as they examined the merchandise. I saw a few with kids on their backs, baskets on their heads, and goods over their shoulders. It was a balancing act worthy of applause. Children also ran to and fro, getting into mischief, trying the patience of their mothers.

The selection in the ancient outdoor mall was incredible. I saw nearly every food item you could think of. Ears of corn were stacked higher than I stood. I saw many grains, all kinds of fruits, and numerous varieties of beans and squash sitting in baskets in the middle of the street or piled upon blankets. I saw pumpkins. In fact, dried pumpkin seeds in little cloth bags were sold to hungry shoppers as a snack. There were also stands selling a kind of hot stew boiled in kettles. Walnuts and peppers were the only other food varieties I recognized.

Sellum grabbed a pear from one of the baskets and took a bite. The merchant saw him. On impulse he called angrily at Sellum. Sellum turned abruptly, and sent him a threatening stare. The merchant's expression mellowed immediately. He saw Sellum's feathered breastplate and realized he'd insulted a soldier. Sellum waited until the merchant had stumbled out an apology before we continued. After Sellum's back was turned, the merchant mumbled a few words under his breath that I'm sure were anything but complimentary.

Primitive tools of all kinds were on display—scrapers, choppers, disc-shaped blades, hammerstones. I saw the grinding stones that Garth had called *metates*. There were all kinds of animals, some alive—some dead, skinned and prepared for cooking. Cages were filled with turkeys, foxes and exotic tropical birds. There were also monkeys and "coati" animals, live snakes and snakeskins, live turtles or turtle shells. I finally found out what a peccary was. They looked like little hairy pigs. One merchant was selling wooden cages with small dogs inside. The way the dogs were treated, I got the impression they were not sold as pets. I don't want to think about the alternative.

I watched a Nephite boy under one canopy showing off three jaguar kittens while his father took bids for the animals from five or six anxious buyers. I could only hope it was for more than just the kittens' hides.

I saw a lot of pottery and jewelry—jade, beads, and precious metals. One man came up to us claiming to have an excellent price on beeswax candles. Another displayed brilliant blue-green and red feathers. Sellum brushed them off.

It wasn't all shopping in the plaza either. There were also leisurely attractions. Sellum wasn't too patient with my questions, but he did identify two of the places. One, he claimed, was a steam bath. I could see the steam seeping up from a hole in the roof. The other was a zoo. It was small compared to the zoos I'd visited, yet I would have given anything to have gone inside and seen what kind of animals they had. But besides having no time, I didn't have the price of admission.

Also attracting a considerable amount of attention on many street corners were scores of performers—jugglers, acrobats, and dancers with beads and rattles around their legs and arms. I watched one man bend his legs all the way around his neck and behind his head. He proceeded to walk around on his hands, drawing laughter, applause, and cocoa beans from the crowd.

Finally we reached the section that Sellum was seeking. It was a row of clothing shops—the Nephite version of J.C. Penney's.

Fine quality material was made from both furs and plant fibers. Inside one shade-cooled shop, animal hides of every variety were on display—from rabbit to lizard. There were enormous jaguar hides on sale, if you could afford them.

Sellum chose new sandals for us. This "brand" had backs behind the heels. Our shabby loincloths were replaced with—I hate to call it a skirt, but that's what it looked like. Trust me, it was very masculine. It felt like linen, with red and yellow stitching around the base and the top. Looking around me, I picked up real quick on the "in" fashions and chose some neck beads that I could use to replace Pachumi's tether. I built a real necklace, stringing my silver and jade ornament at the bottom. Back home, I wouldn't be caught dead in such things, but here, it was cool.

The store owner complimented us for our tasteful choices and brought out his measurements to figure up the price.

"Put it on Moroni's tab," Sellum told him arrogantly.

The store owner was frantic. "No, no, no, no—" he said. "This is too much. I've already donated my portion to the state. I'm a businessman. I must make a living."

Sellum ignored him and led us back into the street. The merchant was fuming, clenching his fists as he watched us go.

"Why didn't you pay him?" Garth asked Sellum.

"Being a soldier has its privileges," Sellum winked.

Nobody said anything for a couple of minutes while we made our way through the market crowd. I didn't think what Sellum did was right, but I didn't feel it was my place to tell him so.

An odd thing happened as we were nearing the outskirts of the market plaza. I'm surprised I even remember it. A man called Sellum's name. Sellum stopped and the two made eye contact. Sellum looked as though he were expecting to receive something. But the man shook his head and turned away saying discreetly, "Nothing yet. Tomorrow."

Garth and I followed Sellum to the building referred to as the palace—the palace of the chief judge of Zarahemla.

CHAPTER 12

Two mighty buildings stood within the city walls. The first was the holy temple. It was made of stone, and, surprisingly, a considerable amount of wood. I expected all the important buildings to be tall pyramids, like in all those pictures of Central American ruins. But Garth explained that most of the bigger structures in MesoAmerica were built after 300 A.D., just before the Nephites were destroyed. In fact, as he put it, spacious buildings were a sign of apostasy for the Nephites—the beginning of the end.

The temple had its own high wall. Through the gate, I could see one main building and some smaller ones—we walked by too quickly for me to describe much more. Our objective was to enter the tall fortress that stood before us now.

They called it the palace. On one or two occasions I heard it called the "Palace of Benjamin." Apparently King Benjamin had begun its construction and been its first occupant. Now, it did look a lot like a pyramid. It wasn't a perfect see-saw of steps like the ones in Egypt, but on top of the main structure was a smaller square, topped off by an even smaller square with a window, all of it stone, except for sections of the roof, which were covered with wood and stucco.

I got a bit anxious and took it upon myself to lead the way up the steps, taking two at a time. The steps were a lot higher than they were wide. They were made that way to encourage you to walk with respect slowly to the side as you climbed. It didn't slow me down though. I quickly reached the entrance. Mighty pillars held up a rim that sheltered the front of the palace. Two sentries stood at the doorway, like you'd expect at a medieval castle. They looked displeased with me. Running up the stairs of the chief judge's palace might have been somewhat irreverent. Sellum asked one of them to lead us to the stateroom and added, "Orders of Captain Teancum." Weighing their dislike for us against the possibility of infuriating Captain Teancum made them agreeable. I think Teancum had a reputation for having a nasty temper on occasion.

The palace floor was covered with checkered mats. Every inch was kept scrupulously clean. Many soldiers sat in the hallway—napping, sharpening weapons, etc. They looked at us with the same wonderment as everybody else. Garth's freckles were considered particularly unusual. Moriancum appeared and relieved the sentry.

"There you are," he greeted us. "The council is waiting."

Moriancum led us down the hallway and around the corner, passing all the soldiers. Despite their inactive state, some of those guys were about as burly—generally mean-looking—as any Nephites I would ever see.

"Who are all those men?" I asked.

"Bodyguards," Moriancum said. "Zarahemla is a dangerous city. Some of the captains won't go anywhere without protection."

Down the hall, a certain doorway sent out a stream of dusty daylight. Voices were echoing from inside the room. Two more sentries stood guard outside. Moriancum led us through the doorway. An older man was speaking—not real old, but a little gray on the edges. Our entrance seemed to have interrupted matters. The older man broke off his speech.

Moriancum called this the great council room. There were murals on the walls—Nephite kings and prophets of former days.

Their portraits surrounded a mighty golden sword balanced on wooden holders. Behind the sword was a red curtain. There was a window on the far wall; a corner of the lowering sun shone in, making me squint. Ten men were seated around a magnificent hardwood table, etched and carved with curves and triangles, shapes and circles. Upon the table were several open books with deerskin covers; maps of cities and landmarks within the land of Zarahemla had been sketched on bark stripped from fig trees.

Our presence caused some concern. A word from Teancum calmed the group.

"These are the ones I mentioned," he said.

The older guy resumed speaking. Teancum gestured to Garth and me. Two empty spots on the bench at Teancum's right had been reserved for us. I studied each of the ten faces. There were heroes here—people whose names I would know. I could feel it. I wanted to hear the names attached to the faces. One of them had to be Captain Moroni; another, Chief Judge Pahoran. I was staring into some of the most powerful faces in the Book of Mormon—maybe in all of history.

The older man continued, "We must understand what we're up against. The list of families read earlier is by no means complete. We hear, almost daily, of new families refusing to take up arms. Most of the kinships are unwaveringly loyal, but those choosing neutrality may well be the element that tips the scales against us."

"It's no secret," he went on. "The army is not as loved as it was. A year ago, our chief captains were revered. Too many are now referring to them as villains. In many cases we have brought this attitude upon ourselves. Some districts demand outrageous sacrifices from the people to support their army—tributes and otherwise."

One of the men blurted out, "It's uncontrollable! I've seen many kinleaders abuse their positions, but replacing them causes an uproar in the kinship, and if we crack down, the family will not fight!"

"I understand, Captain Gid," the older man consoled.

Another man interrupted. "Replace them anyway!"

This was the only Nephite I had noticed with blue eyes—bluish-gray to be exact. His voice might as well have had a thunderbolt behind it, the way everyone perked up. This was him—I knew it—the Nephite idolized by every Mormon boy since the Book was written, the chiefest of chief captains, Moroni. Garth knew it too.

Moroni continued, "I will not lead an army whose sub-captains are thieves. Captain Gid, I command you to find one kinleader from an influential kinship in your district—a man whom you are confident is guilty—and convict him for his crimes."

"As far as the law?" Gid asked.

"Yes," Moroni emphasized. "Then publish his punishments abroad. Let his kinship feel the sting of shame. Perhaps we will lose one family, but God willing, the example will send a firm message to the patriots. This is our last chance to purge this army. If we don't take action, an almighty curse will rain upon us, and all the swords between Bountiful and Manti couldn't alter the course of our destruction."

"We could rally the people, as we did when Amalickiah tried to take the throne," the older man suggested.

"We don't have time," Moroni sighed. "If, as Teancum says, Amalickiah's army has begun its attack, they will take every coastal city in a matter of weeks. Our army must march within twelve days, Judge Pahoran."

So this older guy was Pahoran. Only from Garth's education did I recognize the name of the chief judge of the Nephites.

"I'm aware of the urgency, Moroni," Pahoran responded. "But this nation is in more danger from within than from without!"

"I understand, Judge Pahoran," Moroni consoled. "You fear that if the army leaves Zarahemla, nothing will stand between you and the dissenters. I sympathize with that fear, but if Amalickiah's army cuts us off from the narrow pass, the war may be over for us. I will leave as powerful a guard as can be spared."

"What does the Lord say, Prophet Helaman?" Pahoran requested.

A man across the table began to speak. Helaman was a young prophet. His clothing was the most colorful of anyone's in the room: white and blue with the most intricate needlework that I'd ever seen on any Nephite raiment. He wore a breastplate containing many smooth stones—twelve in all. A big cloth "hat" entwined his head and a golden crown fit over his eyebrows. If I'd picked this guy out of a lineup, I'd have guessed him to be a Nephite king. But it was the uniform of the high priest of the Church of God. There were two other high priests on each side of him.

"The Lord has been very quiet on this matter," Helaman began. "He is waiting for the people to speak—to speak for the principles on Moroni's Title of Liberty. Even while the banners still hang from the towers of repentant Kingmen, they seem to have forgotten the words, and I can't seem to jog their memory. When the people have broken their silence, perhaps the Lord will break his."

"What of the Ammonites, Prophet Helaman?" asked another captain.

Helaman answered him. "The generation of Ammon has vowed never to wield another sword, Captain Antipus. They should not be compelled to do so. There is a rising generation among them. These young men talk of organizing their own army. If it is so, I ask permission to oversee and approve such an organization. The matter of enlisting any Ammonites into military service is an issue of the most tender and sacred character."

"I agree with your approach on this matter, Prophet Helaman," Moroni said. "After the eastbound armies have departed, I will issue you an escort to Melek. If the young Ammonites decide to fight, let it be of their own free will. I couldn't bring myself to sway them one way or the other."

"Shiblon will carry out the temple duties in my absence," Helaman announced, indicating the high priest on his right. Shiblon nodded.

Pahoran spoke again. "The Nephite army is already a melting pot. Our conscriptions have never been so widespread. We've never had so many peoples in one army. The ranks are filled with prejudice and misunderstanding. Weaving them into one unified force, under one appointed leader—who may not even speak their language—will be a troublesome task. In some cases as many as three to four interpreters will need to be employed."

"I may have solved this problem—at least for the eastern captains," Teancum declared. "I haven't asked our guests yet, but now is as good a time as any. I cannot explain the gifts they possess. Perhaps Helaman can. It doesn't matter what tongue is spoken to them, they understand every word."

"These are boys, Teancum," Moroni pointed out, "not soldiers."

"They come from the lands northward," Teancum explained, "by ways and means I don't understand."

"Then how do they know our nation's languages?" demanded another captain. His name was Solomon.

"Please stand," Pahoran persuaded us.

We gathered our feet beneath us and presented ourselves before this dignified audience. I remember a school teacher once told me that whenever we see someone's face, even if it's for a split second, the image is permanently burned into our minds—deep inside maybe—but it's always there. What an honor, I thought, to have my image burned into minds such as these.

Pahoran spoke. To us it sounded like English, but we were later told he spoke a specific Lamanite dialect, one used by the coastal peoples.

"What are your names?" he asked.

We answered.

"What brings you to our land?" Moroni inquired, speaking in Jaredite.

Garth kept with our strategy—honest but vague. "We're not sure. We got lost and ended up here."

Helaman added a few words in another language. He was confident he'd be the only one in the room to have been schooled in it. "How is it that young boys could travel so far without being eaten by beasts or cannibals?"

We didn't answer. Not because we didn't understand the question, but because we weren't quite sure what to say.

"Did you understand my words?" Helaman asked in what must have been, to him, the standard Nephite tongue.

I stammered a little, "Maybe they weren't hungry when they had the chance."

Helaman was very surprised, "I spoke in sacred Egyptian. None but prophets are taught this language."

"What is your opinion, Prophet Helaman?" Teancum requested. "Is it of God or of the adversary?"

Helaman was still pondering. "Where do they sleep tonight?"

"They'll sleep in the camp of my kinsmen," Teancum offered.

"Can you bring them to the temple tomorrow?" Helaman asked.

"Of course," Teancum agreed.

Moroni had been massaging his chin, watching my every move with intense curiosity. Finally he dropped his hands to the table. "This is a remarkably odd development."

"Perhaps God is behind us," suggested Teancum.

"With the problem of language barriers now facing a possible solution," Pahoran said, "at least for two of the eastern armies, I'd like to reiterate our most dangerous problem—Amalickiah's poison remains among us. Last month's bloodshed didn't end the dissensions—not entirely."

Another captain mournfully agreed. "I can confirm that with a sad testimony." We hadn't heard from this guy yet. In a whisper, Garth asked Teancum who he was. His name was Lehi.

"Despite our efforts, converts still breed like maggots," Lehi reported. "I've placed ears in nearly every village in the vicinity of Zarahemla. The whisperings are everywhere—in the streets, the markets, even the synagogues. There have been a few arrests. We've learned very little. I feel something is brewing. Something very evil."

Moroni smashed both fists onto the stone table. It startled me.

"We've wasted too much energy on Kingmen!" he shouted. "So much blood has been spilt!"

I was confused. I turned to Garth. I wanted him to hear my question over Moroni's voice, so my whisper was rather loud. But Moroni had paused.

"What do they have against kings?" I asked him.

Every flutter of speaking in the room died like a gunshot. All eyes were burning me. You'd have thought I'd said, "What's wrong with devils?" in a room full of angels.

"Teancum," began Pahoran, "this is a sacred council. We know the loyalties of every man in this room, except those of your guests."

"They are very young," an embarrassed Teancum defended. "They don't know our ways or our problems."

"Educate them on such things, Captain Teancum, if you intend to make them assets to your army," Moroni stated. "From my experience, a boy's heart is loyal to the hand that feeds him. I hope you are able to fill that requirement."

Teancum nodded.

"Are there any questions?" Pahoran asked.

"Twelve days?" Lehi repeated.

"Twelve days for Solomon's armies and ours. Teancum's request to depart earlier will be granted," Moroni confirmed. "How soon will you leave?"

"Five days," Teancum stated.

"Five?" Moroni was impressed. "You've surprised me with your stamina before, Captain. I'm sure it will be done. My intention is to wind up affairs in the capital and merge my own forces with those in the east before the rains return. Captain Lehi and Captain Solomon will be responsible for stepping up the supply line to the east. Antipus and Gid will organize one for Manti and southward. Brief Pahoran on all your arrangements so that he may enforce them. The palace's arsenal has built up an ample supply of obsidian for your soldiers—but don't hoard it."

Pahoran waited a moment to see if there were any more questions.

"This council will convene again the day before Teancum's departure. May we close?" he asked the group as a whole.

Helaman was asked to offer prayer. Everyone in the room stepped away from the table and knelt on the floor. Helaman stood and held his arms upward.

"Oh gracious God, our blessings have been abundant in times past. Let us be mindful of them during these times of heavy heart. We are grateful that such a council as this, with such strong and faithful men, could be assembled this day to represent the will of Thy people in the cause of defending the precious freedoms that Thou hast granted. Please bless each of these, our mighty nation's captains, Moroni, Lehi, Antipus, Gid, Solomon, and Teancum, and bless our honorable Chief Judge Pahoran and his counselors, that they may lead this nation in wisdom and righteousness; that we may conquer our enemies and find peace again within our borders. Help us, oh God, to obtain the victory and help us to live worthy of Thy blessings when it is accomplished. As this great council adjourns, we ask Thy spirit to go with us always, until all Thy works shall be accomplished. Amen."

I said "amen" with the rest. Many of the captains embraced and expressed commitment to the cause. Then Teancum, with Moriancum, led us out of the palace and home to his family camp.

CHAPTER 13

Another deep purple sunset covered the sky when we arrived at the camp of Teancum's family. They called themselves Jershonites. They were one of many kinships that had descended from the lineage of Mulek. There were nearly a hundred Jershonites in Zarahemla. By the look of things, they didn't plan their residence to be permanent. The houses were similar to the palm and clay huts Garth and I first encountered in the jungle.

Teancum had taken the trouble to march his family from Jershon to Zarahemla shortly after the trouble with Morianton, when rumors of a massive invasion were imminent. Many members of his kinship had already resettled here after giving up their lands to the converts of Ammon. Then, when the Ammonites were resettled in Melek, and Moroni made Jershon a base for his armies, the Jershonites returned. Teancum had commanded all the armies in that part of the land for the past seven years. When this newest war was over, the kinship planned to begin a new settlement in the East Wilderness—a permanent one. The new city would be named after Captain Teancum. Garth and I had heard these dreams recounted constantly during our trek over the mountains.

We were a good hundred yards from the center of their neighborhood when a tiny person with a little piercing voice, screaming for joy, popped out and attacked Teancum. Teancum snatched up the tiny fellow and spun him around a time or two. It had been quite some time since the Nephite captain's youngest son had seen his father. The little guy, no more than four, couldn't stop the tears.

"They said you weren't coming home ever again," he sniffled.

"Who?" Teancum asked.

"Jared and Tomoni."

"Well, you tell those boys to come see for themselves. It would take more than all the Lamanites in the Land of Nephi to harm your father," Teancum reassured.

This rugged old Nephite kissed his son on the forehead, drying the boy's tears with his thumb. The boy's high, wailing voice announced to the rest of the camp that the patriarch of the kinship had returned.

Wives, children, brothers, and cousins came to greet us. Moriancum's three little girls and his wife were swarming around him, smothering the poor guy with hugs and other nonsense.

My first impression of Nephite women, upon entering Zarahemla, was that overall, they were a pretty homely bunch— simple clothes, no makeup. I'd been raised to judge beauty by what you see on billboards. It just took some getting used to. I was beginning to recognize the pretty ones. When I saw Teancum's wife coming through the group to embrace her husband, I had a model by which to judge the rest. She was beautiful.

"Are you well, my husband?" she asked, releasing her embrace just far enough to see his eyes.

"Yes, Nuahmi. I'm sorry Teancum the Younger couldn't be here with us," he apologized.

"Gallium told me," she said. "We'll pray for him together— at least for the few days that you're with me."

Teancum introduced us to the group. Everyone, especially the children, showed immediate and aggressive interest in us.

Moriancum's two youngest girls, about six and seven years old, took hold of each of my hands.

"They are from the North," Teancum told them.

"If I looked that white," Teancum's son declared, "I would go to the river, cake my face in mud, and wash it off over and over again until my skin was brown."

"Muleki!" Mrs. Teancum scolded. "That was very, very rude."

"Where are your mother and father?" asked one of the little monkeys clinging to my side.

"At home. A long ways away," I responded.

"Nuahmi," Teancum said to his wife, "we are all very hungry."

More corn, more squash, more beans. Dinner with the Nephites was becoming too predictable. Our plates were prepared by Teancum's mother. She was a sweet old lady—wrinkled, but far from feeble. I watched her crack nuts into a bowl faster than I could have eaten them. Moriancum's family kept bees, so there was honey. When they passed around the hot cocoa this time, I dumped a big glob of honey into my cup and stirred. It made the drink tolerable. Teancum had four children—two boys and two girls. Teancum the Younger was his oldest. His two daughters were both married and living with their spouses in other kinships. Mrs. Teancum described her four-year-old son, Muleki, as a "surprise and a blessing." She'd begun to believe her childbearing years were over.

After dinner, wood was added to the bonfire. It was a healthy flame when Teancum stepped near it, using the light to illuminate his features. The rest of the Jershonites automatically began to wander from their huts. They seated themselves to listen to their kinleader.

Garth and I joined the fireside. Moriancum's two youngest daughters saw me sit down, and danced on over. They planted themselves on either side, each taking an arm. This curse had plagued me my whole life. I'm a real lady-killer to six- and seven-year-olds. Their names were Eddi and Minnikiah. The first one's name sounded sorta funny—like a boy's name in English.

For the first time, I noticed Moriancum's third daughter. She stood at the corner of Moriancum's hut. This one looked close to my age. Her hair was black and long, hanging all the way down her back. I caught her staring at me over the flames. As soon as she noticed that I had noticed, she snatched her glance away and acted as though she'd been giving Teancum her attention the whole time. The captain began his speech.

"My prayers will be full of gratitude tonight. I'm glad to be among you again. As you've all heard, the Lamanites have attacked the city of Moroni. Teancum the Younger and Jerem are in Jershon at this time. I would ask your prayers to be with them and with all our kinsmen still in the East Wilderness."

I caught her looking at me again. We locked stares for a few seconds. It was a contest. She lost and turned away. I laughed inside at the victory.

"When do we leave, Captain?" Gallium asked.

"Five days," Teancum announced.

Sellum commented, "That doesn't give us much time."

"I know it doesn't. I desperately need your support, my kinsmen. Our family and friends in the East Wilderness are under siege at this moment."

I noticed Sellum was about the only bachelor in the crowd. Even Pachumi and Mocum had wives. There were over a hundred people gathered to hear Teancum this night, both old and young, warrior and maiden, family and friend.

I glanced over at Moriancum's older daughter again. I admit, she was rather pretty for a Nephite girl. She looked at me again. The little squirt, Eddi, on my right arm noticed the eye games I was having with her older sister. She began to giggle. Now the older sister really turned away.

"Do you want to marry her?" Eddi asked.

Find a cliff, kid, and jump, I was saying in my mind.

Teancum continued, "We'll travel seven days ahead of Solomon's and Lehi's armies to our homeland of Jershon. There, we hope to learn of the movement and progress of Amalickiah's army. Moroni believes, and I am in agreement, that Amalickiah's goal is to secure the narrow pass into the land Northward, and surround the possessions of the Nephites. Naturally, we will cut him off before he gets that far. God willing, we will be home soon after the commencement of the new year."

Everything else on Teancum's agenda was organizational. He assigned runners and messengers to gather kinleaders under his command to his camp for instruction.

Moriancum's older daughter moved as if to leave. She paid me a glance to make sure I was watching. My mind began searching for an excuse to follow her.

"Do you think they have enough firewood?" I whispered to Garth.

"Probably," he replied. "Why?"

"I think they need some more." I started to stand.

Eddi giggled again. "He wants to follow Menochin," she revealed.

Where's a gag when you need one? I thought.

"Who's that?" asked Garth.

I stammered, "I—I don't even know. I'm getting firewood."

I had to escape that obnoxious giggle. Awkwardly, I stepped over several people, offering "excuse me's," trying not to distract Teancum. Menochin was almost inside the doorway of her father's hut. Moriancum was standing nearby, intently listening to his brother. I couldn't approach while he was there. It just wouldn't look right. At that moment he stepped forward to remind Teancum of certain kinships newly assigned to his jurisdiction from the upper Sidon region. I knew this might be my only opportunity.

Menochin was exerting a lot of effort to ignore me. I maneuvered myself her way. My actions wouldn't have looked any more obvious if I were to stick my hands behind my back and whistle "I Was Strolling Through the Park One Day" while spinning in aimless circles. As I drew close, she threatened to go entirely inside.

"Excuse me," I fumbled. She stopped and acted as if even a moment of her attention was to be esteemed a great honor. Her long black hair whisked across her face and settled again on her shoulders. The firelight danced in her eyes. I was losing my concentration.

"Yes?" she waited.

"Do you know where I might find more firewood for the fire?"

"There's a big pile behind Gallium's hut," she pointed.

"Oh, OK. Right over there, then." I started to back away. "That's a good place for it." I stood there, looking like an idiot. Finally my eyes rolled back in my head. I blew all the air out of my lungs and looked at the ground. "Guess I better get some," I mumbled.

First impressions were not my strong point. I could tell she was trying hard not to crack up. I began to turn.

"There's probably enough already on the fire," she blurted.

I spun back around with the grace of a ballerina. "Do you think so?" I said.

"It'll probably burn all night," she added.

"Oh, well, I watched Captain Teancum throw more wood on, so I wondered if, maybe, he wanted the fire even bigger . . . maybe."

"It's very big. It's hot over there."

"It sure is," I speedily agreed. Good to establish common opinions. "That's why I moved away . . . Then again, I thought more wood, at least on hand, might be nice."

She smiled and my heart melted.

"Your name is Jim," she declared. The way she said "Jim" was so sharp and crisp. It popped from her lips.

"Yeah, Jim," I confirmed. "My real name is Jamie, but I go by Jim. I like it better. Jim." I nodded.

"Don't you like to be called by your given name?" she asked.

I hemmed and hawed once or twice. But she interrupted.

"Among my people, a man's name is very sacred. It is given to him by his father to remind him of who he is or who he should become."

"We do that too," I insisted. "Jamie was my grandfather's name."

"Was your grandfather a great man?"

"Yeah, I guess so. He was a stake president. But see, where I'm from there are a lot of nerds named Jamie, too."

"Nerds?" she repeated.

"For instance, how would you like it if your uncle were named Amalickiah instead of Teancum," I explained. "You'd rather call him something else, right?"

"He would still be my uncle, the great captain," she proudly declared. "There is an evil Lamanite named Jacob. There is also a great prophet named Jacob. When I think of the name Jacob, I think of the great prophet. I will call you Jamie."

The name had never sounded so sweet. Frankly, I wouldn't have cared if she'd called me Rumpelstiltskin.

"My name is Menochin," she said. "It was the name of King Benjamin's queen. She was a great woman. And my grandmother says she was very beautiful. I want to be like her."

"Yeah," I nodded. The way I said it sounded really stupid, as if I was admitting that she was like her already, at least the beautiful part. She smiled. Maybe she blushed. It was too dark to tell. I'd have given anything to know if she had blushed.

Her mother called. "Menochin, get your sisters. I think they're bothering the guest boy."

Eddi and Minnikiah were fumbling all over Garth, exploring his hair and freckles. Garth stared ahead with a blank, frustrated smile. Nobody seemed to notice the girls' antics except Mrs. Moriancum.

Menochin excused herself and retrieved her sisters. Teancum continued:

"Sellum, if you insist on staying in Zarahemla, your responsibilities will be the heaviest. There are at least fifteen kinships here under our jurisdiction."

"That leaves me and my two boys to go to Sidom and Aaron," Gallium offered. "We'll start tomorrow, recruit those we can, and meet you in Jershon."

"Excellent," Teancum praised. "Thank you, Uncle."

Moriancum added, "There may be some confusion about which captain has jurisdiction over the kinships in Aaron."

"We need every able-bodied soldier," Teancum insisted. "I'll confer with Lehi and Solomon and, if worst comes to worst, we'll sort them out in Jershon."

"I understand," Moriancum consented.

"I want all kinleaders in Zarahemla and regions round about who are under my jurisdiction at this fire for council the night after the Sabbath. Pass on the command."

Teancum pointed toward the wide, grassy field north of the Jershonite camp. "Our soldiers will begin to gather in these clearings the following morning. Are there any questions?"

There were no questions.

"Sleep, kinsmen."

With that last piece of advice from their kinleader, the Jershonites began to break up the meeting. Teancum noticed me in the background and mentioned to Sellum about taking Garth and me to the temple tomorrow before he began his rounds so that we might meet with the prophet, Helaman.

Menochin took one last look at me before her mother hurried her into their hut. She smiled after her eyes turned away.

It was a big, open smile. Ha! I thought. She likes me. Yet she kept just enough doubt in my mind to prevent me from getting cocky. I could hear the little girls tease her when they got behind the door. All of a sudden, I looked up. Moriancum was standing over me. His silhouette blocked the firelight. It scared me for a second.

"Sorry to startle you, Jim," he said.

"That's all right," I replied.

Moriancum opened the wooden door on his hut.

"Moriancum," I called. He gave me his attention. "My real name is Jamie."

He looked at me oddly for a second. Then he smiled. "Good night, Jamie."

"Good night," I answered, and joined Garth, who was retiring to Teancum's hut.

CHAPTER 14

I dreamed about Menochin. Strangely, in my dream, I was back in Cody. Menochin was with me. I was taking her out on a date—just as a friend. I wanted to go to the movies, but I was worried. Menochin had never seen one before, and I didn't want to offend her with some gory horror film. Fortunately, *E.T., The Extra-Terrestrial,* was playing at the Cody Theater.

Next thing I remember, we were inside. The movie was starting. Slater and Jack-O were sitting behind us, pointing at Menochin's clothes and laughing. I threatened them. They started throwing popcorn into Menochin's long black hair. We were a couple of minutes into the movie. It was the scene around the table; they were playing games. Despite the popcorn, Menochin was watching the story with great interest. One of the characters on screen said a cussword, and did something sort of crude. Nothing major, I thought, but Menochin started to cry. She got up and pushed her way past everybody's legs, clumsily, because her hands were covering her eyes. I followed her. Everybody in the theater was throwing popcorn at us. It looked like a blizzard. When we got outside, she asked me how I could watch such vulgar things. I was speechless.

Mrs. Teancum rescued me from my dream with an awakening call. Garth and I washed our faces and wrapped the tethers of our Nephite shoes around our ankles. Sellum was waiting for us outside.

We walked back through the Zarahemla neighborhoods, down the main city road along the river. Though it was still early, about seven a.m., most of the townspeople were already up and hopping—doing chores, cooking, or faithfully working in the field. There were farms right in the middle of the city. Roadside merchants were setting up their wares. Not all goods were sold in the market plaza. Merchants along the road operated their stores like highway mini-markets. For people who only needed the basics, it suited their purposes. The salesmen were just as aggressive as usual, even this early in the morning.

After an hour of steady walking, we stood within the inner city, looking through the temple gate. Sellum left us there, explaining that he had much business to conduct. He said he'd return to take us home later that afternoon. "Ask any one of the priests where you might find Helaman," instructed Sellum before he disappeared.

The temple was a massive square building with a wide doorway. There were Nephite inscriptions all over the walls above and around the entrance. I couldn't read them. We were given the gift of tongues while among the Nephites, but not the gift of translation. A big red curtain blocked our view to the inner chamber. The building was adorned with gold on the corners, the pillars, and the rims around the roof and windows. A fire was burning within and smoke escaped through an opening in the wooden roof. A high stone porch went all the way around the temple. Except for the stairway climbing up to the door, the sides had sheer walls.

There were other buildings. Between us and the temple were rows of neatly thatched rooms connected together like little offices, or prayer closets. There was also a small stone building to the right of the temple and an even smaller building to the left.

Monk-like servants were tending the gardens and hurriedly running various errands.

"Tomorrow's the Sabbath," Garth reminded me.

The gardens were beautiful—multi-colored and prickly. One of the men, a priest perhaps, was coming toward us with a small smile—the kind of smile adults usually give kids before they tell them to run along. As he got closer, he began to look at us with familiarity.

"Has Teancum sent you?" he inquired.

"Yeah," I said.

"Then you've come to see the prophet?"

"That's right," Garth answered.

"Come this way."

We were taken to the building on the right. This, I discovered, was the residence of the high priest, who, of course, was Helaman. Helaman greeted us warmly. He invited us into his garden and we sat on some smooth stone benches under the shade of several bushy trees.

"Jim and . . . Garth," Helaman reminded himself.

"Yes," Garth confirmed.

"I spent a considerable part of last evening pondering the things you said in the council. I feel confident that your presence among our people is good—not evil. Teancum will be pleased to know. It is clear you have come from a place very far away, but I don't believe you have answered fully when you say that you are from the North."

"No, we haven't," Garth admitted. "We've tried to explain before, but nobody could figure out what we were talking about." Garth got right into it. "We come from another era, over two thousand years in the future. A time when people build great machines—even machines that can travel to the moon. A time long after Jesus Christ's earthly ministry. In fact, the people of our day anxiously wait for Christ to come again. Our prophets tell us it's very soon."

"Then you were born during the last days? How can this be?"

We shrugged our shoulders. Garth said, "We kinda hoped you could tell us."

"And then we hoped you could tell us how we can get back home," I added.

"Have any adults made this journey with you?" inquired Helaman.

"No," I told him. "Only my little sister was with us."

"And where is she now?"

I bowed my head. "We don't know. Amalickiah has her. We were all captured. Garth and I got away, but she—"

My voice cracked. A tear tried to escape my eye. Helaman curled his hand around my head and pulled me into his shoulder.

The prophet looked upward and began to ponder and reflect. "I have never experienced, nor heard of such a miracle. There must be a reason. God does not act without a purpose." Helaman looked into my eyes. "But I'm afraid I don't have any answers for you right now, my young brothers."

"We have a book," Garth said, "with stories about your people. Your name is in that book. So is Captain Moroni's and Teancum's and many others that we've met. A man named Mormon compiled the book over four hundred years from today, just before the Nephites were destroyed." Garth looked embarrassed. "I guess I should put that in future tense."

Helaman nodded. "You have been blessed to know many things. My father, Alma, told me in the days before he died about the destruction of this people."

Garth went on, "Mormon's son, Moroni, was the last Nephite prophet. He buried the book in a hill. In the last days, a man named Joseph Smith was led to the hill, and he translated the book into our language by the power of God. Joseph Smith was a prophet, like you. There's a period of history that we call the Dark Ages when there were no prophets. Joseph Smith was the first prophet with God's authority in over a thousand years. He restored the Church of Christ, just like your grandfather, Alma, restored it to the Zeniffites."

Garth grew enthusiastic, and Helaman hung on every word. He asked many questions, trying to get clear a picture of things. Garth told Helaman about Carthage Jail and the wagons west, the growth of the Church and the missionaries. He told him about modern-day temples, the gathering of Israel, and the future gathering of the whole Church.

They got into a doctrinal conversation, and Garth mentioned the three degrees of glory in heaven and baptism for the dead. Helaman interrupted Garth, "You haven't taught these doctrines to my people, have you?" Helaman's voice was very stern.

"No," Garth said, hoping he hadn't said something that would get him into trouble.

"These things have been revealed to many prophets," Helaman admitted, "but we do not write them. The people are not ready to receive them. Many would rebel at such knowledge, and the work in our day would be crippled. I'm glad to see that a time will come when all men may know and ponder such truths. But for now, I would urge you to keep these mysteries in your heart."

Mysteries? I'd known about the three degrees of glory all my life. Baptism for the dead was taught almost as much as baptism for the living. It was a curious change of policy indeed.

We ate lunch with Helaman and the rest of the priests. Before digging in, I listened to the longest blessing on the food that I've ever heard. I thought I'd die of starvation. Later, Garth commented on how beautiful the prayer was. I should have expected as much.

After lunch, Helaman walked us to the temple gate. Tomorrow was the Sabbath, he said, and there were many things yet to be prepared.

"I will inquire of the Lord concerning you," Helaman stated. "I will ask him why you are here, and I will ask him how you might return. After I've arrived in the Land of Melek, I will send word. In the meantime, will you accept Teancum's invitation?"

"To be interpreters?" I said.

"It would be a great service to the Nephite armies."

I answered, "I don't know."

Garth was shocked. He looked as though he might push me behind him and apologize for my ignorance. "What do you mean, you don't know?" Garth demanded. He turned to Helaman and stood straight. "If my services are requested by the Nephites, I'd be proud to give them."

"In return, would the Nephite army help me find my sister?" I requested.

"That would be a fair exchange," Helaman agreed. "But it's a matter you'll have to take up with Teancum. Thank you for coming here this morning, my new friends. God willing, we will have many more conversations. Were you brought to the city square by an escort?"

"Yes. Teancum's cousin, Sellum," Garth told him.

We looked around for Sellum.

"He's running errands," I said.

"If you'd like, I could have one of my priests take you back to Teancum's camp."

"We'll wait here a while," I insisted. "If he doesn't show up in a few minutes, we know the way."

Helaman thanked us again, said good-bye, and called us "friends" one more time. What an item to tell the other kids and Old Man Simonton back in Sunday School. The Prophet Helaman considered us his friends. We watched the ancient prophet, now anything but ancient, walk across the grounds, climb all the way up the temple steps, lift the curtain over the doorway, and go inside.

We had no idea when Sellum might show up. We agreed to look for him, and went out into the busy marketplace. The temple grounds had been an oasis from the hustle and bustle of the market. It was intense today—like Saturday at the mall. We grew discouraged quickly. There were so many faces that even if Sellum were within twenty feet, we might miss him. The noise made it equally confusing. Prices and bargains were continually called back and forth.

All at once my eyes stopped scanning. One of the faces stood out. I almost didn't recognize him, but this was the guy that Sellum had briefly spoken to yesterday, after we had gotten our clothes. He was purchasing something from one of the craftsmen and waited as it was wrapped in a bundle similar to cheesecloth. I remembered he and Sellum had plans to get together today, though I didn't know why. He hadn't seen us, and my instincts told me I preferred it that way. Garth noticed I was staring. I pushed him behind a chubby shopper at a jewelry stand to keep him from acting obvious.

"Who are you looking at?" Garth had to know. I pointed.

The chubby woman looked at us rudely, put the bracelet she'd been examining back on the wooden holder, and stepped away.

Sellum's friend now had the bundle in hand and was making his way through the crowd. We started after him.

"Who is he?" Garth insisted.

"We saw him yesterday. Sellum spoke to him, remember?"

"Yes," Garth protested, "but why are we following him?"

"He told Sellum he would have something for him today. They were planning on getting together," I responded.

"Why don't we just ask him where Sellum is, instead of behaving like spies?"

"Because it doesn't seem right."

Garth crinkled his nose and sent me an expression that said I belonged on another planet. "It doesn't seem right? What are you talking about?"

I didn't know how to answer Garth, so I didn't bother. After a while, both of us got into the spirit of the thing. It was a game. When he looked as though he might turn our way, we pretended to examine the merchandise. Our chase took us all the way to the other side of the market. This guy was acting very nervous—even guilty. He clutched that little bundle like it contained illegal drugs. The scene would have fit right in on the television show *Miami Vice*. Reaching the gates of the city square, he turned one last time, as if he suspected he was being followed. But Garth and I, having mastered the art of acting inconspicuous from dozens of mystery movies, escaped his attention.

Sellum's friend left the square. We kept on his heels. He led us into a neighborhood left of the gate, where the stucco buildings were old and peeling. The structures were built close together, each having many rooms. Today must have been a holiday. The buildings were mostly empty. The voices of the market crowd had diminished to only a hum in the background.

I could hear his footsteps occasionally as he crushed a dried palm reed. We stayed hidden, poking around the corner at the last minute to anticipate his direction. When it was almost too late, it occurred to me *he* could hear *our* footsteps as well. The man stopped and listened for several seconds. Garth and I crouched behind a stone fence, hardly breathing.

Somewhat satisfied, he went on slowly. We had to keep a greater distance, and we probably would have lost him entirely if it hadn't been that he'd reached his destination.

As we crept along a certain wall, we heard sounds inside— shuffling and mumbled words. We felt certain Sellum's friend had gone into the front entrance. Garth and I crawled into the shadows between two buildings. One of the walls was collapsing and created a nook that was particularly dark. The first building's wall was unplastered. Many of the wooden planks had half-inch spaces between them so we could see inside.

Quite a group was gathered. Thirty people, maybe more. Our angle made it difficult to tell. The men were very quiet at this moment, sitting cross-legged on the floor, their backs to us. Slits in the ceiling and walls covered the room with stripes of sunlight. At the other end, a man stood behind a table. Sellum's friend, having just made his entrance, was called forward. He passed the bundle over the table to the man.

This was a dismal place to hold a meeting, I thought. Cobwebs dangled above each head. There was only a single candle on the table.

With bony fingers, the man behind the table proceeded to untie the twine that held the bundle together. Sellum's friend returned to the audience. Garth and I watched the package unravel and the contents were revealed. They were knives of glossy obsidian. The blades were sleek and sharp.

"Seven knives, seven men," said the man behind the table. He arranged the knives upon the cheesecloth in a straight line, with the blades directed toward himself and the handles toward the audience.

"Rise," he instructed, and the front row—seven men—stood on their feet, blocking our view of the knives and table.

Suddenly a hand tightened around my shoulder and startled me. It was only Garth. He pointed into the room.

"The third man," he said in a whisper so quiet that I read his lips more than I heard his voice.

I looked at the third man in the row of seven. It took a moment for me to recognize him with his back turned. But after a moment I knew. It was Sellum.

The man behind the table continued his instructions. "Each of you will take the knife before you and swear with an oath to accomplish the task assigned to you. As you recite the oath, you will cut your own arm between the wrist and the elbow so that the blade may taste of your blood. That way, it will know whose breast it must pierce if you fail."

The spirit of blackness was so heavy, I could actually feel it, and its pressure kept me from budging a single centimeter.

I watched the first man of the seven reach forward and take a knife. "With this knife, I, Riboloth, son of Levi, will cut short the breath of Pahoran, son of Nephihah, before the Sabbath breaks or the breath that is cut short will be my own."

I saw his right shoulder tense up and his left shoulder shift sharply. The man had drawn blood from his own arm.

The second man took the next knife. "With this knife, I, Sidon, son of Hiddoni, will cut short the breath of Moroni, son of Moroni, before the Sabbath breaks, or the breath that is cut short will be my own." He too sliced into his own flesh and let it bleed onto the blade.

Now Sellum reached forward and took the third knife and recited his own terrible oath. "With this knife, I, Sellum, son of Coriantor, will cut short the breath of Teancum, son of Jershon, before the Sabbath breaks, or the breath that is cut short will be my own."

My heart was beating so loudly I was afraid it might give us away. It was all I could do to turn my head enough to sneak a glance at Garth, whose eyes and ears were riveted on each man as he recited a murderous vow. Lehi, Gid, Antipus, Solomon— every one of them was marked for assassination within the next twenty-four hours.

I wanted Garth to make the next move. I didn't think I had the strength. The way I was trembling, it was as if the ground were rumbling. It was my misfortune that the builder of all those cobwebs should crawl across my hand when I was in this state of mind. I never saw the spider. I only felt its tickling legs on my knuckles. I swung my hand and snapped my wrist, propelling the creature into the air. In doing this I slapped Garth's arm—just a little—but it caused a sound.

Only two or three of the men on the back row actually heard it, but when their heads turned, it caused a chain reaction. Everyone in the room was facing the wall through which we peered.

"Somebody's there!" a voice called. We heard the audience erupt.

Garth made the first move, as I had hoped, and led me between the buildings and out the space on the other side. As we emerged into the thin street, men started coming around from the front of the building. Their pursuit was desperate. Garth and I knew it had to be. I was moving fast, but, like in a bad dream, I felt as though my legs were kicking in slow motion. We ran between two more buildings. There was lumber propped against the corner. Garth pulled down several strips, creating a barrier, but the men broke through it like a herd of cattle through a twig fence.

We turned into a new street. The pursuers had gone around the other way and gotten ahead of us. Though still a good ten yards away, their arms were already outstretched to seize us. We were forced to run to the left. The walls in that direction came together into a square. It was a dead end—yet my feet refused to stop. Garth had the same problem. We ran smack into the center wall. Our arms were the only thing cushioning the impact. I turned back. The way into this little inlet was choked with men scrambling toward us, their eyes blazing.

"Here!" Garth screamed.

He'd found a window on the right wall and was already hoisting himself through it. I helped him, pushing his feet with such force that he lost his balance and fell inside. I only had time to swing my left leg through before the clutching hands held my right knee and my hip. My free arm swung viciously, but without effect. They began dragging me back. I might have fainted in terror at that moment if I hadn't been shaken by the scream of Garth's voice. He'd picked up something—a broken post—something. He swung it with all his might, like a hammer onto an anvil. It came down on the arms that held me and broke their grips. It probably broke a few arms as well. I fell inside. Men were already struggling through the window as we rushed through the front door, around one more building and into another street that was cluttered with garbage and rotting food. We saw people ahead. Many people. The main street that led into the city square was less than a hundred yards away.

Charging toward the main street, we could still hear the panicked voices of our pursuers, though none were in sight.

We reached the street and splashed into the crowd. They continued walking mindlessly in one direction or the other. We couldn't avoid colliding with a few, causing their purchased goods to tumble onto the ground.

As we looked south toward the square, many of our pursuers had also reached the street. We saw them pointing toward us. Our first thoughts had been to seek refuge at the temple or the palace. Now that way was blocked. We ran north, heading for the bridge that brought us across the Sidon River. The crowd separated for us. We were drawing a lot of attention.

"Stop them!" I heard one of the conspirators call out. "They are thieves!"

One of the townsfolk had the nerve to grab Garth by the scruff of the neck.

"Hold on, boy!" he ordered Garth.

Garth pleaded, "They're going to kill Moroni! They're going to kill everybody!"

The man smiled. I think I might have heard other onlookers laughing. Were his words so preposterous? Maybe they were all in this rebellion together.

"Don't let him go!" a conspirator called while ruthlessly fighting his way through.

I took action. I kicked Garth's assailant in the spot I knew would give the best results. Garth was set free immediately and the man collapsed. Everyone's eyes were drawn toward the fallen man long enough for Garth and me to escape. We went up the road, and at the right moment we slipped into a cluster of buildings on the opposite side. A block later, Garth and I were staring over a dike into the slow and shallow waters of the Sidon. We needed rest, and this appeared to be our only opportunity. Looking back one last time to make sure we were unseen, we lowered ourselves over the dike and stood up to our waists in the brown-green river. The dike had uneven inlets which protected us from view both up and down the bank. Garth braced himself against the wall, panting heavily, massaging the back of his neck where he'd been bruised. I sucked the air into my lungs. My heart refused to soften its beat. We said nothing to each other for several minutes. Then Garth asked simply, "How long should we stay here?"

I answered, "Until it's dark. Or until we're found. We don't have any other choice."

CHAPTER 15

By the time the sky grew dark enough, Garth wasn't sure he had the strength to pull himself up and out of the river. My own legs were stiff and frozen. The water hadn't seemed all that cold when I first plopped into it. As time went on it grew colder and colder. I'd been listening to my teeth chattering for hours. Each time I reached under the water to feel my legs, the numbness had grown worse. The scabs on my knees had washed away.

"We have to try," I encouraged Garth.

I'd set the example. I was barely tall enough to grip the top of the dike. To find the leverage I needed to pull myself up, my legs would have to jump. Making the attempt, my feet performed like cement. They didn't even come an inch off the river bottom. Leaning my forehead against the dike with the cool wood offering some relief, I mouthed a short prayer and rehearsed the act of jumping, over and over, in my mind. Leaping, hoisting—it was like learning how to do it all over again. I tried a second time— gave it all I had. Somehow, my wavering elbows held my weight. By rolling my body, I awkwardly dragged my lower half over the edge of the dike. I rubbed and pressed my calf muscles for several minutes until I could feel them again. Bending my knees to stand felt wrong, as if legs were never meant to bend.

I heard Garth's impatient whisper, "Jim! Where are you?"

Limping back, I reached down to grab Garth's arm below

the shoulder. "Jump!" I told him.

His first attempt wasn't much better than mine, but with our strengths combined, Garth came to a landing on dry ground. Ten minutes passed before we felt ready to walk. Now the question was, where could we go? Attempting to reach the city square was out of the question. There were only two entrances, and certainly both of them would be untiringly watched.

This was the Sabbath. We couldn't see any fires glowing, and Zarahemla, of course, didn't have streetlights. Passing cracks in the doors, we could see the flicker of a candle now and then, but that was the only light—except for the moon, almost fully round. I never realized how bright the moon could make things with no other light to assist it. Buildings and other shapes were very distinct.

We made our way toward the main street. We knew they would be watching it as well, but there was no other route back to the Jershonite neighborhood.

We could hear faint voices all around us, chanting prayers, singing, or laughing. When we reached the main street, we stood still, watching the shadows, trying to sense any movement. We couldn't be sure it was safe, but we took a chance, crossed the street, and walked along the row of buildings on the opposite side.

The streets were completely empty, where only hours before they had been bustling with hundreds of pedestrians. A few minutes into our journey, we passed an open door. Leaning in the doorway was a Nephite gentleman, elegantly dressed—a successful businessman perhaps. His voice startled us.

"Children!" he called. "Come in and rest. It's not proper to be out and about on the Sabbath."

I began to run. Garth followed. We didn't trust him. We couldn't trust anyone. The man called to us twice more, the last time angrily. Then he decided, I suppose, not to bother with us.

We ran a hundred yards or so. From then on we seemed more inclined to walk in the center of the street. There were too many shadows, too many corners on either side.

About five minutes later, I thought I saw something move. Glancing back, I could swear I'd seen a figure dart behind a building. It was a good ways back. It could have been anything. Both Garth and I began to hear rustlings—like birds in the bushes, unseen. We walked faster.

In another moment, we could clearly see the silhouettes of several people. One of them was running alongside us down a parallel street, trying to get ahead of our position. The others were stalking us from behind, moving in slowly. A man to the rear crossed the road and disappeared. Needless to say, we started running again.

So did they, calling to one another, "Move in!" and "Go around!"

Like a ghost, one of them stepped into the street ahead. Gripping a club, he patiently waited for us to come to him. We were a little more agile than he expected and skirted off into a lot full of high bushes and shrubbery on the right. Rather than follow us alone, the man decided to wait for his companions.

"In there!" I heard him shout.

We found ourselves in the midst of many tents—a campground of sorts. Garth tripped on a basket of fruit and fell with a grunt. I stopped and pulled him up. It was clear to me that if we went much further in this direction, we'd end up completely lost. We had to hide. Looking back through the bushes, I saw torchlights coming toward us. Where did they get the torches, I wondered? They had been preparing for this hunt since this afternoon. The obvious hiding place would be the nearest tent. We found the opening, and fell inside.

I felt somebody's leg. It wasn't Garth's.

"What's going on?" mumbled a sleepy voice in the darkness.

My first impulse was to run again, but Garth wouldn't do it. He pleaded with the tent's occupant.

"Please, help us! They want to kill us!" Garth begged.

"Why?" the stranger asked.

Our pursuers were closing in. Garth implored one last time.

"Please," he whispered, "We're innocent! Please believe us."

The stranger cleared his throat—it was an awful sound—then he climbed between us and went outside.

Our lives were in his hands. Garth had no right to give him this power. For all we knew he was on their side. We could still run, I thought. No we couldn't. It was too late. They were among the tents.

"Look at what's happened!" we heard the stranger yell. I'm assuming he discovered the mess Garth had made of his basket of fruit.

"Where are they?" I heard one of our pursuers demand.

The shine of the torches showed through the tent's weavings.

The stranger continued ranting, "Who will pay for this? Who are you chasing?"

"Two boys," a third voice informed him. "Did you see them?"

I heard other stirrings around us. Some of the other tent dwellers had also been awakened.

"They ran right on through," lied the stranger.

The men went on. The torches faded away. For some unknown reason, the stranger had decided to protect us.

He called after them, "Whose boys are they? Someone will have to pay!"

It occurred to me that these tents belonged to the street merchants. The section of highway nearby had been thick with salesmen this morning.

The stranger waited a moment, allowing the other sleepy merchants to retire again into their tents. Then the tent's flap was pulled back. He looked at me, looked at Garth, and came inside, crawling back between us. Sitting now in the spot where, a moment ago, he had enjoyed a peaceful slumber, the stranger folded his arms and took a deep breath.

"Now, what can I expect in return?" he asked politely.

"We don't have any money," Garth admitted.

"What! Not even a single cocoa bean?" His tone wasn't polite anymore. "Maybe I should call them back again."

He moved as if he were going to get up and do just that.

"Wait!" Garth grabbed his arm. "We can pay you later. We have some very important friends."

"Oh, you do? And who might they be?"

"Captain Teancum," Garth told him. "Moroni, if we have to."

As expected, the stranger laughed. "Don't try and con an old con. Certainly you can be more creative than that."

"No, it's true," I insisted. "If you take us to Teancum, there'll be a worthy reward waiting."

"And what would an army captain want with boys?"

"We're his special interpreters," Garth stated.

He laughed again, this time in a manner of exasperation. "Oh, forget it. I'm tired. Just remember that old Tugoth has a place in his heart for little cons. Out, out!" he said and brushed us off.

I wanted to do as he'd requested. Garth had it set in his head to earn this guy's confidence.

"No, please!" Garth begged. "You have to believe us. We heard some things that we shouldn't have heard. Terrible things. That's why they're after us."

Tugoth grew impatient. "I was sleeping, boy! Be grateful that I'm too dizzy or I'd lash you myself."

Garth told him, "They plan to murder some very important men before the Sabbath breaks."

Tugoth sat up again, "What did you hear?"

"We overheard their oaths," I decided to add. "We were hidden, but they found us."

Now our host was genuinely frightened. "You mean those were Kingmen? And they're after you? And I helped you?" The realization hit him like an ulcer. "Oh, how could I be so stupid?"

"We have to get to Teancum. You have to help us," Garth insisted.

"I can't!" Tugoth stammered. "I'm a member of a minor trade order. Once my wares are gone, I'm headed west. Zarahemla's problems are not mine."

"Are you a Nephite?" Garth asked.

"So my mother told me, yes."

"Then they are your problems. The Lamanites are invading Nephite lands even as we're talking."

Tugoth put his hands over his face, "You two are just a bad dream. If I shake my head, you'll be gone, right?"

"They're watching for us everywhere," I said. "If you could just tell Teancum we're here. Bring him to us."

"I liked it better when I thought you were little cons," Tugoth sighed.

Someone was standing outside the tent. The flap was stripped open. A Kingman crouched outside, peering in with thin white eyes. His lips widened into a grin. Tugoth crawled out of the tent, cowering. He walked on his knees. His hands were pressed together, held upward, in praying position.

The Kingman threatened him with his club. "So you lied to us!"

"No! I was holding them for you. I was about to call you back." Tugoth's begging was pitiful. I wanted to club the miserable flake myself.

The Kingman looked again into the tent, turning his back to Tugoth. That was his mistake. Tugoth had a weapon hidden between those prayerful fingers. He knew exactly where to place it. The Kingman cried out and fell onto the tent, collapsing the walls around us. As we climbed out of the mess, we heard Tugoth chanting, "Now I've done it. Now I've really, really done it."

The Kingman had been alone when he'd decided to backtrack, but his shriek brought the torches that had wandered several hundred yards away, moving back in our direction. It woke up the whole community as well. Men were popping out of every tent. They looked at the bleeding body.

"Why have you done this, Tugoth?" asked one of his fellow tradesmen.

"I wish I knew," Tugoth lamented.

Garth and I took off running again, back toward the road. Tugoth, seeing no other option, followed right on our heels. We reached the street. My first impulse was to go in the direction leading toward Teancum's camp. Everyone accepted my decision for a while, then Tugoth expressed other ideas.

"I know where we can hide! Follow me!"

Tugoth didn't leave any opportunity for discussion. We veered left, into another neighborhood—simple houses of wood. A few minutes later, Tugoth stopped us.

"Here we are," he announced.

Tugoth led us into an animal pen with a low, splintered fence. There were no animals here at the moment, but within the pen, a small shelter had been built to protect the animals from the rain and weather. We climbed under it.

"A business associate of mine raised dogs here," Tugoth said. "We can hide here for a while. Then you're on your own. Thanks to you boys, I'll be leaving town tomorrow morning."

"What about Teancum?" Garth reminded him. "Bring him! We'd go ourselves, but they'll be watching for us."

"They'll be watching for me, too!" Tugoth said.

"No. You killed the only one that would even recognize you," said Garth.

"What possibly makes you think Captain Teancum would come? Now, I've accepted that you may have overheard something you shouldn't have. But that gibberish about having important friends—you made that up, didn't you?"

We both shook our heads.

"It's true," I assured him.

"Who are you?" Tugoth demanded. "Government brats? Is your father some kind of official?"

"We're Jershonites," I told him. "Teancum is our father."

Garth's eyes bugged out, but fortunately, Tugoth wasn't looking at him.

Tugoth huffed, "That makes him a little more than a friend, wouldn't you say?"

Garth caught on to what I was doing and added, "Yes, but we'd just met you. We didn't know if you could be trusted."

"Well, that's something you still can't be too sure of, my little con men," Tugoth sneered.

"Will you do it?" I pleaded.

Tugoth looked away and sighed again. "The children of the great Captain Teancum, eh?" Tugoth still sounded skeptical. He turned to me quickly. "How many sisters do you have?"

I knew he was trying to trip me up. I tried to remember. "Two."

"Two?" repeated Tugoth. He watched my eyes. "Maybe you're right. I wouldn't know anyway. All right, little con men, I'll go. First thing in the morning."

"You have to go now," Garth insisted.

"I'm tired!" Tugoth roared.

"Seven men might die before morning. Teancum, my father, is one of them," I told him.

"All right! I'll go! If I'd known tonight would have ended like this—killing a man, running through the streets, disturbing army captains in the middle of the night—I might have aided my slumber with poison. At least I wouldn't have been awakened. Which sons shall I say request his presence?"

"Jim and Garth," Garth said hastily.

"Jim and Garth? What kind of names are those?" Tugoth lifted his hand. "Never mind. If I'm not back in an hour, you'll have cause to worry."

"Do you know the way?" asked Garth.

"Everyone knows the Jershonite neighborhood—at least any trader who's dirtied his hands in the weapons business." Tugoth climbed out of the shelter.

"Only bring Teancum," I called after him. "Try not to awaken anyone else."

We watched Tugoth's shadow for a long time. He went across a garden, through a cornfield , then faded out of sight.

Garth and I were alone again. It was getting chilly. I missed the mild nights in the jungle on the other side of the mountains.

"What time would you say it was?" I asked Garth.

He guessed, "Between one and two."

We didn't say any more for a few minutes. A swarm of gnat-like insects made their way into the shelter. We swung at them with our arms. The swarm broke up a little, but never entirely moved on.

I asked Garth's opinion. "Do you think we should have told him about Sellum, so he could warn Teancum?"

"I wondered about that," was all he said.

I answered my own question. "I didn't think he'd believe a story that accused his own cousin of such evil, if he heard it from a stranger."

"I knew what you were thinking," Garth replied.

Garth tried to sleep a little. Time passage is really confusing when you're watching an imaginary clock in your head. It was a very, very long hour. I kept looking across the field, expecting Tugoth to return.

I tried to sleep. I wasn't blessed with Garth's ability to find peace of mind. "I don't think he made it," I finally blurted out.

Garth opened his eyes. "Give him a little longer."

He closed his eyes again and let his mouth hang open. I pulled my knees tighter into my chest. I deserved to catch pneumonia for the way I'd treated my body today—soaking in the Sidon River all afternoon, shivering in a dog hutch all night.

At least another half hour passed. Finally, I began to see the shapes of two figures making their way toward us, across the cornfield. I lifted my shoulders in anticipation. My movement awakened Garth.

Sure enough, it was Tugoth and Teancum. They crossed the garden, leaping over the fence into the pen.

"Jim? Garth?" Teancum called. What a strong, welcome voice.

We hopped out of the shelter. Teancum was armed with his silver sword and a javelin.

"I'm glad to see you're all right," Teancum sighed. "At first light, I was prepared to release an envoy of troops to search for you. Where is Sellum?"

"He never came back?" I asked.

Teancum was confused. "No. I told him to send word to the Zarahemla kinships about the meeting tomorrow night. Then I asked him to take both of you to Prophet Helaman. I haven't seen him since."

"We saw something—" Garth began.

"Yes, this man, Tugoth, tells me you've gotten mixed up with the secret plots of Kingmen. Tell me from the beginning."

We told him about the man we followed in the market. We told him about being led into the empty neighborhood.

"There were about thirty men," I continued, "They were gathered around a table. Seven of the men cut themselves with a knife and swore they would each kill one person before the Sabbath breaks."

Garth filled in the names. "You were one of them. Also Moroni and Pahoran. The rest were Lehi, Gid, Solomon, and Antipus."

"Who were the assassins?" Teancum demanded, "Did you hear their names?"

"Yes," said Garth, "I made it a point to remember every one of them. The man who was supposed to kill you was Sellum."

Teancum's jaw dropped. It was the only time I ever saw the great captain surprised by any news. He looked down, mournfully. "My own cousin," he gasped.

Then Teancum grabbed Garth's shoulders. I'm sure he didn't mean to, but in his frustration, he shook Garth as he spoke. "Who are the others? Tell me every single name!"

Amazingly, Garth remembered every name, and every father's name that had been spoken in that dreary room. Teancum seemed to recognize them. He released Garth.

"Every one of those men is in a position to accomplish exactly what he intends. Riboloth is one of Pahoran's judges. Libnah, son of Jacobi, is an advisor to Lehi. We have to get to Lehi's camp. It's not far from here. Can you boys still run?"

I felt like I'd been endlessly running for the past seven days. If I ever got home to Cody, I swore I'd never run again.

Tugoth came with us. He recited all his troubles to Teancum. "I lost everything when I stepped forward to save these young men's lives," Tugoth panted. "All my merchandise, my whole life's savings!"

"I'll see to it that you're compensated," promised Teancum.

Teancum was right. It wasn't far, only a fifteen-minute run, to Lehi's camp. We traveled southwest, climbing a road cut between two hills. The road opened up atop a plateau, revealing a host of tents.

Outside Captain Lehi's tent, guards watched us approach and stepped forward. They lowered their swords when they saw it was Teancum.

"Captain Teancum!" a guard exclaimed. "Is there an emergency?"

"Arouse Captain Lehi!" Teancum requested. "Libnah, son of Jacobi—is he here?"

"His tent is back there," a guard indicated.

"Arrest him immediately!" commanded Teancum.

The guards were hesitant. "Will Lehi confirm this order?"

Just then, Lehi stepped out of his tent, wearing only a tunic. He tied a sash about his waist. "Yes, I'll confirm it," he said. "There must be a good reason for it, if Captain Teancum has come to make such a request at this hour." The way Lehi said it made it clear he demanded an explanation.

Three of the guards departed. Lehi looked at his fellow commander with great curiosity. "What's going on?"

Teancum explained, "There is a conspiracy, Lehi. A residue of Kingmen will try to murder Pahoran and all of the chief captains of the Nephite army before the sun sets again. Libnah is part of it."

"Libnah has been at my side for over a year, Teancum," said Lehi. "He's one of my finest strategic advisors. There must be a mistake. Who discovered this conspiracy?"

"These boys overheard a private conference revealing the scheme yesterday afternoon," said Teancum.

Lehi studied us and spoke to Teancum. "You've placed a lot of faith in the testimony of two very young men. I hope this affair doesn't end in embarrassment, Captain."

The guards were returning. They held a grumbling Libnah by each of his arms.

"What's the meaning of this?" Libnah demanded. "Dragged out of my tent in the middle of the night? Captain Lehi, I deserve an explanation!"

Garth and I had been temporarily hidden from Libnah's view, behind Lehi's tent. The moment our eyes connected with Libnah, he stopped square in his tracks, unable to breathe. He looked up at Captain Lehi, whose expression grew very stern as he watched Libnah's panicked reaction. Libnah struggled to escape from the hold of the guards. He succeeded in freeing one arm. That was all he needed to reach inside his tunic and pull out a black obsidian knife. Our view of the struggle was hampered when the rest of the guards rushed onto the scene to help subdue him. Libnah was wrestled to the ground. Teancum and Lehi moved in for a closer look. They pulled the guards away from Libnah's body. The conspirator wasn't moving. Teancum turned him over. Libnah's hand clutched the knife's handle. He had buried the blade into his own belly.

CHAPTER 16

Things were very busy in Lehi's camp after the assassin's death. Alarms were sounded, soldiers were awakened, orders were shouted. Armed messengers were dispatched with missions to inform all five of the remaining leaders about the impending plot. Teancum and Lehi personally led a troop of soldiers to the city square to warn Pahoran and Moroni. As for Garth and me, we were given an armed escort back to Teancum's camp.

Tugoth remained in Lehi's camp. He agreed to help identify the men he had seen, if they were captured. Maybe tonight's events had inspired some kind of Nephite loyalty in Tugoth, or maybe he was just doing it for a price. Either way, we owed great thanks to the bumbling merchant. We found an opportunity to express it to him just before dawn, as our escort was preparing to depart.

"I knew you weren't really Teancum's children," Tugoth insisted, "but I figured if you were willing to carry the story that far, I'd better do as you asked."

"I hope we'll see you again," I said.

Tugoth chuckled, "I'll have to think about that one. Good-bye, little con men. Today's the Sabbath, and I believe I'll sleep all the way through it."

Tugoth had the right idea. When we got back to the Jershonite neighborhood, it was all we could do to stay awake while explaining to Moriancum and the rest about what had happened. Finally, Mrs. Teancum brought us inside her hut and arranged a shady corner in her front room for us to crash.

When my eyes opened again, I was staring into what I thought were the eyes of an angel. Menochin was running her fingers through my hair. When she saw me stir she moved her hand away.

"I'm sorry. Did I wake you?" she asked.

Never before had waking been something I regretted so much. If only I could have pretended to be asleep a little longer and savored the attention.

"No. I mean, it's okay," I told her.

I looked for Garth. He was gone. "Where's Garth?" I asked.

"Outside."

"What time is it?"

"It's late in the day," she said. "The sun will be setting soon. You missed the whole Sabbath."

"How long have you been here?" I asked.

"Only a few minutes," Menochin admitted. "Everyone knows what happened last night. They say you saved my uncle's life, and many other lives as well. You and your friend are heroes."

I thought to myself, if waking up to her face was my reward for being a hero, I should definitely be a hero more often.

Mrs. Teancum was preparing a meal near the hearth. "Is he hungry, Menochin?" she inquired.

"Are you hungry?" Menochin asked me. I nodded.

"Yes, Aunt Nuahmi. He's very hungry."

Mrs. Teancum had a big spread of food prepared for me— meat and warm vegetables and cold cocoa, sweetened with honey.

Halfway through the meal, Garth burst through the door. "Teancum's coming back!" he yelled.

I ran outside with Garth, greeting the captain as he returned. A handful of Lehi's men were at his side. His youngest boy was the first to reach him, as usual. Teancum gathered the toddler in his arms. Moriancum reached him next. Teancum put his son down at that moment and engaged in serious conversation with his brother.

"The conspiracy has been all but crushed," Teancum told Moriancum. "They're still making arrests. Captain Moroni wants every effort made to find and punish the offenders. Garth and Jim will be needed to identify the few who refuse to confess."

"What's become of Sellum?" inquired Moriancum with some hesitation.

"He's still at large. Sellum is the only designated assassin that is not in custody or dead."

Teancum's tone was unchanged. I'd never have guessed he was speaking about his own cousin, or that he was aware there still might be some danger to his life. You had to look at everyone else to see evidence of the tension that existed over the issue.

"I have other grave news," Teancum continued. "We didn't reach Captain Solomon in time. He's dead."

"Captain Solomon? What will become of his army?" asked Moriancum.

"Lehi and I have already discussed it. He will lead Solomon's men to Jershon. There, we will divide his soldiers equally between both our armies. Only two armies will march east before the new year commences. Moroni approved it."

Teancum saw his wife waiting in the doorway. As he started to go to her, he noticed Garth and me. The captain sent us a painful smile. From that gesture alone, we knew how grateful he was. Yet in that smile we could also feel the weight of stress the day's events had brought upon him. His cousin, a companion since his childhood, had betrayed him.

Teancum embraced his wife. Before retiring into his hut, he turned to address the gathering family.

"I know everyone is anxious for more information, but it's still the Sabbath. I intend to take advantage of what's left of it."

It was only an hour before the sun went down and the Sabbath would be officially over. Just before dark, kinleaders began arriving in Teancum's camp from all over the city of Zarahemla. Of the fifteen kinships, each had two to four representatives present. After including all the Jershonites, it made tonight's fireside pretty crowded.

Teancum began by clearing up false rumors that had been circulating. Some had heard that Moroni had been murdered. Others had heard that Teancum's cousin had fled the country. One had even heard that Pahoran was behind the conspiracy. That rumor angered Teancum. He rebuked the man who reported the rumor for even considering it could be true.

"Now more than ever," Teancum roared, "we must unify the army both physically and spiritually. Any false rumors must be crushed. The character of any leader dedicated to the cause of freedom must be defended!"

Many kinleaders agreed with Teancum and took the time to express their commitment. One after the other bore his testimony of God and family, and reassured Teancum of the loyalty of his kinship. Listening to them raised my spirits and did a lot to dispel the gloom. I'd started to think nobody could be trusted anymore.

When the talk turned to details—provisions, assembling, that sort of stuff—I got up and wandered away from the fire. If I missed anything important, Garth could fill me in later. Restless, I wandered out into the clearing. Tomorrow, soldiers from all over the territory would pitch their tents here. Thoughts about home came to mind.

If it was Saturday night there, like it was here, I'd be bumming money off my dad to go roller skating about now. As Dad was reaching into his pocket, Jennifer would appear and ask to come along. I'd tell her, "No! You'll only cramp my style." Then Dad would hold his wallet high in the air and declare that if I didn't take my sister, I'd get no money. Of course, I'd start to complain and moan, but I'd always give in. Then I'd ditch Jen on the way there. I yearned for a chance to apologize to her for all the mean things I had pulled.

I turned around and looked back at the fire, a good hundred yards away now. Someone was coming toward me. The fire was positioned right behind the person's head, causing a dark silhouette. But I could tell by the long hair, dancing as she jumped over obstacles, that it was Menochin.

As she got near, she put her hands behind her back.

"I saw you walk away from the fire," she said. "Were you bored?"

"No," I assured her, "I was just . . . thinking."

I sat down on the ground, hoping she'd follow my lead and keep me company. She sat right next to me.

"Do you miss your home?" she asked.

She was a pretty perceptive girl. "Yeah, I guess so."

"Who do you miss?"

"My brothers and sister," I said, "Mom and Dad."

"Anyone else?"

Boy, that was a loaded question. I knew what she was getting at, but I'd learned from my years of social experience not to make it obvious that I knew.

"Like who?" I asked innocently.

She got right to the point. "Like a girl?"

"Like a what?" I teased.

"You know, a fiancée. You're old enough to marry now. Do you get to choose who you will marry or does your family decide for you?"

"We decide for ourselves!" I defended. "You mean *you* can't marry whoever you want?"

"Sometimes we can, if, during the courtship years, we find someone we love. If we don't, then our parents find someone for us."

"What are the courtship years?" I asked.

"Thirteen to fifteen," said Menochin.

"You're kidding! We're not even supposed to date until we're sixteen!"

"Sometimes the men will wait that long," Menochin admitted. "The prideful ones."

"To answer your question, no, I don't have a fiancée or even a girlfriend."

"There are many Nephite girls," she said. "I'm sure you've met a lot of them by now—some that are very beautiful, I suppose."

"I've only met one I'd describe like that," I uttered.

By the end of my statement, I was looking right into her eyes. I'm such a suave kind of guy, I thought. I can't help myself sometimes.

She smiled in a shy way—a way that made my chest well up inside like there was a tidal wave trying to come out. Then Menochin scared me to death. She leaned forward a little and closed her eyes.

I'd seen this moment in the movies. It was some kind of cue, right? I was supposed to kiss her, right? I'd never done this before. I didn't even know how my lips were supposed to move. Do I breathe in or out, or what? I couldn't carry this out! Yet something inside me, something very male, told me if I failed, I'd be an eternal shame to my sex.

She'd opened her eyes, just a squint, to see what I was doing. I moved forward, very slowly, and stuck my lips out. Just before contact, Menochin had the nerve to grin, snap back, and leap to her feet, laughing. She went running back across the clearing.

"Where are you going?" I called.

"I'm afraid of snakes!" she laughed. After a few more steps she turned around. "Come on!"

That's it, I said in my mind. Never again! Girls were exasperating by nature. I'd known that since the first grade. How could I have been so foolish as to think otherwise, even for a moment?

Menochin was running through high weeds back toward the fire. Reluctantly, I got to my feet and went after her. By the time I reached the high weeds, Menochin was almost back to the fire.

I was startled by a rustling on my left. A dark shape was propelling toward me. I tried to leap sideways to dodge him, but I fell into the weeds and a powerful hand reached around my throat. I looked up into a wild and desperate face.

"Sellum!" I cried.

Menochin turned around to see what had happened. I heard her scream. Sellum stood me up and clamped one arm across my chest. In his other hand, he held a knife—a glossy obsidian blade. He began to walk backwards.

"You've destroyed me, boy!" he cried.

Menochin screamed several more times. She finally got the attention of everyone gathered around the fire. Sellum held the knife so close to my eye, I couldn't focus on it.

"I wouldn't have done it!" he continued. "I knew even as I was reciting the oath, I couldn't do it. But no one would believe that now, because of you."

"Then why?" I choked out.

"I was chosen," he shrieked, "because of my proximity to him! If I had refused, I would have lost my life then, instead of tonight!"

They were coming now, rushing across the clearing. Sellum fell to his knees. His grip on me didn't loosen.

"Tell them that," I urged him. I didn't think they'd believe it, but I'd say anything if it might convince him to spare my life.

He mumbled, "It's too late."

They were arriving now. I saw Moriancum and Garth among them, and many of the kinleaders. Sellum placed the blade against my throat.

"Don't come any closer!" he commanded.

The crowd stayed back, but began to surround us. Bows were loaded.

"Stay in front of me!" Sellum cried.

Teancum stepped through and stood before us. He held out his hand toward Sellum.

"Don't do this, my cousin," said Teancum calmly.

"Don't mock me, Captain! I have no cousins. I'm as alone as a man can ever be," he said mournfully, then barked, "Don't get behind me!" Teancum waved back the men that were creeping around through the weeds. "Keep back! All of you!"

Teancum looked back at Sellum. "You're not alone, my cousin. Your God will always be your God. And we will always be your family."

"God?" said Sellum, "There's no God for me."

"Don't believe that. It's Satan's lie," Teancum told him.

"No. Maybe once it was a lie—"

"It's still a lie!" Teancum roared.

The captain carefully stepped forward, his hand still extended. I hoped he knew what he was doing.

"Hand me the knife, Sellum," coaxed Teancum.

Teancum was getting close enough that Sellum could slit my throat, toss me aside, and complete his evil mission just by lunging forward. Teancum had no defense. His sword was still in its sheath.

"Come back to us, my cousin."

Tears had trailed all the way down my cheeks. I felt one of them fall. Judging by where Sellum was holding the knife, I'm sure the tear splattered on his hand. My tear triggered something in Sellum. He started to weep, and dropped the knife. It bounced off my thigh and fell into the dirt.

Before I knew it, Teancum had pried me from Sellum's grasp. A half dozen men seized Sellum from all angles. He was bound and taken back over by the bonfire. There, with Teancum and Moriancum sitting close on either side, the broken cousin confessed to everything and recounted the details of his being recruited into the league of the Kingmen.

He said he had grown disillusioned with the Nephite cause when they refused to invade the Lamanite lands when they had the chance. The Kingmen talked about seizing this kind of glory. They painted a vision of the Nephites becoming the most powerful nation on the face of the land and they made him many promises. Some of their causes Sellum believed in, some of them he didn't. Sellum hoped, in time, the policies he felt were foolish would die. But he soon learned they wouldn't let him go halfway. By then, he was in too deep. It was impossible to escape.

Some of the kinleaders agreed to take him into the city square to join the other imprisoned conspirators. Before they departed, I watched Teancum embrace his cousin. Then he watched the escort of soldiers head down the street, fading into the night.

"Will he ever rejoin the kinship?" Moriancum asked.

"I will hope . . . one day," Teancum replied.

CHAPTER 17

"Will you make me a promise?" I asked Teancum early the next morning. "If we help you now, when it comes time will you help me rescue my sister?"

Teancum set down his breakfast bowl and looked at me squarely. "I will," he promised.

They began arriving shortly after sunrise. Hundreds of them—some wearing no more than a loincloth, no sandals. Others toted meager homemade weapons. Many were barely older than Garth or me. Yet others looked as if they had been warriors all their lives. Their weapons were coarse and worn. Some were stone-tooth swords with bloodstains dyed deep into the wood. This wasn't their first march, and I don't think they expected it to be their last.

There was a feeling of excitement, especially among the younger soldiers. They wrestled with each other and made a lot of ruckus. The older, seasoned warriors seemed impatient with them. Cooks arrived shortly before noon. They brought a train of servants carrying corn, beans, dried fruit, and other supplies in baskets fashioned into burdensome backpacks.

Moriancum organized the distribution of new weapons and shields from the government arsenal. He gave out swords and spears, axes, and a kind of stick that threw darts. Garth called these sticks *atlatls*. Soldiers had been trained for certain weapons and were assigned to specific positions in battle. Being a bowman was considered a privilege. Men competing for this position shot arrows into targets, while sub-commanders made selections.

Carriers from the palace filled a shelter near Teancum's hut with protective clothing: breastplates, headgear, armgear, and leg gear. The breastplates looked very similar to the ones I'd seen among the Lamanites. Garth explained that Moroni had developed the clothing and the Lamanites had copied the design.

Even though many of these boys seemed green, none of them were entirely untrained for battle. Zarahemla had many schools for military education, established long ago and expanded by Moroni. Boys had been attending these schools for years. I watched the skill some of them exhibited when demonstrating their weapons and felt envious. I wished my school had trained us in such things.

To be honest, I spent most of the morning watching Menochin rather than the soldiers. I helped her with her chores: washing pots, gathering food from the garden, and feeding lunch to her two little sisters. Naturally, she had to endure more teasing from the little runts, but I guess, in Menochin's mind, I'd become worth the persecution. After lunch, Menochin and I were alone. I watched her weave a blanket on a loom stretched and tied from the roof of her hut down to the ground. It seemed like we spent most of the time talking about me. It's not that I'm conceited. She just kept throwing questions at me, wanting to know about my family and my land. It was hard to explain specifics without talking about modern concepts she wouldn't understand, so I only told her stories that made sense in both time frames.

Menochin was incredible—in perfect control of her world. It surprised her that I seemed to know so little about everyday

Nephite tasks, like preparing corn by soaking it in lime, or knowing which plants could be used to make rope.

Sometimes, while watching her, I'd imagine a scene in which we were married. She would take care of me in this strange world, cooking my meals and making my clothes. I would return from hunting and she'd be waiting for me in the doorway of our little hut, the same way Mrs. Teancum waited for the captain. We would plant the garden side by side, and teach our children about life and God. Maybe I never would get back to Wyoming. Maybe everything I was imagining would one day come to pass. It was flattering and yet frightening to see in Menochin's eyes that she was thinking the same thoughts from time to time.

Later that afternoon, Teancum informed Garth and me that an escort from Moroni's headquarters had arrived to take us into Zarahemla to identify some of the conspirators. The soldiers who brought us into the city explained that there were very few common criminals within the prison walls. Nearly all of them were dissenters who sided with the cause of Amalickiah. Just over a month ago, they said four thousand men had been killed fighting Moroni's troops in a bloody street battle. Now I understood why Moroni was so stressed about the subject of Kingmen when it was discussed in the council.

When we got inside, we were taken to a room equivalent to the warden's office. Captain Moroni was there with his private staff of officers and servants.

"We have brought the witnesses," Moroni was informed by a member of our escort.

"Good," I heard him comment. "Let's settle this matter and get on to more important business."

The legendary chief captain of all the Nephite armies walked right up to us, held us awestruck with his pale blue eyes, and congratulated us for our bravery.

"Captain Teancum told me the whole episode," he said. "Your presence among our people has become something valuable indeed. We're very grateful to you."

If I'd been warned that Captain Moroni would be thanking us personally this afternoon, I would have at least practiced saying "You're welcome." As it was, I squeaked out a feeble, "Uh-huh."

Moroni smiled and looked away. "Line up all of the accused—immediately!"

The only things missing were the bright spotlights and the one-way mirror. About twelve accused conspirators were herded into a blank, cold chamber of the prison.

"Now look at them," Moroni instructed us, "and tell us which ones you saw that afternoon, whether they were taking oaths of murder or simply in company with those taking such oaths."

As the guard moved down the line from one Kingman to the next, one of Moroni's officers asked us, "Did you see this man?" "Where?" "What did you see him do?"

I identified most of them. Garth was able to remember the faces of every single one. Among them was the man that we had followed in the market. There was burning hatred in his eyes. He spat in our direction. Another prisoner used profanity and called us "eaters of snakes." To me it was a silly sounding insult. I guess, to them, it was considered pretty low. These were not people I wanted to meet in dark alleys in later years of my life.

"That's all," Moroni finally said. "Take the boys out."

I was glad it was over. An officer gently led us from the room. Not even a minute later, Moroni came out as well.

"I'm sorry you had to endure that," apologized Moroni. "I've shed many tears to God wondering how these times could have produced such men."

"There were others," Garth told him. "We saw over thirty men in that building."

"I'm sure there are others," Moroni told Garth. "I can only pray this last defeat has broken them. I hope in the wake of Amalickiah's defeat, their hearts will change. The testimony you boys have given was crucial. Once again, we thank you."

Moroni turned to our escorts. "Take them back."

With that, Moroni left us and was immediately surrounded by his staff. They turned Moroni's attention to other pressing matters and followed behind the captain as he left the prison ahead of us. I'm not sure if this will make any sense or not, but after he walked away, dignified, a long metal sword at his hip, the air felt different. It wasn't hotter or colder, just different—emptier.

Garth and I went back to Teancum's camp, arriving soon after the sun went down. Soldiers kept arriving late into the night. Dozens of tiny fires dotted the field.

Menochin had made boiled corn tamales for Garth and me. It was another of the thousand ways the Nephites had for preparing corn. As we ate, Garth began talking.

"You remember the banners we saw hanging from the tower when we first arrived?" Garth asked. "Those were Titles of Liberty. After the battle with the Kingmen a month ago, Moroni forced the dissenters who weren't killed to either take up the sword in defense of their country or be hewn down. Flying the 'Title' shamed them in the eyes of their peers. That way, even if they rebelled again, the other dissenters might sooner kill them than trust them. Pretty clever of Moroni, don't you think?"

I was barely listening to Garth. Menochin had my mind rather occupied. She kept going back to the hearth and finding more food for us, smiling at me each time she returned.

"Anybody home?" Garth waved his hand in front of my face.

"I'm sorry," I said. "What'd you say?"

"I said, 'Pretty clever, don't you think?'"

"Yeah, yes it was," I admitted.

Garth sighed, "I've got a feeling three is becoming a bit of a crowd around here. I think I'll find Teancum and ask him what our duties will be."

"You're a great cook," I told Menochin after Garth had left.

She blushed. "I'll have to work very hard to be as good as my mother and my grandmother."

"I wish I could have you over for dinner at my house sometime. My mom makes great spaghetti."

Then I had to explain what spaghetti was, but the only item in the recipe she even recognized was tomatoes.

After dinner, we went outside and sat next to the bonfire. Tonight it burned without any audience except Menochin and me. Teancum, Moriancum, and the kinleaders were out among the troops.

Menochin taught me about the stars, how they moved around the sky from season to season. She pointed at a certain cluster in the southern sky and asked me to promise that I would return from battle before the cluster was in that position again. While she waited for me to make the promise, I grew very uneasy. Reality settled back onto my mind.

"I don't know if I can make that promise," I said.

"Why?" she asked.

"Because," I began, "I might have to go home to my own people before then."

"When will you know if you have to go home?"

"I don't know," I mumbled.

"When you return, I will go with you," she insisted.

I laughed, "That would be a good one. No, that wouldn't work."

Tears started to well up in Menochin's eyes. I realized I'd insulted her. Feeling lower than a toad, I grabbed her hand.

"If I do come back, I probably never will go home. Then, I promise, I'll come for you . . . I, well—I love you, Menochin."

Okay, I admit, at thirteen years old, I wasn't sure I knew what love was. Gosh, I'd only known this girl for a couple of days. But to me, right now, the feeling was real. It seemed like older people made love too complicated—too many games and stuff. Maybe what I felt right now was as pure and simple as love ever got. After all, this was my first.

There was a ring on her finger. She pulled it off and placed it in my hand. The stone in it was blue and smooth.

"I want you to keep this," requested Menochin.

"I can't take it," I told her.

"Yes, you can."

"No, this is yours."

"Take it or I'll hit you over the head!" she barked.

I took it. It slipped onto my index finger just fine.

"You'll think of me when you look at it?" she asked.

"I will," I promised.

I wanted to give her something that would fulfill the same function. The only thing I had was the jade and silver necklace I had picked up that first night in the jungle. I removed it, handed it to her, and made her make the same promise.

Thinking back on this moment, I should have kissed her right then. She certainly gave me another opportunity. But I got really self-righteous for a moment. I knew God was watching and I thought to myself, if ever I tell this story to my kith and kin, I should set an example for all modern boys and girls to follow, and forgo any youthful osculation. Silly decision, but my heart was in the right place.

When I finally went to bed, Garth was already lying there, staring at Teancum's ceiling.

"Anything the matter?" I asked.

Garth said, "I'm going with Lehi tomorrow to be his interpreter. There'll be another council meeting tomorrow afternoon. I'll go to the palace with Teancum, and that'll be the last time you see me for a while."

"Really?" I said, and climbed under Mrs. Teancum's blankets.

It took a while for the whole impact of Garth's statement to sink in. When it did, I got very uptight inside. Garth had been with me nearly every moment of this adventure. Could I make it without him? I needed Garth. He was my only link to what was real. Both of us stared at the ceiling for some time.

In a moment, Garth said, "I may have been too anxious when I told Prophet Helaman I'd do anything to help the Nephites. I don't think we should be separated. I need your strength, Jim."

"You're kidding! My strength? This humidity must be rotting your brain."

"I guess you're right," Garth teased.

Mrs. Teancum came in from the other room and added wood to the fire in the hearth.

"Good night," she whispered to us.

"Good night," we answered. She blew out the candles and left.

Garth knelt and said his prayers. I closed my eyes and said mine. I prayed that Garth would be okay. Mostly, I prayed that I would be okay without him.

The next day the scene was pretty much the same—massive gatherings of soldiers. By noon there must have been ten thousand Nephite warriors in the clearing. For the first time, my services were required as an interpreter. Several kinships had arrived from the wilderness of Hermounts, southeast of Melek. Many of them were not direct descendants of the Nephites, but had been converted to Christianity by the missionary efforts of Alma the Younger. They had a good working knowledge of Hebrew, but Moriancum wanted my help to make sure, when he gave his instructions, that all of his meanings were clear. I would be in greatest demand, Moriancum told me, when we met up with Gallium in Jershon. The army they had assembled from the Sidom and Aaron regions might speak two or three different languages.

I was depressed all day—torn between spending time with Garth or Menochin. Neither of them was very good company. They were as depressed as I was. At least Menochin put a lot more effort into pretending she wasn't depressed.

All at once, Garth's dreaded hour was upon us.

"We're ready to go to the palace," a messenger announced through the doorway of Teancum's hut.

Garth looked at me and tried to smile, while at the same time biting the inside of his cheek.

"Look at it this way," he said. "I'll only be one week behind you."

"Sure," I responded. "I could always lag behind and wait for you, that is, if I have a hard time sleeping and need to hear one of your history lessons."

"Yeah, and if I get the urge to let you lead me into another life-threatening encounter, I'll run ahead of Lehi's army and catch up to you," Garth added.

He held out his hand for a friendship shake. We locked thumbs, locked fingers, and hit down upon one another's fists.

"See ya in Jershon, bud!"

Garth was gone. Menochin walked over to me, held my hand and admitted she loved me too. Together we watched the sun go down that night. We made more promises to each other. I suppose if I were to describe the scene, it would sound really corny, so I won't go into detail.

I was planning to stay up with her all that night, but she wouldn't hear of it. "You'll be marching the whole day tomorrow," she reminded me, "and I won't keep you from getting your rest."

We said a prayer together before the evening ended. Menochin said the words. She prayed that the war would end quickly and that I would be safe. She also prayed for her father, her uncle, and her countrymen.

While we stood together outside Moriancum's hut, procrastinating the moment of separation, Menochin's mother finally called for her daughter to come inside. Menochin looked at me one last time with tear-filled eyes and gave me a smile that beamed with so much love that I said the heck with setting an example for kith and kin. I laid a big kiss right on her lips. And I'm not ashamed to admit, it felt great. I doubt I'll ever feel anything even half as wonderful ever again. Besides, how many times in a boy's life does he get the opportunity to kiss a beautiful Nephite girl? You just don't pass up things like that—not if there's a brain in your head.

CHAPTER 18

I heard whispering in the other room. The noise woke me up. Last night I had slept alone—and not altogether soundly—so I was sensitive to any noise. It was Teancum's voice. He and his wife were kneeling together in solemn prayer one last time before the captain would again leave his family to command a legion of troops on another long march. The words were tender and private.

I squinted and tried to determine the quantity of daylight outside. There wasn't much. It was very pale and dim, like the morning we'd escaped from Amalickiah. The flame in the hearth was burning low. Teancum emerged from his bedroom, followed by his wife.

"Would you like breakfast, my husband?" she offered.

"No. I'm afraid I haven't time," Teancum said regretfully. "My commanders are probably already waiting for me."

Mrs. Teancum struggled to hold in her emotions. She knew this march was different than others she'd watched depart over the last seven years. It wasn't just a repositioning of men. Nor was it something as simple as pursuing rebellious countrymen, the majority of whom were unarmed.

"Muleki will be sorry he didn't get to tell his father good-bye," she said.

"I'll kiss him," whispered Teancum.

I watched him move over to the opposite corner and lean down to kiss his four-year-old son. The little fellow acted as if he'd been wide awake and waiting all along.

"Hi, Daddy," I heard the sleepy voice yawn. Muleki extended his arms to hug his father.

"Hello, little Muleki."

The child gave Teancum no choice but to lift him into his arms.

"Are you going away again?" the voice peeped.

"Yes, but I'll be back soon. You'll take care of your mother and your grandmother, won't you?"

Another yawn. "Yes, Daddy."

The tiny body dropped limply again over Teancum's shoulder and fell back asleep. Teancum held the boy for a moment longer, then placed him gently back into his hammock.

Mrs. Teancum stepped next to her husband and got her own hug.

"You'll stay in one piece for me, my captain?"

"As long as you're praying for me, my wife," Teancum assured her. "Awaken Jim. Feed him if he's hungry, and send him to the northeast end of the clearing to find me."

"Yes, Captain."

"I love you, Nuahmi. Keep a fire burning in the hearth until I return."

They embraced one last time, and then, without looking back, Teancum was out the door.

After taking a moment of repose against the hearth to collect her emotions, Mrs. Teancum called out my name. I ate a quick breakfast and thanked her for all she'd done. Because she'd gotten into the habit this morning, she gave *me* a hug too. Teancum's wife had woven Garth and me our own bedrolls. She placed mine in my arms. I hung it over my shoulder while she commanded me to take care of myself and, if I found opportunity, her husband as well.

I was one of the last people awake. The tents had been taken down, tied into bundles, and strapped upon the backs of every third soldier. The columns of men, now adorned in full battle regalia, began their formal assembling at the bellow of shell-shaped trumpets. Soldiers dodged around me, scrambling to find their positions.

An ancient Nephite army was a little more complex than I imagined. At the rear of the columns were all kinds of personnel—everyone from cooks to physicians. The number of men that carried food, water, extra weapons, and extra protective clothing almost made up an army in themselves.

The troops traveled together as kinships as much as possible, but also according to weapon position and field time. The more skilled and experienced a soldier was, the closer to the head of the army he would march.

To find Teancum I followed the sounds of the trumpets. After walking down the assembling columns, I found him standing boldly before his army, Moriancum at his side. The Prophet Helaman had troubled himself to arrive at this early hour and personally offer a blessing upon us before departure.

"We're about to pray," he told me. "Stand down the ranks and repeat my words. Because of your gift, the men will hear the prayer in their most common language. It will be a powerful way to begin the march."

I went down the ranks as far as I could without putting myself out of hearing range of Helaman's voice. The prophet motioned this massive host to kneel upon the ground. Like ten thousand dominoes, the men closest to the front kneeled first, then everyone behind them caught on, and followed. I was concerned that my young voice wouldn't carry as far as Helaman hoped and therefore, lack the power he anticipated. To my surprise, my words rang out as though I were upon the rooftop of the palace.

These were the words of Helaman's blessing:

"Oh gracious God, mover of mountains and skies, on this morning the hearts of these men, and the hearts of all thy faithful children, pour out thanks unto thee for the strength we have been given to assemble in thy holy name to march in defense of our country and our religion. We are grateful to the mothers and fathers of these valiant men that they have been raised up to fear thee and to love thy word. We pray they may return to their families with all their strength and faculties. And if it be thy will that some of these men must return to thy presence, we ask that thou wilt reward them generously in the world in which thou wilt take them.

"We ask, oh God, that thou wilt move this army with the same ease that thou couldst move any mountain. Bless the captains who watch over them. Inspire them with knowledge, that this campaign may be shortened and no further bloodshed will persist. Bless them with the humility and faith to seek thy guidance in all their decisions. With the deepest pleading of our souls, we ask thy spirit to go with us always, until all thy works shall be accomplished. Amen."

I echoed Helaman's every word. After the prayer closed and I lifted my eyes, many of the men were looking at me as they rose to their feet. My voice *had* touched them, as Helaman knew it would. The distance was still too great for many of them to hear everything, though from that moment on, ten thousand men seemed to know who I was.

Once again the trumpet blared, this time in a more direct pattern. Teancum spun on his heel and took the first step forward. The wheels on this glorious steam train of men started to churn. The march east had begun.

I waved as I passed Helaman and received a wave in return.

Since we were finally underway, I figured Teancum might be able to breathe a sigh of satisfaction, but the chief captain never got a moment's peace. Soldiers were constantly running to and from his presence, receiving various orders. Arrangements still had to be made with supply lines behind us and recruiters ahead. Scouting parties were dispatched as well. After journeying to assigned points ahead of the army, they would backtrack and report their findings to Teancum and his commanders.

We crossed the Sidon River. There were no bridges. Even if there had been, this army wouldn't have had the patience to use them. They plunged in as if the water couldn't hinder their pace in the least, walking up to their waists in the sluggish current. Fortunately, this section of the Sidon was free of the squirmy gifts that the murky river in the East Wilderness had attached to us. "If only all the rivers in our path were as kind and shallow as Zarahemla's Sidon," commented Moriancum.

We climbed into the high country above the Zarahemla valley. There were children on the rim again. They followed along with us as they had a few days ago, pointing and yelling with more excitement than ever, for now they had much more to gawk at.

Around noon, the army rested. We were offered a simple lunch of corn patties and dried fruit. I ate alone, sitting on a mound of stones next to the road. Being as young as I was made me an item of interest, and everyone treated me very politely, but when it came right down to it, I was just a kid and not a fellow soldier. I missed Menochin, and I missed Garth. I feared this march would be dreadfully lonely. These thoughts hadn't troubled my mind for more than a minute when I observed a certain warrior shyly studying me. He was one of the younger ones, sixteen or seventeen at the most. Finally, he got up the courage to come over.

"They say you're from the North—the far North. Is that right?" he asked.

"That's right," I answered. "The far, *far* North."

"I find that fascinating," he said. "Astoundingly fascinating!"

"Astoundingly?" I repeated. "Why?"

"On account of my great-uncle, mostly. He was of the society of long-distance traders. I'll bet he traveled farther north than any other Nephite. When I was little he told me stories. Most of them exaggerated, I'm sure. At least I think they were exaggerated. He's dead now, so I'd consigned myself to the possibility of never knowing, unless I were to go there myself."

"What kind of stories did he tell you?" I inquired.

"Oh, cities of gold, magnificent waters and fountains, tribes that were half-men, half-dog, deer as big as houses—that sort of thing. I'm sure he was exaggerating." The soldier looked up at me slowly with one eye. "Wasn't he?"

"A little," I admitted. "All but the deer part. We do have a lot bigger deer where I come from."

"How I'd love to hear all about it. I'd even pay you—if I had any cocoa," he offered.

"You don't have to pay me," I said.

"I couldn't thank you enough. I will repay you someday. Just name the favor."

Strapped on this guy's back was a Nephite sword. The blades were wrapped in deer leather.

"May I see your sword?" I requested.

"Certainly."

The soldier put his shield on the ground and brought the sword forward. Unwrapping the skins, he revealed the weapon's deadly sidegrooves set with obsidian blades. It was a nasty-looking thing.

"I'll make you a deal," I decided as I felt the sword's weight in my hands. "I'll talk your ear off about the North if you get me one of these swords and teach me how to use it."

"Now there's an excellent trade. It's a deal!"

"We'll shake on it," I offered.

Shaking hands in the manner I was used to wasn't a common custom among the Nephites, but it only took a second to show him how.

"Allow me to introduce myself," the soldier announced. "My name is Hagoth. I come from a family of traders and ship-builders on the West Sea. I admit, their operation is a humble one. But when I return, I have high ambitions—very high ambitions. Let's get you a sword, my friend."

We journeyed to the rear of the columns, back to the supply carriers. Hagoth pointed out the man to see. He displayed a selection of swords. I chose one from the dozens he had on hand and held it out for Hagoth to examine.

"Too big," he said. "Remember, you have to carry it, wield it—sleep with it. It should stand no higher than your hip, and for you, the lighter the wood, the better—as long as it's not prone to cracking. With your height, you'll need skill, not force."

Hagoth chose one for me. "Try this for size."

Its blades were very sharp and long, jutting out on both sides.

"What if I fell on it?" I asked.

"It would cut you in two," Hagoth declared. "That's why you wear it on your back and properly wrap it. And even then, don't fall backwards. If a heavy whack will rip through a breast-plate, you know it'll rip though this."

He tossed me a strip of deer leather with some tethers and showed me how to tie it comfortably upon my back, alongside my bedroll. Then he selected a feather-studded breastplate, just my size, and a round shield for my left arm. I wore it all in proud display. Thus ended lesson one.

"Tonight I'll show you a few defenses," Hagoth promised. "By the time we reach Jershon, you'll be a master, Jim, my friend."

I walked with Hagoth the rest of that day. He introduced me to the soldiers in his kinship. I found two of them particularly easy-going—his second cousin, Jenuem, and his friend

Benjamin. Hagoth's "kinship" was a hodgepodge of warriors from a particular coastal area, some related, some not. The kinleader was a guy called Ridonihah. He wasn't directly related to anyone in the group. He was a professional soldier assigned by Moriancum to lead these men.

In fulfillment of my end of the bargain, I told Hagoth and his companions all about the North.

"It snows a lot," I explained. "In fact snow and ice covers the ground almost half of the entire year."

"I've never seen snow," Benjamin admitted.

"You're not missing much," I said. "Except for skiing. Then I like it. Mostly it's cold and miserable."

"What is *skiing?*" Hagoth asked.

"Well, you strap two strips of wood on your feet, go to the top of the mountain and—whoosh!—all the way to the bottom."

"Sliding? How do you keep your balance?" Jenuem asked.

"It ain't easy. You gotta practice," I bragged.

"I don't believe any of it," huffed one of Hagoth's more haughty companions named Loromish. His first impression of me wasn't all that positive.

"Well, it's true," I insisted. "There's nothing more exhilarating than to zoom down a mountain at full speed with some good loud music blaring in your ear."

"There are musicians on the mountain?" wondered Hagoth.

"No, no, no." I was going a little too fast for these guys. "It's hard to explain. You'd have to be there. You folks like music?"

"Loromish is a singer," Hagoth revealed.

"Sing us a song, Loromish," I encouraged. "I haven't heard music in so long, I might go nuts soon without it."

"Well . . ." Loromish pridefully hesitated. "All right. I'll do it tonight."

"What about now?" I asked.

"While we're marching?" Loromish winced. You'd think I'd asked Beethoven to perform in a low class nightclub.

"Sure! That's the best time."

I began to sing, "When Johnny comes marching home again—Hurrah! Hurrah!" and I wound up with, "And we'll all feel gay when Johnny comes marching home!"

I was a hit. About a dozen guys started applauding me.

"Wonderful!" Hagoth commended. "Very unusual music. I insist that you teach me some of the songs of your people."

"Okay," I accepted. "I'll teach everybody a song—right now."

I proceeded to sing the theme song from *Gilligan's Island*: "Just sit right back and you'll hear a tale . . . ." This was a style of music they'd never heard before. I forced them to learn the lyrics for a second go-through. They loved it!—Well, all but Loromish. He was offended by it all, and didn't mind telling me so. Hagoth muttered something equivalent to "lighten up," and the singing was allowed to continue. Frankly, a pond of bullfrogs sounded better than my Nephite choir. I was making them use their vocal chords in a way that was totally foreign to them.

Next I sang the Beatles' "Twist and Shout"—complete with rock 'n roll-type screams, but it didn't go over too well. Too many weird notes, I guess. They felt much more comfortable with "You Are My Sunshine." And after a little practice they didn't sound half bad. (I wasn't judging too harshly.)

By the time we stopped for the night, we'd only come about three-fourths of the distance we had covered when our group traveled this route alone. With ten thousand men, that was to be expected.

Before it got dark, Hagoth and Benjamin showed me some moves with my new sword and shield—mostly maneuvers to keep me from getting smashed by the other guy. I caught on pretty quickly, if I do say so myself.

"Tomorrow, the lesson will cover offensive thrusts," Hagoth said.

Then he spent a few minutes showing off with his own sword, tossing it from hand to hand and taking it around his head like a baton.

"I'm impressed," I told him.

"If you're gonna practice stuff like that, use a plain club, without any jags," he warned.

After dinner the kinships settled into their own intimate groups to relax and converse. I was asked if I would sing one more song. I thought for a moment, then moved into the middle of them all so they could see my hand gestures.

Book of Mormon stories that my teacher tells to me,
Are about the Lamanites of ancient history.
Long ago their fathers came from far across the sea,
Given this land, if they lived—righteously.

I sang all the verses. They were somewhat confused by the words, but seemed to enjoy the hand gestures.

After my performance, Loromish kept his word and sang for us. To me, it was kind of a simple song—very "Indian" (though that description might leave something to be desired). The Nephites became very peaceful. Whereas my songs were a novelty, this was their heritage. The ballad told the story of the lost kingdom of the Jaredites—

In a certain era,
Which no one can reckon,
Which no one can remember,
There was a government for a long time. . .

When Loromish was finished, Ridonihah organized a prayer circle. I thought it best to find my way back to Teancum's tent, so he wouldn't wonder where I was. But I promised Hagoth and the rest of my new friends I'd march with them the following day, ready with a fresh batch of stories.

Over the next few days, I got pretty close to Hagoth, Jenuem, and Benjamin. Hagoth and Benjamin taught me everything they knew about the obsidian-edge sword. I can't say that I performed with the same grace they did, but my training was adequate.

"You've come a long way," complimented Benjamin.

"Indeed," Hagoth agreed. "Any Lamanite would consider you a formidable foe."

I really didn't expect to participate in any battles. That wasn't my job. Knowing that fact made it safe to imagine what might happen if I did. Among the Nephites, warriors who were valiant in battle were given their own plots of prime land. The kind of heroics I daydreamed about would have earned me an entire valley.

As the week passed and we got closer to Jershon, the reality of the destined conflict grew more and more real in my mind. Once, in the middle of the night, the whole camp was alerted. Amulonites had crept in and stolen some food and even went as far as killing one of the carriers for a measly basket of grain. Several guards admitted they remembered seeing the intruders walking through the tents prior to the assault, but they walked with such ease, with such an attitude of belonging, that they were passed off as restless soldiers. The thieves were vigorously pursued until three had been struck down. At first I thought we were under a surprise attack from Amalickiah's entire army. After that event, my daydreams ended.

I finally told Hagoth about my sister. He felt very sorry about the situation and said some discouraging things.

"Prepare your heart for the worst, Jim, my friend."

I lost my temper. "I don't have to prepare for anything! Teancum made me a promise—and he'll keep it! If he thought the worst, do you think he'd make such a promise? Do you think he's a liar?"

Hagoth made a hasty apology. I apologized too. He said he understood my anguish and hoped, intensely, that I was right.

In spite of Hagoth's apology, it didn't take the echo of his words out of my mind, and I was depressed for some time. It heightened my suspense and my eagerness to know that tomorrow we would be in Jershon. There I might discover something specific about Jenny's whereabouts, as we learned how far Amalickiah's ruthless invasion had progressed.

CHAPTER 19

Someone mentioned that we had crossed into the land of Jershon. Scattered throughout the jungle were the remains of tiny settlements built by Lamanite converts, more often called Ammonites. The structures had been left to rot and crumble in the heavy rains.

"They've been gone for five years," Jenuem told me. "When Moroni declared this valley a base for his army, he ordered the Ammonites to move to Melek. They knew it was for their own protection."

"They must have gotten awfully sick of moving," I concluded.

"They're the best Christians I've ever known," said Jenuem. "If Moroni had asked them to sail back to Jerusalem, they would have done it. Actually they like the fresh mountain air in Melek. They originally came from the highlands."

We wandered through one Ammonite ghost town with almost thirty jungle-choked buildings. As we looked at all the cut wood and cleared land, it was obvious the Ammonites were a hard-working people when they were in Jershon.

The jungle was thick, but there were many open plains between the trees, so I was spared the feeling of suffocation I'd had before. Around noon we emerged from the forest. In the middle of a particularly wide clearing, a city wall crossed the skyline. This was the army base of Jershon.

Trumpeters, perched on the highest towers, made everyone aware of the approaching army. Maybe they suspected us to be an advancing Lamanite battalion. But our own trumpeters returned the signal and the latches on the city gates were lifted.

Most of the buildings outside the fort were situated along the edge of the jungle. A few remaining inhabitants, mostly old people, poked their heads out and wandered over to greet us.

There were actually three walls of defense around Jershon. The first two lines were piles of stone. The innermost wall consisted of a deep mote with timber set against the inside edge and packed in with dirt. If an army thought it could get in by digging a tunnel, they'd be quickly frustrated. To make it even more impregnable, the timbers had been sharpened into spikes—which made going up and over an equally discouraging idea. If I were a Lamanite captain, I'd have sooner attacked Zarahemla than this place.

I caught up to Teancum and made myself available. The space within the fort looked rather confined. Ten thousand troops could have stuffed themselves into it if they had to, but unless they were defending it, it wasn't necessary. To make things less cramped, Teancum chose to keep us stationed out in the open.

"Tell the men to start pitching their tents," Teancum called.

They wouldn't keep the soldiers outside the city for long. They knew there'd be an open marketplace in Jershon. The prospect of fresh meat and drink had ten thousand mouths watering.

Teancum and Moriancum were overjoyed to see that the first man waiting inside to greet them was none other than their stalwart Uncle Gallium.

"I knew you'd arrive today! If you hadn't, we might have marched into battle without you!" Gallium declared.

"How are you, my uncle?" Teancum called.

"Strong, Captain. Better than ever," said Gallium.

"Where's my son?" Teancum asked.

"I'm sure he and Jerem heard the trumpets. Mocum and Pachumi should also be around here somewhere."

"How went the recruiting?" asked Moriancum.

"Sidom and Aaron were very generous, I think," said Gallium. "We arrived with 2,754 men. How about yourselves?"

"We left Zarahemla with just under 10,000 men," reported Teancum. "During the march we may have recruited another 600."

"There are still a good two thousand reserves stationed in Jershon," estimated Gallium. "All together, we should face ol' Bloodeye with a force nearly 16,000 strong."

Teancum nodded and drifted off in thought.

"Is that enough?" Moriancum asked him.

"It's never enough," admitted Teancum. "But it's all we'll need."

As we proceeded into the fort, Captain Teancum's face brightened. His son, Teancum the Younger, came toward us, followed by Jerem, another of Teancum's cousins. The father and son embraced. It was a high-spirited reunion.

"And how are you, Jim, my boy?" asked Gallium as he mussed up my hair. "I'm assuming since you're here, your call as interpreter was approved. Where's your spotted companion, Garth?"

"With Lehi," I said.

"Well, I guess we couldn't have both interpreters—not that we wouldn't have use for them. A lot of our recruits don't speak a word of Hebrew. If they hadn't understood what I meant by pointing my finger toward the land of Jershon, I might not have gotten them here at all."

"Bring all kinleaders together for council tonight," Teancum announced.

Moriancum sent several men into the ranks to spread the word.

When Gallium said that his recruits had come from Sidom and Aaron, he was speaking generally. Actually, they had come from many cities and communities in that vicinity. Sidom and Aaron happened to be the only two that had significant Christian populations, though all the cities accepted a certain, though weak affiliation with the government in Zarahemla.

Gallium's men had pitched their tents inside the gates of the city. They gawked at us, probably saying in their minds, "So this must be the great Teancum."

To those who also seemed to be saying, "Who's that pale-looking kid with him?" I returned their stares with a glance that served to say, "His personal, private, executive interpreter—in case you were wondering."

Teancum the Younger told his father that he and Jerem had made it to Jershon two days after they separated.

"We reached Nephihah that same night to warn them," young Teancum reported, "but it made very little difference. Nephihah has since fallen to Amalickiah."

"Nephihah has been taken?" Teancum mourned.

Moriancum was surprised. "But Nephihah was one of the better fortified settlements in the East Wilderness."

"Many other cities have fallen as well," regretted young Teancum. "Lehi, Morianton, Omner, Gid—a team of scouts, arriving last night, claim Mulek is under siege as of yesterday. They didn't expect it to hold out much longer."

"And all in less than thirty days," mumbled Teancum.

"It's the largest army Amalickiah has ever assembled," said Jerem. "He himself commands the Lamanites in every battle."

"As I guessed," said Teancum, "he's headed for Bountiful to seize the pass. We can't wait for Lehi. By then, it might all be over. I want to speak with these scouts."

The inner part of Jershon looked much like the inner part of Zarahemla, except there were no buildings as beautiful as the palace or the temple. Still, there was a government complex and a synagogue situated in the same general places. The market was considerably smaller. I'll bet at any other time it was only set up once or twice a week. But in anticipation of all these armies passing through, the local merchants pulled out all the stops and gathered every thread of merchandise they could find.

Teancum, Gallium, and young Teancum headed for the government complex to meet with the local leaders, many of whom would be kin to the Jershonites. The rest of us went shopping, gorging ourselves with all the fresh fruits and vegetables we could swallow.

The gate to the settlement started to bottleneck with all the trailworn soldiers. If they'd been cattle you could have called it a stampede. I could see anxiety on the merchants' faces as they tried to hastily secure their goods.

I spotted Hagoth, Jenuem, and Benjamin among the masses and went to greet them. They wanted to hear about the cities that had fallen. I told them we'd probably march again tomorrow to cut off Amalickiah's conquest of Bountiful.

"It's nice to have a friend that moves in upper circles," Benjamin told me. "Instead of hearing the rumors, we can spread them."

I happened to glance over at one of the shops, surprised by what I saw.

"I know that man over there," I said.

At a certain canopied stand, a handful of soldiers bought papaya from an old blind man. Hagoth and the rest followed me over. There was a young boy helping him—ensuring that he didn't get anything snatched from under his nose. Even so, the old guy seemed pretty capable all by himself. He slapped a soldier's hand with his cane as he tried to pick up one of the papayas.

"I'll hand it to you!" he snapped. "You trying to cheat an old man? How many do you want?"

The soldier asked for five and placed several cocoa beans into the blind man's palm while he mumbled, "Someone ought to teach you young folks patience."

"Who's next?" he asked. "Only one at a time."

I stood at the counter and announced my presence. "Onin?" I asked.

Those old eyes started to shine, just the way I remembered.

"I know that voice," Onin said. Then he thought real hard, rapping his fingers on his chin. "You're one of the boys from the North!"

"You're right," I told him.

"Of course I'm right! My, my, my," he chattered, "I thought the Lamanites would have cooked you for sure."

"We escaped," I said. "All but my sister."

"Well, they won't cook her, I don't believe. A young girl makes a useful slave. When she's older, a useful wife."

"We left you in the jungle. How did you get here?" I asked.

"Walking on my sandals, just like you. After you children got hauled off, I had a cuss of a time getting back to my hut. I got there though, the next morning. Had to travel all night, but it don't make much difference to me, you know. Then some ornery Nephite soldiers, retreating from the city Moroni, found me and told me I had to come with them. I told them I didn't want to come—liked it where I was. But those boys wouldn't take no for an answer. So I made 'em a deal. If they carried three baskets of papaya for me, I wouldn't make a fuss. They did, and I'm here. Papaya's almost gone though."

"That's too bad," I said. "You've got a lot of new customers."

"Well, take a few before there aren't any to take," Onin invited. "My treat."

Seeing Onin brought this whole adventure full circle for me. It also brought back images of the last time I saw my sister. Onin also let Hagoth, Jenuem, and Benjamin have a free sample of his wares. Then he told me to tell Garth he was still available if we ever needed a guide.

"I'll make you a promise. Next time, we'll get to where we're going. You can take old Onin's word for it."

Teancum's army needed a day of R & R. They had grown tired and they had become grumpy. It was time to let off some steam. Several fights broke out among the men. They were only squabbles, but it all went to emphasize Pahoran's point that these soldiers were an unusual melting pot of cultures. I'd come to learn that even from one city or valley to the next, the Nephite peoples had many different customs and differences in dress, speech, and education.

Rain kept drizzling for most of the afternoon. Toward night, the sky cleared and the men started to settle down. They began to kindle fires and roasted duck and turkey.

My presence was requested with all the other commanders and kinleaders in a conference outside Jershon's government complex. There were more than five hundred men surrounding the platform upon which Teancum spoke. It had become a very hot, muggy evening and I heard much grumbling. This crowd of inlanders didn't much care for the weather on this side of the mountains.

Teancum began his speech by telling us everything he knew about Amalickiah's invasion thus far. He paused between sentences, while I stood by and repeated every word.

"I estimate that we'll clash with the enemy within two days," Teancum announced. "At this moment Amalickiah is storming the city of Mulek. By now it may have fallen. From there I'm certain he'll advance on Bountiful. Therefore we'll march into the borders of the land Bountiful and cut him off while he marches out in the open. From this moment on, we'll march in strict battle formation. The bowmen will march as a group. Experienced swordsmen will march at the head of the army. Inexperienced will remain in the rear. It is the responsibility of the individual kinleaders to designate their own men into one category or the other. Each kinleader will also choose one to three warriors from his own kinship that he feels exemplify the greatest fighting skills and have them report to my presence at first light. These men will spearhead the army and I will personally lead them into battle. The kinleaders may not include themselves as front linemen without my approval. I would prefer them to stay behind so that the army's flank won't be lacking in leadership."

As I repeated the last part of Teancum's instructions, I felt myself swallow. I knew Teancum would keep me with him at the front of the army in case he needed an interpreter. This wasn't what I'd mentally prepared myself for. When the mighty armies met, I had hoped to be soaking rays somewhere behind the lines. After the meeting adjourned, Teancum confirmed my suspicion. But he comforted me by saying ten men would be assigned to serve exclusively as my bodyguards.

"You're too valuable to my army to leave unprotected," he said.

"Can I choose some of the bodyguards myself?" I asked.

Teancum agreed. "As long as a kinleader has pre-qualified them to be among his finest warriors," he added.

I went off to find Hagoth's kinship to see who Ridonihah would choose to be part of the spearhead group. When I got there, Ridonihah was in the process of making that selection. He informed Hagoth and Benjamin that they would go to meet with Teancum at first light. It was a bittersweet honor. Jenuem offered them his congratulations. I wandered into their group and added mine as well.

"I'm not so sure it's something I should be congratulated for, Jim, my friend," Hagoth admitted. "Maybe you should be giving us your condolences instead."

"I'll be right beside you," I said. "Or should I say, you'll be right beside me. Teancum gave me permission to choose ten bodyguards. I want you guys to be among the ten."

Hagoth grinned. "We'd be honored. Not that you need us. As well as you've mastered that sword, I'm sure you'll be a bodyguard for the ten of us."

"See you at first light," I said, smiling.

I wanted to sleep near Teancum's tent tonight, for my own security, I guess. Walking back through the rows of tents, soaking my feet in the mud, I tried to recall all the war movies I'd ever seen. The truth was, I had no idea what to expect. I hoped between now and morning, Teancum would tell me two or three more times how valuable my life was and how intensely he intended to look out for my safety.

CHAPTER 20

The rain started pouring during the night, joined by thunder and lightning. Like most of the men, I started out the night sleeping under the stars, but after the first few drops fell, I asked Moriancum if I might join him in his tent. "I thought this was the dry season," I whimpered.

"In the East Wilderness, it's always wet, only some seasons are wetter than others." Moriancum rolled over and fell asleep.

An hour after the downpour began, the edges of my blanket were soaked and my sleeping pad was floating in mud. I achieved a total of two hours' sleep. Despite the conditions, and my tossing, Moriancum never stirred once.

Around four or five a.m., when the rain finally stopped, I wasn't even grateful. My shivering kept me from lying on my back any longer. I ended up dozing the last hour of the night in a sitting position, with my chin on my chest.

I heard Teancum rise before dawn. Moriancum awakened a moment later and quietly crawled out of the tent, trying not to disturb me. Young Teancum arrived on the scene shortly thereafter. I figured sitting in the mud wasn't doing me much good, so I climbed out of the tent behind Moriancum and joined the gathering crowd.

"Good morning," young Teancum greeted me. "Sleep well?"

"Don't tell me you did," I grumbled.

"I did," he said. "One thing my father taught me when I was very young: a new soldier will gripe and complain when weather interferes with his comfort. a seasoned warrior sleeps soundly in spite of everything. He's come to learn the value of sleep—and when it's offered, he takes advantage of it."

That was all I needed to hear this early in the morning—a speech scolding me for my attitude.

"My father has told me all about the courageous things you've done for us. When we first came upon you and your friend in the jungle, I knew there was something important about you," said Teancum the Younger.

If he was trying to butter me up after telling me I had a sour attitude, he was on the right track.

As the morning light began to glow, the soldiers assigned to march with Teancum began to arrive, taking their position at the head of the army. Hagoth and Benjamin stood close by, ready to defend my life at the cost of their own. The first thing I wanted them to do was select another eight men to act as my bodyguards. I was ashamed to select them myself. Many of the warriors were not much older than me, and couldn't have had much more training than I'd been given, yet had to stand bravely on their own.

After Hagoth's selection was completed, I whispered in his ear, "Are any of them wondering why I deserve such special treatment?"

"Of course not, Jim," he assured. "They've all seen you interpreting. They know your value to the army as well as Teancum does."

"I feel a little guilty," I said.

"It's all in your head," Hagoth told me. I felt like everybody was criticizing my attitude this morning.

The entire army, almost sixteen thousand strong, stood ready to march into battle. Because of a mist of fog that had risen from the earth, I couldn't see the end of the column. When the trumpets sounded, the army appeared as though it were marching forth out of the clouds of heaven.

There was very little conversation in the ranks. No one was in the mood for my stories. The army was much more somber, and very determined in its pace. Somewhere through the jungle ahead, over those hills, and across those plains, another army was lurking. That army had already shed a considerable amount of blood, and the satanic man who led them kept them anxious to shed considerably more. With every new vista that opened before us, I squinted to see if a host of men was crouched in the underbrush, waiting to ambush us.

During our lunch rest, several of Teancum's scouts returned, reporting that Mulek had fallen. Amalickiah was presently marching along the coast toward the land of Bountiful—just as Teancum had predicted. After that announcement, lunch was over, and Teancum heightened the army's pace even more, causing us to jog. We maintained this pace for twenty or thirty minutes before Teancum let us walk again. But twenty minutes later the jogging was reinstated. This was the pattern that we endured for the rest of the day.

By late afternoon we were a sweaty and sore mass of men. At the hour when we would normally set up camp, Teancum kept us going. Finally, just before the edge of the sun touched the distant hills, we came to a halt. I noticed a new smell in the air, fresh and salty.

We had stopped only because lookouts noticed another group of scouts scampering toward us across the plains. They informed Teancum that if we continued we'd reach the coast of the East Sea soon after dark.

"Where is Amalickiah?" Teancum demanded.

"You've passed him," the scout reported. "His troops are camped a half-day's march up the coast."

Teancum looked out over the lowlands that stretched before us, touching the ocean. It was a clear strip of open land with trees, marshes, and patches of jungle.

"He'll bring them through there," Teancum observed. "We'll be waiting."

A runner from the back of the army hastily approached. "Captain Teancum, the rearmost column has broken away in pursuit of three Lamanites. They claim the spies have been following us most of the afternoon."

"Make every effort to capture them!" Teancum commanded. "Pursue them into the night if you have to!"

A few minutes later, another messenger reported that one of the spies had been slain and the other two were in bonds.

"This may be the edge we need," mused Teancum. "Old Bloodeye loves surprises."

Teancum ordered Moriancum to stay in the hills with half the army, while the remainder of the troops, including the spearhead battalion, would descend into the lowlands and wait, meeting Amalickiah head-on.

"When the battle commences," Teancum commanded Moriancum, "sound the charge and come out of these hills with thunder, hitting Amalickiah's flank with the fury of God. We'll drive them into the sea."

While 8,000 men started pitching their tents, the other 8,000, including me, had the fun of marching another half hour after the sun had completely disappeared. As the stars were starting to glimmer, we positioned ourselves behind a jutting of woods that cut into the lowland plain. If Teancum's plan went correctly, the Lamanites wouldn't discover us until their march brought them right under our noses.

No fires were kindled. After eating what we could from the small supply of food we'd carried with us, we laid out our bedrolls in the damp grass, having no time for tents. If the rains started again, we'd simply grin and bear it. After what Teancum the Younger said to me this morning, I was determined to sleep soundly like a seasoned warrior—even if it snowed! The rains didn't return.

In the morning, I was almost the last to awaken. The sun was already peeking over the horizon when Hagoth roused me. All ten of my bodyguards had saved me a portion of their breakfast rations, and Hagoth had the task of bringing the food forward.

"I can't eat all that," I said, staring at a couple of pounds of cold corn biscuits and jerky.

"You'll insult us if you don't," Hagoth winked.

I started stuffing corn bread into my mouth while Benjamin, Hagoth, and the rest looked on.

"Is anybody still hungry?" I asked, with a corn biscuit in each hand and more of the same in both cheeks.

They all shook their heads until I begged for mercy. After having a laugh, they moved in, gathering up the remainder of my meal for themselves.

The rest of the morning was spent waiting. I watched the clouds drift by. I watched a bee decide upon a certain flower then suddenly fly away. Perhaps it had a premonition and decided it was best to find a different field to seek its pollen—a part of the world where the flowers would be tall and untrampled tomorrow as well as today.

The day grew hotter and hotter. It must have been close to eleven o'clock when men began running back from their lookout positions on the other side of the woods.

"They're coming!" one of them said. The adrenalin started to surge through my body.

Teancum commanded us to hold our positions. I repeated his command. That was the last sentence anyone uttered that wasn't a whisper. My eyes focused down the row of trees, staring into the open, empty plain—waiting for the first Lamanite warrior to walk into view. A few minutes passed and I could hear them. Thousands of footsteps grew steadily louder as they marched onward, trampling the plain beneath their sandals. In another moment, I could hear their voices—Lamanite commanders calling random orders to their men.

Then, all at once a thousand tiny figures entered our frame of vision. They were a quarter-mile distant, between us and the hills. At the front of the Nephite host, I watched a single silver sword rise into the air.

"Attack!" Teancum cried.

The column of Lamanites stopped cold in their tracks. Trumpeters from the Lamanite ranks were sounding the alarm as I came to my feet. Hagoth called at me to sit tight, but I had to see it. I just had to see the moment of impact. To avoid being trampled by thousands of Nephite warriors as they charged past me, I moved in closer to the trees with Hagoth, Benjamin, and the rest of my bodyguards following closely on my heels. When I reached the edge of the woods, the entire expanse of plains opened up to my vision. It seemed like the columns of Lamanites never ended. Their numbers were at least double that of Teancum's army.

My first thought, looking out upon the enemy as their ranks started dispersing to meet Teancum's charge, was how sorry I was Lehi and Garth were a week behind us. My faith that I would see the end of this day was starting to waver. My second thought was rather unusual. I thought about the war in heaven before the world was created, and the one-third of all souls that fell away with the adversary. How could the Lamanites fight in the campaign of a man as wicked as King Amalickiah? Yet this startled Lamanite army had raised thousands of swords to defend—even die for—his evil cause.

The impact came. Weapons began to clash, and the two armies started to mix. I could hear the cries of men as they were cut down in the barrage of arrows and darts. It was clear that Teancum's charge had caught the Lamanites off guard, and despite the difference in numbers, the Nephites were pushing them back. But like a wave coming in from the ocean, the Lamanite hordes were moving quickly in my direction. Since they knew they outnumbered the Nephites, they were trying to spread out and involve more soldiers in the conflict.

There was a drumbeat rumbling in the hills and a flurry of trumpets. I looked up to see Moriancum's 8,000 men, with timing comparable to the cavalry of the American West, rushing at full speed to meet the Lamanite flank.

Hagoth was finally bold enough to grab my arm and lead me back into the security of the woods, as the violence was now within a stone's throw. Hagoth, Benjamin, and the other eight bodyguards surrounded me on all sides within a tight cluster of trees. It finally occurred to me to unwrap the cloth from around my sword and stand ready in case it was needed.

All my life, whenever kids would get together and talk about what they feared most, my answer was always "death." But for some reason, the prospect wasn't frightening to me at this moment. It all seemed like such a natural part of the cycle of life and, if it happened, I was confident it wouldn't be so bad. My bodyguards didn't share my feelings. Their determination was to do anything but die—and if they were to die, they were set on taking others with them.

The woods were full of soldiers now, both Lamanite and Nephite. Arrows and darts were flying through the trees. One dart hit Hagoth square in the chest. Moroni's breastplate design really worked! The sharply barbed missile stuck there but didn't penetrate, and Hagoth knocked it down with his hand. This shipbuilder from the West Sea owed his life to the breastplate's designer.

Several of my bodyguards returned fire at our offenders with their bows and eliminated several warriors that threatened our position. But more were coming. Many more. Moriancum's charge was driving them east, just as Teancum planned, but it was forcing many of them to run right past us. My bodyguards were forced to raise their swords to steer away or strike down Lamanites who had come into our vicinity. One of my men was hit in the shin with an arrow. The arrowhead went right through the flesh. He buckled under, shrieking in pain. Benjamin helped him break the shaft and remove it.

Seconds thereafter, Benjamin's attention was drawn away by another Lamanite as he lunged forward, heaving an axe. Benjamin raised his shield, successfully defending against the blow. Then, striking his foe across the shoulder, he knocked him to the earth.

A moment later, I stood alone. Each of my bodyguards was engaged in combat while I hid in the middle of a triangle of trees. A dart cut into the bark above where I had placed my hand. I saw the Lamanite who had hurled it. His eye was watching me carefully as he loaded another dart into his atlatl. As I moved behind the biggest tree for protection, Hagoth noticed the man threatening me and surged forward to cut my attacker down with his sword. The Lamanite abandoned his aim before Hagoth could strike, and followed his fellow soldiers in retreat.

Dozens of Lamanites were fleeing past us, not even interested in conflict—on the contrary, doing everything to avoid it. Perhaps they felt they could regain a position of advantage farther east. One of my bodyguards was still fighting. He had been drawn away from the rest of us considerably. Three Lamanites were slain at his feet, and three more had combined their efforts to avenge the dead. Several of my men, including Benjamin, rushed to his aid, but not before the blows he had received were more than he could endure. Benjamin and the others scattered his opponents, killing two, and dragged the Nephite warrior's lifeless body back to the tight cluster of trees.

Benjamin checked him for signs of life. Discouraged, Benjamin looked at me, sighed, and returned to a defensive stance on the edge of the cluster. This was the second man in this land who had given his life for me—a stranger. I whispered a prayer in his behalf, asking God to fulfill Helaman's request that great blessings would await righteous soldiers in the life to come.

Nephites made up the majority of warriors charging past us now. They fiercely pursued the Lamanites as they retreated toward the ocean. We had them on the run. The Nephites' spirits rose into a furor as they chased down the slower of the enemy's soldiers to either slay them or force them into surrender.

We left the security of our little cluster of trees and ran to the other side of the woods. There the trees opened up into another plain where the fighting at that moment was most heavy. Teancum was fighting among the soldiers in that vicinity. When I saw him for that one brief moment, he was unscathed and ferocious, though, like everyone else, his body was drenched in sweat. The sun had turned these damp lowland plains into an oven. Teancum found one brief moment to rest. He saw us.

"Stay within the trees!" he called to us. That was all, and then Captain Teancum went back into battle with more than fifty fellow Nephites behind him.

My eight remaining bodyguards followed the action with me for quite some distance along the edge of the woods until a deep swamp kept us from going any further. I watched the Lamanites continue to flee eastward. I hoped I might spot Amalickiah's supply train. If Amalickiah had kept his harem at his side in the scrublands near the city of Moroni, he might burden his men with the hassle of taking them wherever he went. That meant Jenny might be within a couple miles of where I was standing. Apparently, at the first signs of battle, the supply train had departed for safe ground, probably the beaches of the East Sea.

The battle persisted most of the day. The Nephite soldiers continued driving the Lamanites to the ocean while there was light remaining. As far away as the fighting was, I could still hear the terrifying cries of dying men carried in the wind.

The word spread that Teancum's army would pitch their tents a couple of miles southwest and resume fighting the next day. Hagoth suggested that we start to make our way back to the encampment.

As Teancum had commanded, we stayed within the trees all the way back, the same as we had done coming. The woods were casting long shadows now and the farther westward we walked, the quieter our surroundings became—except for those terrible cries I could still hear in my mind. I was certain I'd still be hearing those cries in my sleep.

Hagoth and Benjamin restrapped their swords onto their backs and guzzled a drink from their water pouches. I'd been carrying my own sword and shield for so long today, I'd come to accept them as part of my arms. I patrolled slightly ahead of the others, with my sword at my side, trying to relieve them of the burden of looking out for my welfare for a few minutes.

Then I learned that if you're looking for trouble, the chances are good that you'll find it. A wounded Lamanite heard us coming and waited to lunge at the first Nephite who passed by. I heard a rustling in the bushes and turned to see a desperate man with his sword held high overhead. I could see the blood dried on his face. He had one open eye, the other was swollen shut. Heaving forward, he yelled.

For a moment I was frozen. But only for a moment. Instinctively, I hoisted my sword into the defensive position and obstructed the Lamanite's blow. The weight of his strike brought me onto one knee, but I was unharmed. He stepped back to strike again, but I blocked it with my shield and took advantage of an open opportunity to swipe him in the leg. My maneuver brought down the Lamanite, but it did very little to restrain his determination. Using his one good leg to thrust his body forward, he attempted another feeble strike, but by now at least four of my bodyguards had been alerted and stepped into the action. He swung again, but this time Hagoth's sword landed first. The Lamanite fell back for the last time and his weapon dropped into the dirt.

Panting and shaking, I held my head between my hands. All the bodyguards begged my forgiveness for their incompetence. I nodded that I would forgive them, and took a moment longer to regain my composure.

Hagoth knelt down beside me and smiled. "You wielded your sword and shield most skillfully," he complimented. "You've proven my point, Jim, my friend. If it came down to it, you could manage as bodyguard for the rest of us."

CHAPTER 21

For the first time, I considered the Nephite sunset to be a foul thing, a gruesome color. It reminded me too deeply of the blood I had to pass by as we walked across the plain toward Teancum's encampment. Physicians and their aides were scurrying about the lowland, seeking Nephites that had been wounded and left in the scorching heat while the battle moved eastward. Soldiers gathered the dead, laying them side by side in designated places. For every Nephite killed, there were three, maybe four Lamanites slain. The contest was shamefully unbalanced. Lacking sufficient strength, skill, and equipment, an average Lamanite warrior was no match for a Nephite.

The soldiers would have gathered the Lamanite dead as well, but limited time forced them to be partial. However, if a Lamanite was found wounded, he was treated and added to the rest of the prisoners. At least four hundred Lamanite soldiers had been captured this day, and were kept under close guard on the far side of the camp.

The last weary Nephite soldiers were coming back now, worn and fatigued, trudging in from the battlegrounds near the ocean. They reported that Amalickiah was making his camp on the beaches of the East Sea. The day had been one of victory, and they were grateful, until they considered what Amalickiah might have in store for them tomorrow.

Nearing the encampment, we came upon the largest gathering of Nephite dead. Walking past the rows of the slain, we listened to the bitter chants of mourners who had found the remains of friend or kin. They paid final tribute to the dead with tears, oaths of vengeance, or both.

Where the rows of the slain ended, a silent mourner knelt over the body of a young warrior. I shuddered when I recognized who it was and a part of my spirit turned into itself, refusing to accept what my eyes were reporting. The mourner was Captain Teancum. Over his shoulder stood his brother and his uncle Gallium. With tears welling and overflowing, I left Hagoth and the rest of my bodyguards behind. The young warrior over whom Teancum mourned was his son, Teancum the Younger.

I dropped on my knees beside the captain and looked into the face of Teancum's firstborn. The eyelids had been closed by his father. If it hadn't been for the wounds, I might have thought he was only sleeping. There was no tension in the warrior's face. If his silent features somehow told of his circumstances in the next world, then Teancum the Younger was truly at peace.

I couldn't read the face of Captain Teancum. There were no signs of weeping. His expression was emotionless. If it hadn't been that he tenderly held his son's hand, I don't know that I would have sensed his sadness at all. Teancum might have thought he had no time for remorse. His son was dead, but the battle that began this morning was far from over. He still had a war to fight. Tomorrow's strategies had to be organized. For the captain of such an army, even the few minutes he took now to gaze at his lifeless son was time selfishly spent. The thought made me sadder still.

"I'm sorry," I told him.

My voice was the means of breaking his concentration. He sighed and began to stand. "I'm not the only father who lost a son this day," was all he said. Rising, he refused to make eye contact with a single soul, but motioned us to follow him back to his tent.

Teancum called his sub-commanders together. I translated while he laid out an extensive plan to divide the remaining army into two units. Three-quarters of his men would attack Amalickiah from the north. The other fourth would march toward Mulek and cut off Amalickiah in case he attempted to retreat. The details of the plan were revealed without the vigorous enthusiasm I'd come to expect from Teancum. Everyone decided it was a reflection of the pain he felt over the death of his son. I read something more. Even as he was announcing his strategy, I felt as though he hoped the particulars of what he was describing would never be executed. This seemed to be "Plan B." I even heard him slip once and say "if" when it should have been "when." There was another plan brewing in his mind, but he was not ready to confide it.

The sub-commanders were dismissed. Exhausted, many wounded, they wandered away from Teancum's fire, leaving Moriancum, Teancum, and myself alone.

A new shape began to form on Teancum's brow—an expression I'd never seen on his face before. The fury of the flames danced wildly in his eyes. The muscles in his chin grew taut, and his teeth were clenched.

"I faced him," he said, "I looked right into his blood-red eyes. He knew who I was. I held his gaze for a long time while the fighting raged around us. He had placed at least a dozen Lamanite servants between us. I held aloft my sword and challenged him to come forward to meet me alone on the plain. Instead, he sent his servants, and before I could cut my way through them, he was gone. I always had a firm conviction of his evil. I gave him credit for his cunning and praised him for

CHRIS HEIMERDINGER

his grasp of strategy. But until this day, I had never judged him to be a coward. Now that I know the truth, I can end this war."

Moriancum was perplexed by the unusual strain in his brother's face. Perhaps if the expression had been present tomorrow morning, he wouldn't have wondered. But the day was over. The determination expressed in Teancum's eyes wasn't something that would wait until the rising of the sun.

"You need rest, my captain," Moriancum urged.

"I'll not rest tonight," said Teancum coolly.

"What do you intend?" asked his brother.

"Moriancum," began Teancum, "this has not been a war between the Nephites and the Lamanites. It's been a war between the Nephites and Amalickiah. If I cut out the source of poison, it will cure the entire body."

"What are you saying?" asked Moriancum.

I knew what he meant.

"You're going there tonight," I revealed, "to the Lamanite camp on the beach."

"That's right, Jim," admitted Teancum. "I am."

"That's irrational!" Moriancum charged. "You would risk your own life and the fate of this army on a foolhardy, unplanned assassination?"

"Unplanned? No, my brother," defended Teancum, "I've contemplated the details in my mind ever since the night the Amulonites walked into our camp to steal grain. If a servant had not cried out and been killed, we might have never known a crime had taken place. In the morning we'd have found we had one less basket of grain, probably misplaced.

"Foolhardy? I don't think so," he continued. "The mission is so simple, so unexpected. And I wouldn't call it irrational. Tonight is the night when irrational events send the Lamanite priests and sorcerers into irrational panic. Isn't tomorrow the first day of the new year? Their apostate religion bases their whole outlook for the future on the events of the first day. They would consider the assassination of their king to be the worst possible omen. The entire war might end. If not the war, at least Amalickiah's drive to the narrow neck would be thwarted. But it has to be done *tonight*."

"Then send one of our front-line warriors," begged Moriancum. "We have many that could do it, walking as silently as you could—if not more—"

"My son is dead," Teancum interrupted. "Very few men could proceed with a will as fixed as mine. I wouldn't charge the task to any other man."

"I can help you," I offered.

Teancum smiled. "Jim, my ever-faithful servant, your skills as interpreter are not required."

"My sister might be in that camp," I pleaded. "I have to find out."

"It's not a mission for two men," discouraged Teancum.

"I know which tent is Amalickiah's," I revealed. "I remember it from the night we were captured. You need me there."

My arguments at least moved Teancum to silence. He pondered my offer. Then I threw in the clincher.

"You made me a promise."

Teancum heaved another sigh. "Find your sword, Jim. Wear a breastplate and arm protection. But leave the headgear behind. It gives us away as Nephites. I'll not carry my own metal sword for the same reason. I'll bring only my javelin."

As we stood, so did Moriancum.

"I can't agree with this, my captain," stated Moriancum, for the record.

Teancum put his hand upon Moriancum's shoulder. "My brother, we played together as children. You've fought at my side since the day we enlisted. You know me well enough to know that I'm not acting irrationally."

"Father knew, despite your talents, you were still the most impetuous of his children. That's why his last pleading to me before he died was to keep you in line. Consider what might happen if you were killed or captured. What would we do?"

"You would carry these men to victory, Moriancum," Teancum commanded.

"If you're killed, what's to prevent that ill new year's omen from crushing the spirit of our own men?" Moriancum asked.

"Their faith in God," Teancum replied.

I gathered the items Teancum requested. My breastplate was strapped to my chest; my sword hung across my back.

"Come," Teancum called to me.

I hesitated. "Captain, maybe we should say a prayer?"

Teancum nodded his agreement. We knelt with Moriancum. I said the words and asked God for protection. In fact, I asked him to make us invisible to them. I prayed that Jennifer would be among them, and that I would find her safe and well. I closed in the name of Jesus Christ.

Reluctantly, Moriancum saw us off. We followed the smell of the ocean. Our journey took us past the bodies of many Lamanites who had fallen in the battle. The awful sight still sickened me. As we neared the East Sea, the wind had picked up considerably. At first it felt good and cooling, but soon it became a nuisance, making our advance more difficult. Before long, we could hear the waves crashing against the beach. Climbing to the top of a hill overlooking the ocean, I imagined Christ and his apostles somewhere out there, floating in a tiny fishing boat, tossing in the surf. In spite of the fear that the Apostles felt for their lives, the Savior slept soundly, knowing his safety was in the hands of God. The thought strengthened me. Looking west, we saw the tents of the Lamanite camp. Their tiny campfires were almost smothered by the wind.

"Don't hide and don't sneak," Teancum instructed. "It's essential that you act as natural as possible. Do you understand?"

"Yes," I nodded.

We stepped down the rise and toward the camp of Amalickiah, acting as if we were Lamanite warriors who had lost our way in the battle and had only now found the opportunity to return. As we drew nearer to the first tents, the place seemed mysteriously still. Fatigue and weather had sent the Lamanites hiding inside whatever shelter they could throw together. Nothing stirred. A little further, we saw sentries on guard, crouching out in the open, cloth shielding their faces from the gusting sand. Making no effort to avoid them, we walked within ten feet of their position. Only one of them even lowered the garment protecting his eyes to look at us. Teancum waved without faltering his pace in the least. The sentry shrouded himself again and faded back into his grumbling world, wondering why he had to stand sentry duty at all. Who would ever attack on a night as miserable as this?

The blowing sand stung every inch of my exposed flesh. It collected in my mouth and in my nose. With one hand clutching the strap hooked to his breastplate, I relied upon Teancum's lead, walking deeper into the heart of the Lamanite camp. If anyone watched us through the flap on their tent, they had the same attitude as the sentries—the same as the Nephite guards the night the Amulonites had stolen food. Our mission was too unexpected, too profound.

My head was lowered against the blowing sand, my eyes directed at the ground. Teancum only forced me to look up once. He grabbed my arm and pointed through the dusty darkness at a circle of tents situated in the middle of the camp.

"That's it," I whispered, making my voice just loud enough for him to hear me over the screaming wind.

"Which one?" demanded Teancum. He needed me to be specific.

To point out Amalickiah's tent, I had to lead the way inside the circle. Now Teancum chose to walk a little more cautiously. He stopped me at an outer tent, and curled his neck slowly around the corner to investigate. Three Lamanite guards had each built themselves a modest lean-to as protection against the elements during their watch. But the exhaustion of the battle was too much for them. They were fast asleep, their heads drooping awkwardly. I was surprised at the sloppy negligence of the king's own guards. They must have had an awfully short job interview. The circumstances were God-sent.

I pointed at the center tent, its sides and roof flapping violently in the tempest. It wouldn't have surprised me to see the whole thing collapse suddenly. But it held firm while Captain Teancum gripped his javelin and forged ahead toward the entrance.

We paused in the calmness beside the doorway. It was all too easy. They were waiting inside to ambush us, I thought. Or maybe Amalickiah wasn't here at all. Those were the only explanations I could come up with for the ease of our mission. How could Teancum have guessed so right? Something had to go seriously wrong, I decided, and it had to be now.

Teancum quickly opened the flap of the tent. We slipped inside with the same ease as a turtle's head slipping into its shell. There in the blackness of the dragon's lair, we listened. Servants were breathing all around us. There were at least five men sleeping in the lair, muttering, snoring. One of them had to be the dragon himself. Square in the center, a low-set cot stretched before us. Buried in the soft, quilted furs, a man lay dreaming. What kind of dreams came to such a man while he slept, I wondered? Was this his time to receive counsel from the demons that inspired him? It seemed the visions that haunted him now were no less than nightmares. His breathing was very unsteady. Air passed into his mouth in little gasps. And even from where I stood, I perceived tiny twitches, almost convulsions, under the lids of his eyes.

This man must have hated sleep. It was the only time he wasn't hailed as king. The characters in dreams tell us who we really are. In the quiet of the night, even Amalickiah couldn't have fooled himself. He was only a man—a child of God whose parents wept. A man who sought adoption to another parent. That parent promised him the glory of the world, and covered a treacherous grin as he accepted.

Teancum crept toward his bed and brought the javelin over his shoulder. He paused over Amalickiah for only a moment. Then, gripping the javelin before him in both hands, he uttered words I could barely distinguish: "For my son."

The end of the javelin rose toward the ceiling. His movement from there was very quick—one thrust downward, then up again. Amalickiah didn't make a single sound, not even a gulp in the throat. But the unsteady breathing ended and Teancum stepped away. The wicked Nephite dissenter, the conquering king of the Lamanites, was dead.

Without delay, the captain motioned that it was time for us to leave. We stepped back out into the gale. The guards still slept. The sand still stung my face.

"My sister," I reminded Teancum.

"Which tent houses his harem?" Teancum asked.

I tried to remember. That night seemed so long ago. "That one, I think."

"We have to act quickly," warned Teancum.

He led me swiftly toward the designated tent. Reaching the flap, Teancum turned to me.

"Find her and come back out as quickly as you can," he instructed. "I'll wait."

The captain opened the flap and watched me creep inside. The smell of flowers was thick. It was perfume, I guess. There were many curtains separating several chambers in this tent. It made the place darker than it had been in the tent of Amalickiah.

There was no way I could find her. I'd have to call out her name, and that would wake everybody. I went back outside and told Teancum the problem.

"What's your sister's name?" he asked.

"Jennifer."

"Say these words," instructed Teancum. "'His Lord Amalickiah requests Jennifer's presence.'"

I went back inside and called out Teancum's words as loud as any king's servant would.

I heard stirring, but no one approached me. I called out the words a second time. This time a curtain was tossed aside and a Lamanite woman stepped up to me. She was very intimidating, approaching rapidly as if she might punch me.

"The king has agreed to let us nurture her. She's not to be touched. Why does he want her?" she barked.

This woman was not one to be tangled with. I tried to reply with some authority, "He just does."

She studied me. "You're not one of his servants. Who are you?"

Another shadow had slowly crept out from behind the curtain.

"Jim?" whispered the tiny voice I knew so well.

"Jen?" I whispered in return.

She lunged forward with embracing arms, blubbering even before she got to me. My sister hadn't changed. Jenny was always blubbering. If I shed a tear of my own, it's not something I have to admit.

Maybe I should have feared the actions of the Lamanite woman, but her defenses melted when she heard Jennifer say my name. As I relished the hug from my sister, she broke it up and encouraged us to leave immediately.

"Go!" the Lamanite woman urged. "You don't have much time."

Jenny turned and looked lovingly into the eyes of this woman. She couldn't curb her impulse to give her a farewell embrace.

"I'll never forget you," she cried.

"Don't be foolish," she admonished. "You must go!"

I was all for that. I lifted the flap of the tent, and was about to rush outside, dragging Jenny after me. Fortunately, I stopped in time.

Teancum wasn't there. Across the circle, the guards had been awakened and were climbing out of their lean-tos. Three new guards were in the process of replacing them. Where could Teancum have gone? Would he leave without me?

Then a waving arm caught my attention. Teancum was standing against the neighboring tent, protected from the guards' line of sight. He signaled me to hold tight for the moment while the sentries assumed their positions. The exchange was made quietly, properly. The former guards went inside a tent near Amalickiah's, and the new ones crawled into the lean-tos and hid from the wind.

Wasting no time, I ran to Teancum, dragging Jenny behind me while she waved one last time to the Lamanite woman who remained standing in the darkness to watch our departure. The three of us stood in the shelter of the tent for a moment.

"Jenny, this is Teancum," I introduced. "*The* Teancum. I'm talkin' *Captain Teancum*. You know who I mean?"

"Uh-uh," Jenny said.

Totally typical of the sister I loved.

We left the Lamanite camp as quietly as we'd arrived. Standing on the hill that overlooked the ocean, I turned back, in spite of the wind, and looked one last time at the tiny fires and the ten thousand tents.

Maybe, just as I had prayed, God had truly made us invisible. At least that's the way I want to remember it.

"Happy New Year," I said to Teancum.

CHAPTER 22

Moriancum had been pacing since the moment we left. I'll bet the expression on his face was worth a picture when he saw our figures emerging from the darkness—marching from what might as well have been our graves. Jenny was barefoot when I rescued her, so, to ease the pain of walking upon naked feet, she rode triumphantly into the Nephite camp upon Teancum's shoulders.

The sleeping Nephite army was alerted by trumpet blasts. At first, they thought the Lamanites were launching an early attack. But the news of Amalickiah's death moved swifter than had the ocean wind. Within three minutes, not one man in all these thousands could avoid hearing an account of Teancum's assassination.

The command spread that all Nephite warriors were to stand in readiness. Any moment, Amalickiah would be found cold in his bed, and the embittered Zoramites might incite the Lamanites to seek vengeance.

But when morning came, the scene was exactly the opposite. Teancum's prophecy of chaos held true. The murder of Amalickiah on the first day of the year was seen by their priests as a deadly omen. The Lamanite camp erupted into hysteria. Before the sun could climb an hour into the sky, the frenzied ranks started retreating southward toward the city of Mulek, where they could cower in its fortifications. Teancum had hoped to cut them off in the event of such a retreat, but they'd scattered faster than even he'd anticipated.

We pursued them all the next day. During the march, Jennifer told me all about her experiences among the Lamanites. The woman whom she had embraced the night of her rescue was named Shimono. Many years before, the king's guards had abducted her and several other Lamanite women. The women had been shopping in the market of the Lamanite capital of Nephi. They were paraded before Amalickiah and those he approved of were adopted into his harem of concubines. Before the abduction, she had been a bride, newly married. They told her that her husband was rewarded and given a post of leadership in a nearby township, but she suspected Amalickiah had killed him out of jealousy. Either way, she never saw her husband again. Though everyone told her being chosen by the king was a great honor, she wasn't comforted. Only because she knew no other course did she accept her fate.

Shimono had protected and defended Jenny while she was imprisoned, both from Amalickiah and from the harassments of Amalickiah's other concubines, who had even tried to cut off her blonde hair while she slept. She and Shimono grew very close. Comforting Jenny many times, Shimono had taken on the role of a second mother, and had listened while Jenny told her about me, her family, and her home.

Jenny boasted that she never had to walk from city to city during Amalickiah's invasion. Servants carried all the women in their own private coaches, a hooded chariot of sorts. Her friendship with Shimono and riding in the chariot were the only positive memories she carried from her captivity.

Upon reaching the walls of Mulek, Teancum decided it would be futile to try and retake the city at this time. The Lamanites had enough manpower inside to fully service all of its fortifications—fortifications originally designed by the Nephites.

Word reached Teancum that Amalickiah's brother, Ammoron, had inherited the throne. When the Lamanites retreated, Ammoron hadn't stopped in Mulek. He continued his escape with a small body of warriors and instructed the Lamanite forces along the way to defend all captured Nephite possessions to the death. Rumors claimed that he was on his way back to the Lamanite capital to organize more reinforcements. It was clear that Ammoron intended to further pursue the war begun by his brother. I was there when Teancum heard the news of Ammoron's ambitions. He was fuming.

"I could have killed Amalickiah and his twisted brother in the same night!" he lamented.

Taking a deep breath, Teancum sat calmly and contemplated the future. "There'll be another time," he nodded. "Another night just as windy."

We spent the next week building walls, digging pits, and constructing many other defenses around the city of Mulek in anticipation of the day when the Lamanite army would have to come out. Mostly I served as an interpreter to relay Teancum's instructions, but I found plenty of time to get down in the dirt with Hagoth, Jenuem, and Benjamin, heaving stones and cutting timber. We made quite a team.

One afternoon, another army of Nephites came marching into the borders of the Land of Mulek with Captain Lehi at its head. Marching proudly at Lehi's side was a young, freckled boy. Garth, Jennifer, and I were now reunited.

Late into the evening, Garth and I tried to top each other with tales of what had befallen us since our separation three weeks before. He had to admit that Teancum's assassination of Amalickiah and my rescue of Jenny topped them all.

After I introduced him to Hagoth, Garth anxiously pulled me aside. "That guy's in the Book of Mormon!" he insisted.

"He is? Where? What did he do?" I questioned.

"Didn't you ever listen, even once, to the Sunday School lesson?" scolded Garth.

News of Teancum's victory in the borders of Bountiful reached Captain Moroni. Moroni composed a special letter to be delivered to Teancum. Messengers carried the letter from Zarahemla to Jershon, then passed it on to Lehi. Lehi delivered it to Teancum.

The letter praised Teancum for turning the tide of the war and commanded him to retain all Lamanite prisoners—even build a facility to hold them if it was necessary. Moroni intended to use them as ransom against the many Nephite prisoners—men, women, and children—held by the Lamanites. He hoped an exchange could be negotiated.

He ordered Teancum to personally march a portion of his army to the land of Bountiful to fortify it against any future efforts by Ammoron to secure the narrow pass. In addition, Moroni requested that he and Lehi expend all the energy they could to fortify the cities and forts that were still under Nephite control. If an opportunity to retake any cities arose, Teancum's instructions were to act immediately.

Moroni regretted that he was unable to add his own army to those of Teancum's and Lehi's in the East Wilderness. He was preparing to go against another Lamanite invasion force that Ammoron had organized along the coast of the West Sea.

With the letter, Moroni had added a note from the Prophet Helaman. It referred to Garth and me.

The note read, "I, Helaman, request that your interpreters, Jim and Garth, be escorted to the Land of Melek, and meet me there, while I am communing among the Ammonites. Please provide an escort for them at once, and make other accommodations to fill the positions with which they have been entrusted. I would not make this request if their presence in Melek wasn't urgent."

The next morning Teancum brought the note to Garth, Jen, and me, personally. After reading it to us, he summed it up. "You're all going to Melek," he announced, "and I'm going to Bountiful. I've organized an escort. You'll leave this afternoon."

Our feelings toward the news were mixed. Helaman had promised he'd send word the moment our course and fate were revealed to him. That meant he might know a way for us to get home. At the same time, the good-byes would be very painful. There wasn't much time to make the rounds.

I knew when I was shaking Hagoth's hand that it was the last time I would ever see him. "Good-bye, my friend," I told him. "I'm going home."

"You'll see me again," he promised. "One day I'm going north. I want to see the great cities you've spoken of. I want to taste snow, and I want to learn to ski."

Garth was standing behind Hagoth, rolling his eyes at me. Later he said to me, "According to scholars, Hagoth won't make it much farther than Acapulco. Some still believe he reaches Hawaii, but either way, I don't think you should have promised him he'd find a ski resort."

Each farewell twisted my insides worse than the one before. Benjamin and Jenuem were next. I embraced them and asked them to give my regards to all the soldiers in their kinship.

I was about to give Gallium a big bear hug when he told me it wasn't necessary to say good-bye just yet. He and his sons, Mocum and Pachumi, would lead our escort to Melek.

"Will we go through Zarahemla to get to Melek?" I asked Gallium.

"I'm afraid not," Gallium apologized. "It would be four days out of our way. My orders are to have the three of you in the Prophet Helaman's presence as soon as possible."

That announcement made my farewell to Moriancum very difficult. Not just because I'd miss Moriancum, but because when I said good-bye to him, I was also saying good-bye to his daughter, Menochin. To think, if I were to stay, this Nephite could be my father-in-law.

"Tell Menochin," I stammered, "Tell her I . . . Just tell her I love her and . . . I'll think about her."

"I'll tell her that, Jamie," Moriancum replied.

The hardest moment was yet to come. Garth and I stood at a distance and watched Teancum shout orders to his soldiers who were running back and forth, preparing for yet another march. This time they would go to the land of Bountiful, where the captain would establish his headquarters until the Lamanites were driven from the land. As we approached him, I couldn't stop a lump the size of Yellowstone from forming in my throat.

Teancum saw us coming and interrupted his labors. I looked into the coarse face and gentle eyes of this mighty Nephite for several seconds, pursing my lips, trying to think of words. Teancum was having the same problem. But as I'd come to expect from this great warrior, he regained his composure through his role as commander of the Eastern Armies.

"You've been a fine warrior," he told me. "I hate to lose you. It'll take four men to fill your job."

I looked at the ground. "Thanks for everything," I mumbled.

A nasty little tear escaped from my eye. I wiped it away as quickly as I could. That wasn't the way I wanted Teancum to remember me.

Then Teancum stuttered a little, "You would have been . . . you are . . . your father should consider you a fine son."

Teancum embraced me the same way he had embraced his own son, Teancum the Younger, with a firm hold on both my shoulders. Something told me that wasn't quite enough. I moved in and gripped onto his chest.

Garth told me Teancum was about to shed a tear of his own. The tear would have divided in two as it traveled down the grooves in his cheek—half for me, and half in memory of his son. Before it could fall, he stepped away, said farewell to Garth, and returned to his men, barking more commands, urging them to move faster.

We found Gallium and his sons waiting for us at the rear of the army. Then, with Jennifer and Garth at my side, I followed them into the jungles of the land of Mulek, and blazed a trail toward the mountains of the Land of Melek.

Our journey took five days. After crossing the Sidon River one last time, we passed through the Land of Noah. Leaving the Sidon Valley, we started into the mountains. For three days we traversed many more valleys and rivers, until the first Ammonite settlement stood before us. I recognized the style of architecture in the buildings to be the same as I'd seen in the abandoned ruins of the Land of Jershon.

As we passed, inquisitive families watched us from their doorways. Garth couldn't help but comment, "So these are the converts of Ammon, Aaron, Omner, and Himni." Then later, as we passed a group of young men working in the fields, he said, "Those boys are likely among the 2,060 warriors."

It was reported to us that Helaman was stationed in the city of Lamoni, the largest settlement in this rural stretch of land. When we finally found him, he greeted us enthusiastically. "I've been waiting for you!" He eyed Jenny and asked, "Is this the sister you spoke of?"

"Yes," I told him. "Her name is Jennifer."

Jenny was shy and hid behind my shoulder until I stepped out of the way, exposing her. She did an awkward curtsy. "Pleased to meet you, Mr. Helaman," she said.

"Prophet Helaman," I corrected her. She gave me a quick but rude glance.

Helaman invited us into his home. The Lamanite converts had built it to accommodate his stay. It was next door to the largest of the valley's synagogues. The prophet fed us a large meal, prepared by his own hands.

We talked briefly about Helaman's plan to organize the Ammonite youth into a unit of soldiers. Then Helaman changed the subject. He didn't feel the timing was quite right to talk about political things. Leaning forward, his face illuminated by the fire in the hearth, Helaman addressed the three of us.

"Your visit to this people has been a very wonderful gift," he began. "It was meant to prepare your minds and hearts for the great struggle of the last days. The Lord has told me that the last generation before his final coming will consist of his choicest children since the creation of the earth. But you will face a world filled with much pain and evil. Men like Amalickiah will gain great power over God's children. Youth such as yourselves will have a great responsibility to build up a pure and undefiled people in the midst of all this pain.

"I hope you will take the strength that has been added to your characters and accept this responsibility. It's in your hands, Jim, Garth, Jennifer.

"Now, it's time for you to return to your people. Early in the morning, I'll take you to a certain place that has been shown to me."

Our last night in the Nephite world was spent sleeping in beds prepared by the Prophet Helaman in an Ammonite settlement of the Land of Melek. I lay awake, wondering what I might expect the next day. How would our families greet us? Maybe they had already given us up—had a funeral and everything. Would Mom and Dad look at us as though we were returning from the dead?

I tried to imagine how Helaman might make it happen. Maybe he'd just say "poof" and we'd be home in the twinkling of an eye. In spite of all my various thoughts, I began to yawn and fell asleep rather quickly.

The next morning, Helaman called us for breakfast. Our last meal consisted of beans and mushed corn. It wasn't a grand meal to remember the Nephites by, but it was typical, and therefore, appropriate.

After breakfast, Helaman decided to take us one last place before he would show us the way home. He led us, along with Gallium and his sons, through the town of Lamoni to a humble hut—the last hut along the road leaving the settlement. The place was well tended. Gardens surrounding it had at least a dozen different kinds of flowers. A couple of Ammonites were busy pruning and tending the shrubbery. Two servants passed us on the path leading to the door, carrying what was left of a fine breakfast they had served to someone inside.

We made our presence known. Another servant greeted us at the door and brought us inside. If the guy who lived here was rich enough to afford all these servants, I wondered why he didn't insist on a fancier house. Lying upon a bed of blankets and furs at the back of the hut, an old bedridden man raised his hand to greet us.

"Helaman, my good friend," he said in a voice much stronger than I might have expected from such a frail body. "Come in, come in. Welcome to my home."

Helaman turned to us.

"I'd like you to meet the oldest son of King Mosiah, the last king of the Nephites. His name is Ammon. This is the man for whom the people of Melek are named."

The only thing I can compare with the expression on Garth's face is the expression of a child when he first meets Santa Claus. This was the man whom Garth had once called one of the greatest missionaries of all time.

Helaman completed his introductions. "This is Jim and Garth and Jennifer."

"Come over here and let me see your faces," Ammon requested.

When we came forward, Ammon took Garth's hand. His eyes reminded me of my grandmother's—transparent, yet alive.

"Helaman has told me about you," said Ammon. "As a favor, I asked him to bring you here that I might meet you. I'm most grateful that you've come."

"It's an honor," Garth said.

"It's an honor for me as well. I'm told that you come from another land and another time."

"The same land," I corrected, then I backed up. "Well, a different part of the same land anyway."

"That doesn't surprise me. I've always known this was the most blessed land upon the earth. I should have guessed that children as beautiful as you would have been nurtured upon it." He touched Jenny's hair with a long, slow stroke.

"We know all about you," Garth told him. "You converted King Lamoni."

"You do know many things." Ammon looked at Helaman. "Then everything Helaman has told me is true."

The prophet nodded.

Ammon told us, "I've devoted my life to serving God and his children upon the earth. I've been highly blessed—beyond what I deserve. Your presence here today is greater evidence of that.

"I've come to know, in recent years, the revelations of God concerning the destruction of my people, the Nephites, and of the apostasy of the descendants of Laman. It's been a source of sorrow for me. Oh, I know, I'm only accountable to the people of my own generation, but it has still been frustrating to know that all my work, all my diligence in his name, would not carry on for many generations. Helaman tells me you have a book describing the doings of this people, and that the words of this book teach the people of your day the plan of salvation. Is that right?"

"Yes, that's right," Garth confirmed.

Ammon closed his eyes and smiled, heaving a deep and satisfied sigh. When his eyes opened again, they were filled with tears. "Now, in the twilight of my life, it's given me an overwhelming sense of peace to know that our work will truly bless another generation of God's children. Thank you for bringing such peace to an old man."

Soon after that, Ammon fell asleep. We hovered over him a moment longer, until Ammon's servant informed us that we had to go because Ammon needed his rest. Garth was the last to leave. He savored every moment that he could near Ammon's side. Garth had finally met his hero.

Helaman directed us out of the hut and back to the local marketplace. The prophet told us we might want to pick up some provisions for our journey. I wondered whether he was going to send us off into the mountains or set us adrift in a boat. Neither idea sounded encouraging. I guess I still had a few things to learn about faith.

For the next couple of hours, Helaman led us into the hills above the settlement of Lamoni. About noon, we found ourselves standing at the foot of a mountain. Although it was clouded over, I suspected it was a volcano. He pointed his finger toward the mouth of a cave, dark and awesome.

Among the provisions Helaman brought for us were three torches. While Gallium, Pachumi and Mocum struck up a flame to ignite them, Helaman gave us some unusual instructions.

"Take the passages that lead upward. Climb—and be faithful. The flames of these torches will not die until you reach your destination. Remember, the character and spirit you have gained among our people will never be taken from you, but the clear memories of our land will only remain if you keep them silent—hidden in the confines of your heart. If you reveal these memories to others, the memories will be taken from you, even as they are revealed."

I didn't understand why that annoying little provision had to be part of the deal. But Helaman wouldn't drop the subject until we had all agreed.

Then he handed us a pouch of toasted corn and several pouches of water. Gallium and his two sons came forward and placed the flaming torches in each of our hands. There were a few tears pricking at their eyes, especially the kind, wise eyes of Uncle Gallium.

We climbed up a ravine covered with tiny white flowers until we reached the mouth of the cave. When I turned back, Helaman, Gallium, Mocum, and Pachumi stood watching. We waved and they returned our wave. For the last time, I looked across the landscape that stretched before us, its mountains and hills, checkered with patches of tilled farmland. The sky was bright blue with only a few lonely clouds wandering west with the breeze. I took in my last breath of Nephite air and smelled the Nephite world, green and fresh. Then slowly, I turned and followed Garth and Jenny into the cavern.

CHAPTER 23

We relied only upon the light of the torches, taking any trail that climbed continually upward. Near the mouth of the cave, we used the flame of the torches to break through wall-to-wall spider webs. After five minutes, Jenny was frightened and wanted to turn back, but I reminded her what Helaman had said concerning faith.

Unlike Frost Cave, this was a damp, muddy cavern. Every rock I touched was bleeding water. I could hear a river running through the mountain. It sounded like a sewer under the asphalt—but I never saw it. Nor did we ever pass any "rainbow rooms" with phosphorescent crystal and icy waterfalls. The air was stale and muggy, making it difficult to breathe.

After an hour or so, the cavern started to feel cooler. Inhaling was much easier, and my sweaty skin began to dry. The going got very steep. The next hour, I started to second-guess myself, swearing I'd seen this or that formation before. My uncertainty faded all at once. We entered a place that I recognized exactly. Somewhere we made a transition. I knew precisely where we were, and how far we had to go. I shouted out my realization to Garth and Jenny. Soon they verified my feelings. One of them would say, "Yep, I remember this" at almost every turn. We were invigorated, and we couldn't help climbing faster and faster, our panting sounding like the chugging of a train.

About four hours after our journey began, I poked my head through a hole. I saw the rope, undisturbed, that we had tied to the jutting stone and left to dangle down into the depths of the pit nearly two months before. We doused two of the torches and carefully carried the last one as we grasped onto that rope as if it were our lifeline to salvation. We climbed up and up to stand upon the dusty, dimly lit surface of the central tunnel of Frost Cave. We only needed to follow the imprints of our own tennis shoes back to the iron gate meant to blockade the entrance.

It was dark outside, but using the light of the stars we made our way back across the rickety wooden planks and onto the winding dirt road leading down the eastern face of Cedar Mountain. A mighty thrill leaped in my soul the moment I could clearly see the lights of my home town, Cody, Wyoming. The place was just as quiet and humble as the day we left. The three of us laughed and sang "Home, Home on the Range," followed by "Oh Say Can You See," skipping and kicking up dirt all the way down to the bottom.

Our bicycles were still waiting for us in the same clump of sagebrush, not even dirty or squeaky, as I might have expected. I doused the final torch that had brought us up through the mountain, and we pedaled vigorously down the West Cody Strip. It felt so good to ride a bicycle. The air was warmer than usual for what I guessed was a November evening in Wyoming. The temperature was perfectly suited to our ancient clothing.

I gazed upon all the familiar sights—the motels and tourist stops, the fireworks stands and the Buffalo Drive-In—with the same excitement I'd have had gazing upon the streets of heaven.

We rounded the corner and pedaled that last stretch of highway to the Buffalo Bill Historical Center. At the entrance to the parking lot, we stopped our bikes. As I looked at Garth, his auburn hair dancing slightly in the breeze, it seemed to me I didn't know him anymore. He wasn't the gawky, eggheaded misfit

I used to torment at Eastside Elementary. For a moment, I missed him. But only a moment. As he smiled at me, wearing that Nephite "skirt" that looked so silly in these surroundings, and sitting upon that miserable rusty bicycle, I knew it was still Garth.

"I guess this is it . . . in a way," I said.

"I wouldn't have made it without you, Jim," Garth responded.

From this moment, riding our separate ways, the adventure was truly over. So we hung there—until I decided I'd had enough sentimentality for one day. "What do you want? A kiss good night?" I asked him. "Well, forget it! I'll call you tomorrow."

As Jenny and I rode away, I called to Garth one last time, "We'll tell them all we got abducted by aliens, and visited Neptune!"

The clock on the courthouse said three-thirty. Pedaling that last stretch was difficult. Suddenly I felt so tired. My sense of time seemed distorted. It was hard to believe that just this morning I'd actually spoken with Ammon, the son of Mosiah. It was like an early childhood memory. My little sister looked as exhausted as I was. I thought she might fall asleep at the handlebars. As we rolled wearily down Beck Avenue, I wondered if I even had a bedroom waiting for me.

Nearing our home, all the lights were out except the one above the front porch. It was as if Mom expected us to ride through that front gate someday, and wanted us to easily find the door. Dismounting, I dropped my ten-speed on the lawn. I was so tired, I can barely remember walking down the sidewalk and climbing those three steps up to the porch. My fingers grabbed the handle on the screen, and that's all I remember. Somehow, I must have gone inside and made my way to my bedroom, climbed into my bed and crawled between the soft, cool sheets.

The following morning, my bedroom door burst open. Through blurry vision, I saw my mother standing there. She began to chide me at the top of her voice.

"What time did you and your sister get in last night, young man?" she demanded.

Was this the loving, tender mother who I expected would smother me in hugs and bathe me in tears?

She continued, "Your father was out patrolling the streets half the night looking for you two! I waited up and waited up—I didn't even hear you sneak in!"

I told her we had been abducted by aliens, but it only added fuel to the fire.

"Don't you smart-talk me, Jim Hawkins! Did you know we almost went to the police and filed a missing person's report? Did you?"

I thought, gee, she must not love me an awful lot if it took her two months to come up with that idea. She kept shaking her finger and commanded me to get dressed for church and come to breakfast with a full explanation—"The truth this time!"

She slammed the door.

While I listened to Mom through the doorway, delivering the same lecture to my sister across the hall, it occurred to me—two months hadn't gone by at all. Today was only Sunday! We'd only been gone a single day! No wonder it didn't feel like November last night. It was still September. My book report on *Where the Red Fern Grows* was still due Tuesday.

At breakfast, Jenny and I told them the truth—partially. We admitted that we had gone with Garth Plimpton exploring Frost Cave and got lost. Another lecture erupted stressing how we might have been killed, and how we should never, never go anyplace without letting someone know—etcetera, etcetera. The two of us were grounded for a month. If only she knew how good that sounded. Frankly, as happy as Jenny and I were to be home, we'd have gladly accepted grounding for a year.

Returning to my room, I had to pass Grandma Tucker at the bottom of the stairs. She was looking at me, her face beaming with a loving grin from ear to ear. Grandma gave me a hug—a long hug. Then she released me. I watched her walk up the stairway and return to her bedroom.

Our story at breakfast was the only success Jenny had in keeping the memories to herself. After Sunday School, I listened to Jenny goad a little friend on and on. She knew a secret, she said, but she could never tell. The little friend finally confronted her after church and demanded some juicy details. Jenny revealed one tiny portion after another until she had unfurled the entire tale.

The next day, her friend came over to the house right after school, wanting to hear more about the Nephites and Lamanites.

"What are you talking about?" Jenny asked.

The confused little friend tried to help her remember, but it was futile. Jenny didn't recall anything more about Book of Mormon lands or times. The little friend kept prodding until Jenny got perturbed. As a last resort, her friend requested to see the Lamanite pullover that Jenny had bragged was hidden in the bottom drawer of her dresser.

I spied on the two little girls as they went into Jennifer's room. Jenny threw open the bottom drawer.

"See! No Nephite dress," she cried.

But the little friend reached in and pulled out such a dress. Jenny was just as surprised. She accused her friend of placing it there as a trick. The little friend was disappointed anyway. "That's just a costume," she said. "If it was real, it would be old and frizzy, like in a museum."

I think my mom threw out my own worn and filthy Nephite duds when she cleaned my closet. Garth kept his, though. He showed them to me one last time before he announced that his family would be moving away. His dad had been offered a better paying job in Rock Springs, Wyoming. Before they moved, I remember Garth's dad even came to church once or twice.

The day Garth left, we made a pact to visit one another every summer. It was a difficult parting for me. I'd never have another friend like Garth Plimpton.

Watching Garth's car leave the driveway and roll away behind the moving van, my eyes naturally rose to look up at the summit of Cedar Mountain. I squinted and found the cliff line where, I knew, stood the entrance to Frost Cave.

After Garth was gone, I had to struggle harder and harder to keep the secret of my adventure inside. Though Garth and I never discussed the memories, even with each other, having Garth around was an outlet of pressure for me. Every now and then, we could look at one another and grin, knowing.

Something within me was driving me to tell the story. I knew I wouldn't be able to hold it in much longer. Toward the end of the school year, I decided I would write it down. Then, even if I forgot, as Jenny had, I could still read about it to remind myself.

It was a silly stipulation that Helaman had put upon us. How selfish, it seemed, to have to keep it a secret. After all, telling an adventure can be almost as much fun as living it.

EPILOGUE

Ever since returning from my mission to Oregon and finding this erasable bond manuscript in the attic, the fine line between what are dreams and what are memories has been a constant source of frustration to me.

Before I went back to BYU to begin my sophomore year, I decided I'd stop in a Wyoming mining town called Rock Springs and visit an old friend. I took this manuscript with me.

The friend's name is Garth Plimpton. He had returned from his mission to Guatemala a few months before me. It was a pleasant reunion. Garth was the finest friend I ever had. I'd known him since the first grade, though we didn't become particularly close until my first year in junior high. He and I even made history together. We discovered a mural of ancient hieroglyphics on a wall along the Shoshoni River, just below town, and showed it to a couple of big shot archaeology experts. The affair got our pictures on the front page of the *Cody Enterprise*.

The next year, his family moved to Rock Springs. Except for a few weeks every summer and one Christmas when he came to Cody, we didn't spend much time together. But we kept in touch, especially while on our missions. In a few days Garth would be leaving Wyoming also, to take advantage of a full-ride scholarship in archaeology at Harvard.

Sitting on lawn chairs in the backyard of his home, sipping Hires root beer and reminiscing about old times, I finally showed him the manuscript. I pointed out that he'd find his name stamped on almost every page. Garth was, in fact, one of the main characters in the story. After thumbing through it and reading a few pages, he told me I had quite a healthy imagination. When I told him I didn't remember writing it, he gave me a puzzled look and handed the manuscript back. I asked him if he had an explanation for how it might have come into being. Garth shrugged his shoulders. He offered the same solution I had already considered—the theory that my Grandma Tucker had written it during her final years. I decided to agree with him and the subject was closed. But as Garth sat back upon his lawn chair and gazed off toward the southern sky, it seemed to me there was a distant look in his eyes—something he pondered, remembered. Maybe it was just my healthy imagination.

After saying good-bye to my friend, I drove down Interstate 80 toward Provo, Utah, excited and ready to re-enter the social world I'd had to sacrifice while serving the Lord these last two years.

I thought about all the beautiful coeds who would soon line up at my door, begging for my attentions. While my imagination was thus conjuring, I happened to glance at my hand resting upon the steering wheel, and noticed the ring on my littlest finger—the one with the smooth blue stone. I'd had that ring ever since I could remember. Exactly where I got it escapes me. Seems to me I found it in a park, and thinking it was valuable, I shined it up and wore it. Over the years, I'd had to move it from my index finger to my pinky. I must have seen that ring almost every day of my life, but today, as I drove down the long, empty highway, it struck me differently than it ever had before. For a split second, an image flashed in my mind. An image I couldn't connect with any particular source. An image of a girl, a beautiful girl with long black hair, in a world with eternal sunsets.

ABOUT THE AUTHOR

CHRIS HEIMERDINGER'S FIRST NOVEL, *TENNIS Shoes Among the Nephites*, first appeared in August of 1989. With the twelfth installment, *Drums of Desolation*, the Tennis Shoes Adventure series has sold over a million and half copies on book and audio. Chris is the author of the novel *Passage to Zarahemla*, and producer/director of the feature film of the same name, as well as its book sequel, *Escape from Zarahemla*, which are now officially part of the Tennis Shoes "universe." He is also the producer/songwriter on the album *Whispered Visions*. With *Drums of Desolation,* Chris presents the twentieth novel of his writing career—a creative span of more than a quarter century.

He is married to Emily with their eleven children, the youngest being Hunter Helaman, who is pictured here. Chris lives with his family in Providence, Utah.

TENNIS SHOES
ADVENTURE SERIES
GADIANTONS AND THE
SILVER SWORD

PROLOGUE

I remember the fog, twisting just below the summit like icy white fingers around a helpless victim's throat. The hill was very high, almost too high to be called a hill, and it was blanketed by an Eden-kissed jungle, rife with every life-sound that God ever saw fit to give a single patch of earth. But the summit itself appeared barren, only a tiny cluster of trees, cushioned in a nest of billowing grasses, and silhouetted against an angering sky. In the center of it all was the blackened trunk of a lightning-scarred tree, the fire having long since consumed its branches. This trunk marked the very pinnacle of the hill, nature's totem, jutting skyward to remind us in which direction we might find heaven.

Blinking my eyes, I saw a man standing there as well, a product of the mist. His head was hoary, his features were olive and aquiline, and his garments were reminiscent of an ancient and idyllic age. He stretched out his arm and earnestly beckoned me toward him, as if nothing else mattered, as if my communion were his last vestige of hope. So I began walking, but he never drew nearer. In spite of my determination, and the quickening of my pace, I couldn't seem to reach him.

This was my dream, the only dream of the night, Saturday, August 8th, three weeks before I returned to BYU to face my junior year.

The same night as the accident.

TENNIS SHOES
A D V E N T U R E   S E R I E S
by CHRIS HEIMERDINGER

2. GADIANTONS AND THE SILVER SWORD

Jim and Garth are now in college at BYU, and their earlier adventures in Book of Mormon lands are revisited in a most unusual way when evil men from the past (Gadianton robbers from Nephite times) pursue them and disrupt their lives with danger and violence. This is a spine-tingling, explosive saga that transports the reader from the familiar settings of Utah and the American West to the exotic and unfamiliar settings of southern Mexico and its deep, shadowy jungles, where Jim must take a mystical sword once wielded by the Jaredite king, Coriantumr.

3. THE FEATHERED SERPENT, PART ONE

Jim Hawkins is now the widowed father of two teenage daughters, Melody and Steffanie, and a ten-year-old son, Harry. Jim finds himself embarking on his most difficult and perilous adventure—a quest for survival against unseen enemies and an evil adversary from the distant past. He must also solve the deepening mystery of the disappearance of his sister, Jennifer, and his old friend Garth Plimpton. Once again he returns—this time with his family—to ancient Book of Mormon times; but now the civilization is teetering on the brink of destruction. It's the time just prior to the Savior's appearance in the New World . . . a time of danger and uncertainty.

4. THE FEATHERED SERPENT, PART TWO

Jim and his family continue their perilous adventures in Book of Mormon times, using all of their instincts and resources to find Garth and his family and deliver themselves from the clutches of one of the most treacherous men of ancient America—King Jacob of the Moon. They encounter murderous and conspiring men, plagues, a herd of "cureloms," hostile armies, and finally earthquakes and suffocating blackness as the Savior of the world is crucified. Along the way, members of Jim's family discover their loyalty and love for one another, and the importance of the gospel is in their lives, culminating in the glorious visitation of our Lord Jesus Christ to the city of Bountiful.

5. THE SACRED QUEST

Jim has just learned that his daughter, Melody, now age 20, has a very serious illness. During their last adventure in Book of Mormon times, Melody fell in love with Marcos, son of King Jacob of the Moon, who had been converted to Christianity. Now Jim's son Harry, 15, is determined to go back in time, find Marcos, and bring him back to be with Melody. He and his stepsister-to-be, Meagan, embark on this journey, but are sidetracked and end up in New Testament times, about 70 A.D. They encounter both believers and antichrists, consumed with finding a mysterious manuscript called the Scroll of Knowledge. The epic climaxes with a breathtaking confrontation between Harry, Nephites, and gladiators, but Harry's adventure of a lifetime has only begun.

6. THE LOST SCROLLS

Harry and Meagan continue their heart-stopping adventure as they face the awesome challenges of courage and survival in the hostile world of Jerusalem in 70 A.D. While Meagan and Jesse, a young Jewish orphan, are held hostage by the evil Simon Magus and the Sons of the Elect, Harry and his friend Gidgiddonihah must make an impossible journey to Jerusalem to find the Scroll of Knowledge, which may contain the ultimate power and mysteries of the universe. They have only a few days to find the scroll and deliver it to Simon Magus, or Meagan and Jesse will be killed. Our young heroes face breathtaking danger and high adventure as they encounter flames, swords, desperate villains, and perhaps the greatest loves of their lives in this sixth volume of the award-winning *Tennis Shoes Adventure Series*.

7. THE GOLDEN CROWN

Hang on to your seats as the heart-pounding adventure of Harry Hawkins and Meagan Sorenson in the land of Jerusalem and the world of the Romans races toward its thrilling conclusion.

In a nightmarish twist of events, Harry finds himself in the midst of unforeseen enemies who seek to separate him from all that he holds dear. To make matters worse, Garth Plimpton and Meagan are forced to make choices that threaten to leave Harry permanently lost in time.

Harry's father, Jim, and Meagan's mother, Sabrina, enter the fray to save their families, while Harry knows that to survive he must somehow reach a faraway land where resides a true apostle of the Lord Jesus Christ. "We're all on a golden journey," Harry is told by a very special person from Biblical history. "A journey inspired by golden dreams, and at the end awaits a golden crown of righteousness."

Reenter the reeling world of the first century A.D. in this, the seventh book in the celebrated *Tennis Shoes Adventure Series*. This is also the final volume in Harry and Meagan's breathtaking New Testament trilogy that began with *The Sacred Quest*.

DANIEL AND NEPHI

A Tale of Eternal Friendship in a Land Ripening for Destruction

Welcome to 609 B.C.! In a world of infinite mystery, when caravans rule the sun-swept deserts and mighty empires grapple for ultimate power, the lives of a young prince named Daniel and a trader's son named Nephi become entwined in an adventure that takes them along the razor's edge of danger and suspense as they struggle to save the life of a king—and the fate of a nation.

Join Daniel and Nephi as they learn the lessons of friendship, fortitude, and faith that shape two young boys into great prophets of God.

Carefully researched and scrutinized by scholars, *Daniel and Nephi* offers a breathtaking opportunity to explore the world of Jeremiah and Lehi.

"In Daniel and Nephi, *Chris Heimerdinger has once again breathed life into significant characters in biblical and Book of Mormon history."*

—BRENT HALL, FOUNDATION FOR ANCIENT RESEARCH
AND MORMON STUDIES

EDDIE FANTASTIC

When the Powers of the Universe Are in the Hands of a Teenager

Eddie Fanta is a fifteen-year-old boy entangled in tragic secrets which leave him questioning life, questioning justice, and questioning God. Louis Kosserinski is a savagely scarred and crippled old man who has remained in utter seclusion for the last forty years.

Mysterious circumstances bring these two characters face to face, where Eddie discovers the old man's unprecedented genius for electronics and microcircuitry—a genius which has spawned a series of inventions which could change the universe forever! Although Eddie sees Louis' inventions as an opportunity to improve an imperfect world, he ends up wreaking havoc at every hair-raising turn.

Join Eddie in his incredible journey through time and space, reality and spectacle, until at last he discovers an ultimate wisdom and understanding about our universe's Creator.